Alex Pine was born and raised on a council estate in south London and left school at sixteen. Before long, he embarked on a career in journalism, which took him all over the world – many of the stories he covered were crime-related. Among his favourite hobbies are hiking and water-based activities, so he and his family have spent lots of holidays in the Lake District. He now lives with his wife on a marina close to the New Forest on the south coast – providing him with the best of both worlds! This is his fifth novel.

By the same author:

The Christmas Killer
The Killer in the Snow
The Winter Killer
The Night Before Christmas

THE
KILLER
IN THE
COLD

ALEX PINE

avon.

Published by AVON
A division of HarperCollins*Publishers*
1 London Bridge Street
London SE1 9GF

www.harpercollins.co.uk

HarperCollins*Publishers*
Macken House,
39/40 Mayor Street Upper,
Dublin 1
D01 C9W8
Ireland

A Paperback Original 2024
1
First published in Great Britain by HarperCollins*Publishers* 2024

A catalogue copy of this book is available from the British Library.

ISBN: 978-0-00870681-4

Set in Minion Pro by HarperCollins*Publishers* India

Printed and bound in the UK using 100% Renewable
Electricity at CPI Group (UK) Ltd

MIX
Paper | Supporting
responsible forestry
FSC™ C007454

This book contains FSC™ certified paper and other controlled sources to ensure responsible forest management.

For more information visit: www.harpercollins.co.uk/green

I'd like to dedicate this book to all those readers who have let me know how much they've enjoyed this series of Christmas crime books. Your kind words have encouraged me to stick with it and to put my all into making each edition as riveting as possible.

Introducing DCI Walker and his team

This is the fifth book in the DCI James Walker series. For those who haven't read *The Christmas Killer*, *The Killer in the Snow*, *The Winter Killer* and *The Night Before Christmas*, here is a brief introduction to the man himself and the key members of his team.

DETECTIVE CHIEF INSPECTOR JAMES WALKER, AGED 43
An officer with the Cumbria Constabulary based in Kendal. He spent twenty years with the Met in London before moving to the quiet village of Kirkby Abbey just over four years ago. He's married to Annie, aged thirty-nine, who was born in the village and worked as a teacher. The couple have a daughter, Bella, aged two, and a son, Theo, who is just over eight months old.

SUPERINTENDENT JEFF TANNER, AGED 49
Now based at Cumbria Police HQ in Penrith. James took over from him as DCI. He's married with a son.

DETECTIVE INSPECTOR PHIL STEVENS, AGED 41
A no-nonsense detective who moved up the ladder to replace James as DI. He's married with two children.

DETECTIVE SERGEANT JESSICA ABBOTT, AGED 36
A highly respected member of the team and of Irish and East African descent. She's as sharp as a razor, and not afraid to speak her mind. She, too, was promoted to her current position as part of the department shake up. She's married to Sean, a paramedic.

DETECTIVE CONSTABLE CAROLINE FOLEY, AGED 30
The youngest member of the team, she lives with her widowed
mother in Kendal. Her three-year relationship to another
woman recently broke down.

PROLOGUE

For Stewart Farrell, going on long morning walks with Daisy was one of the few pleasures he got out of life. And he was pretty sure that she enjoyed the experience as much as he did.

Since becoming a widower nine months ago his beloved cocker spaniel had been his closest companion. She was his rock, his soulmate, the reason he gave himself for getting out of bed each day.

As he watched her now jumping around in the snow, he wondered how he would ever cope without her. Last Boxing Day his wife had been with them. Even though she'd recently been diagnosed with a serious heart problem, she had wanted to make the most of Christmas because she'd suspected that it might well be her last.

This first festive period without her had been really challenging, thanks in part to the bad weather. On Christmas Day he'd stayed indoors like most of the other villagers as blizzards swept across Cumbria. Kirkby Abbey was pummelled by heavy snow and brutal winds. Even the tall Christmas tree in the village square had blown over.

But thankfully today was much calmer and hopefully it would stay that way at least until the New Year.

It was ten o'clock when he turned into Maple Lane on the edge of the village. It stretched for about six hundred yards in front of him, the rough tarmac surface covered by a thick layer of pristine snow. Very few vehicles used the lane, which led only to a single detached house and a gate that gave access to surrounding woodland.

Farrell followed the same route most mornings because there was no need to put Daisy on her lead and so she got to move more freely and burn more energy. It always made him smile when she explored the undergrowth, sniffed out the wildlife and barked at things she saw or sensed. She was doing that now, so something in the knee-high bushes to their left must have seized her attention.

As he approached her, she continued to bark and he followed her wide-eyed gaze, expecting to see a frightened rabbit or deer staring back at him. But instead, he spotted something on the ground between clumps of bushes.

It wasn't until he was within a few yards of it that he realised what he was looking at.

'Oh, Christ,' he blurted to himself.

It was a body half-covered with snow. Parts of a red garment were visible, along with an arm and a shoe.

He felt a stab of alarm and the air shuddered in his throat. For a few seconds he couldn't move and the blood roared in his ears. Then instinct propelled him forward and he was soon on his knees and brushing the snow from the figure on the ground.

It was at once evident that the body was that of a man and, to Farrell's astonishment, he was wearing a Santa Claus costume.

But another shock was quickly forthcoming when he cleared the snow from the face and immediately recognised the frozen features of someone he'd known.

Someone who was clearly dead, and most likely had been for some time.

CHAPTER ONE

They were in the living room. All four of them. Annie was sitting on an armchair while breastfeeding Theo. Bella was lying on the floor, her head on a cushion, her eyes glued to yet another episode of *Peppa Pig* on the television. And Detective Chief Inspector James Walker was on the sofa taking it all in with a contented smile on his face.

He could not have been happier. Today was Boxing Day and he'd got to spend Christmas with his family. Plus, he wasn't due to return to work until Monday, which was still four days away. The next few days would be all about enjoying their special time together.

This afternoon they planned to go for a walk if the weather remained calm and he and Annie then aimed to put the kids to bed early and have a quiet dinner together.

It was a far cry from last year when he and his team had spent the whole of Christmas investigating a series of brutal killings out on the fells. Bella was only just over eighteen months old back then and Annie had been five months pregnant with Theo.

James had spent hardly any time with them, and it had made him feel sad and guilty. In fact, since moving to Cumbria from London four years ago, each festive season had been much the same. Plenty of bells and baubles, but also a horrid amount of bloodshed that kept him busy.

Thankfully it seemed that the county had been relatively crime free this year, and the only thing that had dampened the yuletide spirit had been the atrocious weather.

Yesterday blizzards had raged across the north of England and snow drifts had blocked roads and brought down power lines. In some places the temperature had plunged to minus twelve.

Not that it had spoiled their day. He and Annie had spent it opening presents, playing with Bella and her mountain of new toys, and watching Theo finding pleasure in at last being able to crawl.

The birth of their second child in April had been the highlight of an eventful year, which began in January when he told Annie that he had been offered a top job with the National Crime Agency in London. Much to his surprise, she wasn't entirely against the idea, even though it would have entailed moving away from their beloved Cumbria.

For her the upside would have been him stepping back from frontline policing, where he was always at risk. And he would also be closer to his parents and siblings who all lived in the capital, and so would be able to play a bigger part in their lives.

They discussed it for several days but in the end, they agreed that it would be a mistake for him to accept it. They were happy with their life in Kirkby Abbey and the prospect of more money coming in was not enough to convince them that it'd be a good idea to raise the kids in the crime-ridden capital.

Then in March came the dreadful news that Annie's uncle,

Bill Cardwell, had died at the care home in Penrith where he'd been struggling with dementia. He'd been her only living relative since both her parents had passed away and she had no siblings.

Bill's death was followed by more devastating news in July when Fiona, one of James's two younger sisters, was diagnosed with breast cancer and had to have a double mastectomy.

He was hoping that this coming year was going to be less of an emotional rollercoaster, and he was determined to make the most of his good fortune. Not only had he been blessed with a wife he adored and two wonderful children, he also had a job he loved.

He had been promoted to DCI almost two years ago and led a team based in the market town of Kendal. During twenty years as a copper in the Met he'd acquired the skills and confidence to face down all the challenges that had so far come his way. And he was sure that he would go on doing so.

'What time do you want to go for the walk?' Annie asked, breaking into his thoughts.

She had eased Theo away from her breast and was adjusting her shirt.

James looked at his watch. 'It's almost eleven. I thought we might have an early lunch and go out straight after.'

Annie shrugged. 'Or what if we go out sooner for the walk and then have lunch at the White Hart? It'll be another treat for our little madam.'

They had taken Bella to the pub on Christmas Eve after watching the Santa Claus parade and carol singing in the village square. She'd spent over an hour in the recently installed indoor children's play area and had enjoyed it so much that she'd been pleading with them to take her back.

'Sounds good to me,' James replied. 'Then we can snack this evening instead of cooking a meal.'

He told Bella what they were going to do and she got up from the floor and danced around joyfully for a few seconds before asking where her coat was. When James explained that they weren't leaving the house just yet, she ignored him and went looking for it herself.

It didn't surprise him. Like most two-and-a-half-year-olds their little petal had already developed a mind of her own.

It was then Theo's turn to grab their attention by burping loudly as Annie winded him.

James couldn't help but laugh. 'Do you want me to hold him while you get ready?' he asked her. 'We might as well make a move now and keep madam happy.'

She nodded and he hauled himself up from the sofa. But just then his mobile phone started buzzing. It was on the coffee table between them and it sent a tremor of unease through his body.

'Don't assume the worst,' Annie said, as they exchanged glances. 'It might not be work.'

But gut instinct told him that it was, and he was proved right when he answered the call.

'I'm really sorry to bother you, guv,' said a familiar voice. 'I know you're still on leave, but something's happened and I wondered if you're in a position to respond ASAP.'

Detective Sergeant Jessica Abbott was one of the officers who had been on duty over Christmas and given that he'd told her not to disturb him unless it was absolutely necessary, he knew something big must have happened.

'What is it, Jess?' he said. 'Can't you or someone else attend?'

'I'm just about to head there with DC Sharma, but I think you'll want to go as well,' she said.

'And why is that?'

'Well, a man's body has been found and one of the officers

7

who's arrived at the scene has just contacted control to report that he believes the man has at least two stab wounds.'

'So, he could have been murdered there.'

'That's right, but there's more. The body is lying in undergrowth on the edge of Kirkby Abbey. A spot known as Maple Lane. I believe it's within walking distance of your home.'

James felt his insides contract. 'Blimey, Jess. It is. You were right to call me. I'll set off right away. It won't take me long to get there.'

'Before you do, there's something else you need to know, guv.'

'What is it?'

After clearing her throat, she said, 'It was a dog walker who stumbled across the body. The guy lives in Kirkby Abbey and is apparently in no doubt that the dead man is a fellow villager – Nigel Booth.'

It took a moment for the name to register with James and when it did a cold shiver washed over him.

'Do you mean Nigel Booth as in—'

'Yes, guv,' Abbott said, cutting him short. 'As in retired police officer Nigel Booth, husband of our former colleague, Detective Constable Elizabeth Booth. And get this. He's wearing a Santa Claus costume.'

CHAPTER TWO

James closed his eyes, battling the images that suddenly reared up in his mind.

He'd met Nigel Booth numerous times since moving to Kirkby Abbey. The man had been a detective inspector based at Constabulary headquarters in Penrith before retiring from the force some two years ago. His wife Elizabeth, who'd been part of James's team in Kendal, had joined her husband in retirement back in January. They'd recently made it known that they had put their house up for sale and were planning to move to Spain to enjoy their remaining years in the sun.

'I actually saw Nigel on Christmas Eve,' James said to Abbott. 'He was one of a bunch of guys who took part in a Santa Claus parade in the village. I was there with my family. He even showed off to me as he walked past us. I don't think his wife was there, though.'

'Then that would explain the costume,' Abbott said.

'Possibly, but we can't assume that he's been lying there in the snow since then. He might have gone out yesterday for some reason despite the bad weather. Forensics will have to determine time of death.'

'They've been alerted, guv, and should already be on their way there. We'll need to contact Elizabeth. As I recall their home is actually in Maple Lane.'

'I've never been there, but I believe you're right. Let's wait though, until we're certain it's him. Do you know if she's reported him missing?'

'She hasn't, and no new misper cases are on the system.'

'That could be because she thinks he's somewhere he isn't.'

'I guess we'll find out soon enough.'

'Meanwhile, let's get going,' James said. 'I'll see you at the scene.'

He ended the call and turned to Annie who was staring up at him, wide-eyed.

'I heard enough to know that something bad has happened to Nigel,' she said, her voice shaking.

James pulled his lips tight and let out a breath between his teeth.

'A bloke walking his dog has come across a body in Maple Lane,' he said. 'He's told an officer at the scene that it's Nigel. And it appears he may have been stabbed.'

Her jaw dropped in shock. 'Oh, my God. That's awful. But can you be sure it's him?'

'The dog walker is a local so I doubt that he's mistaken. I'll have to go straight there. I'm sorry.'

'Don't be. It can't be helped and at least this year we got to spend Christmas Eve and Christmas Day together as a family.'

'So, what will you do now?'

'I think I should stay in with the kids. I don't feel like going out by myself with them.'

As if on cue Bella came rushing back into the room dragging her coat along the floor behind her.

'I found it,' she exclaimed excitedly. 'Can we go out now?'

Annie gave him a look that said she would break the news to their daughter that their plans had changed, and he nodded and headed to get dressed for work. He was halfway up the stairs when he heard Bella throwing a mini tantrum.

He felt guilty bailing on them, but he had no choice. What had happened here in his own village required his immediate attention.

He had already showered so all he had to do was slip out of his joggers and T-shirt and into jeans and a jumper. It took him little more than five minutes and when he arrived back downstairs, he was pleased to see that Bella had already calmed down and was back on the floor watching *Peppa Pig*, while Theo was asleep in his mother's arms.

'I'll keep you updated,' he said to Annie, who hadn't moved from the armchair.

She wore a mournful expression and looked to be on the verge of tears.

'If it is Nigel then it's not only Elizabeth who is going to be devastated,' she said. 'There's also Liam and his family.'

James hadn't forgotten that Nigel Booth was both a father and a grandfather as well as a husband. His son Liam also lived in Kirkby Abbey with his wife Colleen and their daughter who was six or seven months old.

James had only met them a couple of times, but Annie had got to know Colleen through the mother and toddler group in the village.

James shook his head and dragged in a long breath.

'And there was me thinking that we were going to get through this festive season without another bout of bloodshed,' he said.

'I think that was wishful thinking on your part given what's happened every year since we moved here,' Annie responded.

He crossed the room, stepping over his daughter, and gave both Annie and Theo a kiss. His wife's bright blue eyes were moist with unshed tears and he could tell that she was struggling to hold in her emotions.

'I'll call you as soon as I get the chance,' he said.

Before leaving the room, he gave Bella a kiss too and told her that he was sorry he had to go to work.

'But I'll make it up to you,' he said. 'Just be good for Mummy and I'll be back as soon as I can.'

In the hallway he put on his scarf, overcoat and heavy-duty shoes before stepping out into a bitterly cold Boxing Day.

CHAPTER THREE

As soon as the front door was closed behind him, James decided to walk to the location rather than drive. His car was covered in a blanket of snow and he didn't want to waste time clearing it off.

Maple Lane was on the other side of the village, but it would only take him about fifteen minutes to get there on foot.

Kirkby Abbey was a small village with just over seven hundred residents, a primary school, a church, two pubs, and some shops. And the walk would allow him to mentally prepare himself for what lay ahead.

As he set off, the cold air rushed into his lungs and snow crunched beneath his shoes. But at least it wasn't still coming down and there was no wind to speak off. The sky was grey and oppressive, though, and clouds were gathering over the fells.

After a few yards he glanced back at their four-bedroom cottage which had been left to them by Annie's mother. It was what had encouraged them to make the move to Cumbria, along with the threats James had received from a notorious London villain while working in the Met. Threats that put the fear of God into Annie.

He had no regrets about relocating and, so far, their life in the Lake District had been far less stressful than it had been in the Big Smoke. Except, of course, at this time of the year. As Annie had just pointed out, it had been overly optimistic on his part to believe they would get through this festive season without bloodshed.

The days leading up to his first Christmas in Cumbria were spent hunting a serial killer who'd struck right here in Kirkby Abbey. The following year he found himself investigating the massacre of an entire family on a secluded farm on Christmas Eve. Then, two years ago, it was the murder of a maid-of-honour at a New Year's Eve wedding. Last year he missed spending Christmas Day with Annie and Bella after a killer targeted a group of huntsmen on the fells. That was actually the last case Elizabeth Booth had worked on before she retired at the age of fifty-six. He was reminded now that she'd played a pivotal role in helping him to solve it.

Her face pushed itself into his thoughts suddenly, and knowing that he would have to break the news to her that her husband was no longer alive filled him with dread. So too did the prospect of having to subject her to a barrage of questions.

Have you any idea who might have killed Nigel?

When did you last see him?

Did he go out yesterday in the Santa Claus costume?

Why haven't you reported him missing?

Have you been at home by yourself since Christmas Eve?

14

James felt another spike of dread when his thoughts turned to Nigel. The man had been a highly respected police officer and was awarded several commendations during his long and distinguished career. He was credited with getting some of the county's most prolific criminals sent to jail. They included a man named Eddie Kane, who had established himself as a significant underworld figure with his hands in lots of pies. Nigel managed to get him on a charge of dealing drugs and he was banged up for three years. But after his release, as all too often happens, he went on to expand his illicit empire and became known as Cumbria's cruellest crime boss. James had himself tried and failed on several occasions to put him back behind bars.

Nigel had met Elizabeth when they'd spent a brief period working at the same station and James was pretty sure they'd been married for over thirty years. Having moved to Kirkby Abbey about twenty years ago from Carlisle, they'd become pillars of the community. He'd never heard a bad word said against them and since Elizabeth had retired, they'd seemingly enjoyed a modest and insular life in the village.

On Christmas Eve Nigel had seemed to be really enjoying participating in the annual Santa Claus parade. He recalled Nigel smiling and waving at the crowd, and how when he'd spotted James, he gave him a thumbs up.

So, if he was now lying dead in the undergrowth by the side of Maple Lane, then three questions would need to be quickly answered. *Was he murdered there? If so, when did it happen? And why on earth had he been targeted?*

Maple Lane was actually a cul-de-sac situated on the northern edge of Kirkby Abbey. It was surrounded on three sides by woodland and you entered it from the main road that encircled the village.

As James turned into it, he was confronted by a uniformed officer in a high-visibility vest who was standing in front of a taut ribbon of police tape that was stretched across the lane.

About a hundred yards further on were two patrol cars with their blue lights flashing, and the sight of them sent a rush of adrenaline through James's system.

The officer immediately recognised James and lifted the tape, waving him through.

'We were told you were coming, sir,' he said. 'PC Fisher is up there with the body.'

'Has anyone else turned up?' James asked him.

The officer shook his head. 'Not since we've been here. Some cars have driven past, but that's all. I don't doubt that more than a few curious souls will come along once the word gets out as to what's happened.'

'Is the man who called it in still here?'

'He is. A Mr Stewart Farrell. He lives close by.'

James nodded in recognition. He had met Stewart Farrell several times and recalled that the man had lost his wife when she'd had a heart attack earlier in the year. That was the thing about living within such a small community, you got to know, or know of, most of the other villagers, unlike in London where many people didn't even know their nearest neighbour.

'A quick search revealed that the dead man isn't carrying any ID or phone, but there are three ten-pound notes in his pocket,' the officer said. 'And I'm assuming you're aware that Mr Farrell has told us that he's Nigel Booth. He apparently lived further up the lane with his wife Elizabeth, who we all know.'

'Yes, I've been told,' James said. 'Has anyone been to the house yet?'

'No, sir. We've not had the chance to.'

'What about forensics?'

'A scene of crime team should be here soon. They've been held up by poor road conditions due to the weather between here and Kendal.'

James thanked the officer and hurried along the lane, which was bordered on both sides by overgrown verges layered with snow.

As he got closer to the action, he heard the crackle of a police radio and saw two more uniforms. One was speaking to Mr Farrell, who was holding a small brown dog in his arms, while the other, PC Dan Fisher, was standing on the left side verge signalling for James to join him.

The body was obviously there among the overgrowth and the closer he got the faster his heart pounded in his chest.

The spot had clearly been compromised to a degree, with people stamping over it, but that was to be expected given the circumstances.

'Hi, there, sir,' Fisher said. 'It's not often that you're among the first on the scene.'

'I'm guessing you know why that is,' James replied.

Fisher nodded. 'Of course. It's no secret that you reside here in the village.'

James was close enough now to see the body, which was face up among the low bushes. He was drawn first to the red Santa Claus costume and the dark stain that covered much of the chest area above a wide black belt.

'It's a stab wound,' Fisher pointed out. 'There's another on his right side just below the rib cage.'

James looked at the dead man's face and it made the blood stiffen in his veins. The features were rigid, frozen, and the skin pasty white to the point of being almost translucent. The eyes were closed, lips swollen and slightly parted, and James couldn't be sure how long the body had been here as the freezing weather would have slowed decomposition.

But he was sure that he was staring down at the face of former police officer Nigel Booth.

CHAPTER FOUR

James had a sudden, intense flashback as he stared down at Nigel Booth's lifeless face.

He was watching the man taking part in the Christmas Eve parade, suited up as Santa complete with the classic hat and false beard. It was quite possible that he had been killed soon after that, perhaps as he returned home.

'Bear in mind, sir, that there was a lot more snow on him when he was found,' PC Fisher said. 'Mr Farrell had already brushed some off to see who he was and if he was alive. And then I had to move the body so that I could inform control what we were dealing with.'

'And what do you reckon happened here?' James asked him.

Fisher expelled a puff of air. 'My gut tells me that he was dragged from the lane to this spot. You can see that some of the bushes have been virtually flattened. It's odd, though, that the killer – or killers – didn't drag him further away from the lane and into the woods. And it seems that not much effort was made to conceal the body.'

James nodded. 'Perhaps whoever killed him was in a hurry. Or it could be they didn't care how quickly the body would be discovered.'

'Then there's the question of whether he was killed here or dragged from a vehicle and dumped, having been killed elsewhere,' Fisher said.

It was a good point and one the SOCOs – the scene of crime officers – would have to consider. But James knew that determining exactly what had happened was not going to be easy. The snow that fell yesterday was several inches deep and combined with the strong winds it would have damaged or destroyed potential pieces of evidence, including traces of blood, shoe prints, and tyre tracks.

James dragged his eyes away from the corpse and looked up the lane. It veered off to the right ahead and there was no property in sight. He'd never ventured along it himself, but he'd heard that it was a favourite spot for dog walkers. The woods on both sides were pretty dense and there were no fences that he could see.

'I'll go and speak to Mr Farrell and then visit the Booths' house,' he said to Fisher. 'If reinforcements haven't arrived by then I'd like you to come with me.'

'Just let me know when you're ready, sir,' Fisher replied.

Stewart Farrell placed his dog on the ground as James approached him.

'I gather you two know each other,' said the officer who was standing with him.

'Indeed, we do,' James responded, holding out his hand for Farrell to shake. 'It's a real shame that we're meeting up again in these circumstances, Stewart.'

Farrell drew in a loud breath. 'I can't believe it. Nigel was such a nice man. Why would anyone want to do this to him?'

Farrell was in his mid to late fifties and wearing a heavy parka and a woollen hat that covered his ears. He had a long, sharp face and James could see the tension in his neck.

'I know you've already told my officers how you came by the body, but would you mind running through it with me?' James asked.

Farrell spoke in a thin, stretched voice and described how his dog Daisy had started barking at the bushes soon after they'd started walking along the lane.

'The first shock was seeing someone lying there dressed as Santa Claus,' he said. 'And then, when I crouched down next to him and cleared away some of the snow, I realised that it was Nigel. We'd known each other for years. His wife was a good friend to my late wife. She dropped in on us quite often after Angela fell ill. Does Elizabeth know yet? She'll be crushed.'

'I very much doubt it, otherwise I'm sure we would have heard from her by now,' James said. 'It could be she's visiting someone over Christmas and is assuming he's safe and well. I saw Nigel myself on Christmas Eve at the Santa Claus parade and I didn't see Elizabeth there. I'm about to visit their house, which is in this very lane.'

'Yes, it's the only property along here and I often pass it. But do you think he's been here since Christmas Eve?'

James shrugged. 'That's one of the things we need to establish.'

Farrell bit on his bottom lip. 'It's a terrible thing to have happened, detective, and it's going to shake the village to its core.'

James nodded. 'People might naturally jump to the conclusion that the person responsible is local and lives among them. And it won't be long before the news is out there because we're going to have to move fast. It'll mean drafting in lots more officers to search this area and go door-to-door asking questions.'

'Do you want me to hang around?'

'No. For now we just need your contact details. We'll be in touch later so that you can make a formal statement. Thanks again for bringing this to our attention. You've had a hell of a shock, and I reckon Daisy has too, so I'd encourage you to go home and try to relax.'

James reached down and stroked the dog before turning away. And just as he did so he saw another vehicle turning into the lane from the main road.

He recognised it at once as one of the pool cars from Kendal HQ, and as it drew closer, he saw Detective Sergeant Jessica Abbott at the wheel and Detective Constable Ahmed Sharma next to her in the passenger seat.

CHAPTER FIVE

Abbott and Sharma were two of the most solid and dependable members of James's team. Their arrival at the scene meant he could now kick-start the investigation, and he decided he'd take Abbott with him to the Booths' house and get Sharma to oversee things here.

Once they were parked up behind the patrol cars, they both jumped out. James was still pretty shaken by what had happened, so he had to pull his thoughts together before he started briefing them. However, most of what he had to say they already knew.

'I just took a call from forensics,' Abbott told him. 'They're about five minutes away.'

'Good. We'll need to clear the lane so that they can get as close to the body as possible.' James pointed to the spot where it lay. 'I can confirm that the deceased is Nigel Booth and it appears he has at least two stab wounds.'

He then tipped his head towards Stewart Farrell, who had started to walk away from the scene. 'I've spoken to Mr Farrell, who found the body. He's on his way home and he rightly pointed out that what's happened is going to hit the community hard. Plus, it will be a high-profile case because Nigel was a retired copper. So, we need to prepare ourselves for that.'

James told Abbott that he wanted her to go with him to the Booths' home.

'Where is it, guv?' she said, before biting her bottom lip. To keep her emotions in check?

'It's just up ahead apparently, the only property on the lane. We need to see if Elizabeth is there. If she isn't then we'll have to find out where she is.'

'It's odd that she hasn't reported Nigel missing, assuming he's been here since Christmas Eve,' Sharma said.

James nodded. 'I know and that concerns me. So, the sooner we can establish her whereabouts, the better.'

He then assigned the DC a number of tasks, the first being to get the lane clear for forensics.

'Then arrange for more uniforms to come here,' he went on. 'The area needs to be thoroughly searched. It could be that the murder weapon was discarded by the killer and is under the snow. And get someone at the office to provide us with contact details for Nigel and Elizabeth's family members. Their son Liam lives here in the village with his wife and young daughter. For all we know Elizabeth could be with them.'

'I remembered on the way here that Elizabeth also has a brother,' Abbott said. 'He's a lawyer and I believe he lives in Lancaster.'

'That's right,' James said. 'If she's not at her house or with their son then maybe he can shed light on where she is.'

As James and Abbott started walking along the lane, she told him that the on-duty team had come to believe that this festive period was going to pass without any major crimes being committed in Cumbria.

'We've spent most of the time twiddling our thumbs,' she said. 'A shopkeeper in Sedbergh was assaulted on Christmas Eve and a group of drunken louts vandalised a pub in Ambleside yesterday. But thanks to the bad weather a lot of potential troublemakers stayed at home. We've only made four arrests and things have been relatively calm all over the county. And then this morning this came in and I realised that it was going to be another not-so-merry Christmas, after all.'

Abbott had been with the team in Kendal when James arrived from London as a DI four years ago. She'd worked with him on what had proved to be some of the biggest and most challenging cases of his career. He rated her highly and at just thirty-six she was destined to rise through the ranks if that was what she chose to do.

'What's your initial take on what we're dealing with, guv?' she asked him.

'I'm inclined to believe he was murdered on Christmas Eve after the Santa Claus parade,' James said. 'It ended about eleven in the morning and I have no idea if he hung around before heading home. We'll have to consider the possibility that he was murdered elsewhere and his body was dumped in the lane, but instinct tells me that's most unlikely.'

'I agree,' Abbott said. 'Now, do we work on the assumption that there was just one assailant?'

'I think so, unless we uncover evidence that suggests otherwise.'

'And I suppose there's also a good chance that his killer is local and was known to him. This doesn't strike me as a spot where you're likely to encounter a knife-wielding stranger seeking out a victim on Christmas Eve.'

She was right, James knew, and that was why so many

unsettling questions were whirling around inside his head. Had Nigel been targeted by someone in the village who, for whatever reason, wanted him dead? Or was it someone from his past? Some criminal he had got sent to prison who had come here seeking revenge after being released?

They didn't see the two-storey house until they were fairly close to it. The property was set back from the lane and surrounded by trees and hedges.

The setting was secluded and picturesque, with a gravel driveway leading up to it.

There was a 'For Sale' sign at the entrance, which prompted Abbott to say that she hadn't realised the couple were selling up.

'They've been planning to move to Spain,' James said. 'And given how crap the weather has been here I can see why.'

Abbott nodded. 'It's a nice place and must be worth a tidy sum.'

It was a large, detached house built of local sandstone with a garage and a well-tended lawn. A Land Rover Discovery was parked on the driveway and James recalled Elizabeth telling him once that it was her husband's pride and joy.

The front door was made of polished oak and looked fairly new. The bell was fixed to the frame and James pressed it. When there was no response after about thirty seconds, he pressed it again.

Still no response.

Next, he peered through the letterbox into a small hallway and called out, 'Elizabeth. Are you in? It's James Walker here. Can you come to the door?'

Nothing.

He instinctively grasped the handle and pushed on it to make sure that it was locked, but to his surprise it wasn't.

'That's not a good sign,' Abbott said as James eased the door open and called out again.

No one answered, so he stepped inside and Abbott followed. She stayed behind him as he walked slowly along the hall while continuing to call out to make their presence known.

The door ahead of them was open and gave access to a spacious kitchen. But as they entered it, the scene they were confronted with caused them both to recoil in shock.

Elizabeth Booth was lying on the laminate floor between the breakfast bar and a tall fridge-freezer. She was on her back with her arms outstretched, clad in loose grey slacks and a white Christmas jumper with a large reindeer motif on the front.

And she was obviously dead, no doubt as a result of the ugly gaping wound in her throat.

CHAPTER SIX

James felt a cold numbness envelope him as he stepped closer to Elizabeth's body.

Her bloated face was frozen in a grimace, mouth open, tongue poking through blue, swollen lips. Beneath her head and shoulders the tiles were stained with copious amounts of dried blood.

The room also stank of rotting meat, which told him that the decomposition process had begun. It was a clear indication that she'd been dead for longer than twenty-four hours.

Behind him Abbott exhaled an expletive and when he turned, he saw that her features were screwed up as though in pain.

'Are you all right?' he asked her.

A sharp nod. 'I'm trying to be, guv. It's just that I've never attended the scene of a murder where the victim was a friend.'

James understood completely. He was experiencing the same sense of shock and bewilderment. Elizabeth was someone he had known for four years. He'd liked her. Respected her. And he'd had every intention of staying in touch with her.

'It looks as though there was a struggle,' Abbott observed, referring to the mess on the floor around the body.

One of two breakfast-bar stools was on its side and next to it were the fragments of a broken mug.

There was no sign of a weapon, though, which James assumed had been a large knife and conceivably the same one used to murder her husband.

'The wound looks pretty deep,' he said. 'And clearly the blade wasn't sliced across her throat. It must have been thrust in with significant force. Her larynx would have been severely damaged and I reckon she must have died pretty quickly.'

Abbott nodded. 'The most likely scenario is that she was killed on Christmas Eve either before or after Nigel was attacked in the lane.' She then flicked her head towards a part of the worktop next to the sink. 'Looks like she could have been preparing lunch or dinner when it happened.'

There was a wooden chopping board upon which rested half a loaf of crusty bread along with some cut off slices. Next to it was a butter dish and a toaster.

James reckoned Abbott was probably right, but he knew from experience that it was never wise to draw conclusions at a crime scene until it had been processed by the experts.

'We have to be careful not to contaminate potential evidence,' he said. 'But we also need to make sure that there's no one else in the house. While I have a look around, I'd like you to call Ahmed. Tell him what we've found and if the SOCOs have arrived have him send a couple up here. Then alert control. This case is turning out to be bigger and more disturbing by the minute. We need more backup.'

James pulled a pair of latex gloves from his coat pocket and snapped them on. Unfortunately, he wasn't carrying any forensic

29

shoe covers, but he couldn't let that stop him exploring the house. It was important to establish if there was anyone else here before more officers arrived.

He shifted his attention away from the body to look around the kitchen. It was all beech and granite with matching appliances. And it was tidy apart from the stool and broken mug on the floor, and the specks of blood around the body.

But then his eyes were drawn to a stain on the sharp edge of the breakfast bar. It was dark red and looked like blood.

A thought occurred to him and he switched his gaze back to Elizabeth. The only visible wound was to her throat, but he now wondered if there was another.

Curiosity compelled him to crouch down on the floor for a closer look and the smell emanating from her caused his nostrils to flare.

He felt the acid lodge in his throat as he placed his fingers against the side of Elizabeth's head and gently moved it to the right.

He saw immediately that there was another wound. A gash to the back of the head from which blood had spilled into her thick grey hair.

It made James think that she most likely tumbled backwards onto the breakfast bar after the blade was plunged into her throat, then dropped onto the floor. If so, then she may well have been unconscious before she fell into the icy embrace of death.

He raised his head and flicked his eyes around the room, hoping to see a security camera. But there wasn't one. Not on the ceiling, the walls or on top of any of the units.

As he stood up, he felt a wave of sadness sweep over him. This wasn't how Elizabeth's life should have ended. It was so brutal, so sick, so fucking unfair. He couldn't begin to imagine why someone would have done this to her.

His heart was beating at a rapid rate and he had to force himself to step around the body and exit the kitchen. He needed to check out the rest of the house to see if there were any more nasty surprises waiting for them.

The dining room was next, small and cosy, with a round table and four chairs. The walls were festooned with framed family photos, including several of Nigel and Elizabeth together in their police uniforms. There was also one of Nigel in his Santa Claus suit, which James guessed had been taken at the Christmas Eve parade last year or the year before.

Other photos were of their son Liam as a baby, a young boy, and with his wife and daughter. James was reminded that he had met the lad a few times, but had never had a proper conversation with him.

Next stop was the living room, which contained a fairly tall Christmas tree and an abundance of decorations. Through sliding doors, he could see a neat patio and a mature garden that sloped down to a high fence. Beyond it were woods that obscured what would have been a striking view of the distant fells. The room itself was well furnished with two long, deep leather sofas and a wall-mounted TV. Between the sofas stood a coffee table on which rested a fruit bowl and two mobile phones, which he assumed had belonged to Nigel and Elizabeth.

There were two other rooms on the ground floor, a tiny study and a toilet, and it didn't appear to James that anything in them had been disturbed.

It was much the same upstairs. The two bedrooms were neat and tidy, and nothing looked out of place.

When he returned downstairs to the kitchen, Abbott was waiting for him, her face pinched and tense.

'I called Ahmed, guv,' she said. 'The crime scene team has arrived and he's on his way here with two of them.'

'And I've been through the house and there's no sign of a break-in,' he said. 'It doesn't look to me as though we're looking at a burglary that went wrong. Which suggests that Elizabeth could have let her killer in.'

James then got distracted by something he noticed on the worktop behind where Abbott was standing.

'Take a look at that,' he said. 'Are my eyes deceiving me or is there a blade missing from that knife block?'

Abbott turned, leaning her head towards it. 'No, you're not wrong. There are five slots and only four knives. And I don't see the knife that was used to cut the bread on the chopping board.'

'Then that may well have been the murder weapon,' James said.

CHAPTER SEVEN

It was Abbott who examined the stainless-steel knife block on the worktop, and she confirmed that it was the serrated bread knife that was missing from the set.

They both then checked the drawers, cupboards, fridge and bin, but they didn't find it.

'We'll have to leave it to the scene of crime team to carry out a more thorough search,' James said. 'But if the bread knife was the murder weapon and it doesn't turn up then we'll have to assume that the killer took it with them.'

Just then someone called out. It was DC Sharma and he was at the front door. Seconds later he entered the kitchen wearing a forensic suit, with two SOCOs following close behind.

When he saw Elizabeth's body his eyes grew wide in their sockets and disbelief shaped his features.

'I really didn't think that things could get any worse,' he said.

'You're not the only one,' James responded. 'Unfortunately, the house isn't equipped with a home security system, which does surprise me given who they were.'

He briefed his DC and the two forensic officers on what he believed had happened.

'The bread knife appears to be missing so it could well have been the murder weapon,' he finished. 'It might also have been used on her husband. Hopefully, we'll know with some degree of certainty once their wounds have been examined.'

He was still putting them in the picture when Sharma's phone rang.

It turned out to be a call from one of the uniforms in the lane who wanted him to know that Dr Pam Flint, the Forensic Pathologist, had just arrived, along with Tony Coppell, the Chief Forensic Officer, who would assume the role of crime scene manager.

'I'd better go and talk to them,' James said, and told Abbott she'd be going with him. Before they hurried out of the kitchen, he asked for the two mobile phones in the living room to be bagged up and sent to the lab for analysis.

'If we're lucky the data records will offer up a clue as to what the hell this was all about,' he said.

The scene in the lane was much busier when James and Abbott returned. More uniforms had turned up and were working with a bunch of SOCOs to determine how best to search for anything that could be construed as evidence.

James spotted Pam Flint and Tony Coppell straight away. They were standing close to the forensics van while pulling on their white protective suits.

Before heading over to them, he asked Abbott to check with HQ to see if anyone had come up with contact details for Nigel and Elizabeth's family members.

'And then arrange for more of our team to come here,' he

said. 'It's possible that those who are off aren't aware of what's happened and how big it is. Top of your list should be DI Stevens and DC Foley.'

James was pleased to see that his two favourite experts had wasted no time getting here. Tony Coppell and Dr Pam Flint were among the best in the business and James had worked with them on most of the big cases he'd headed up since coming to Cumbria. He had enormous respect for them.

'Christmas just wouldn't be the same without a big bloody crime to bring us all together,' Coppell quipped as James approached them.

James heaved a loud sigh. 'I take it you know about Elizabeth.'

It was Dr Flint who responded. 'We've just been told. I already feel sick to my stomach. They were a lovely couple and I just don't understand why anyone would want to hurt them, let alone kill them.'

'It certainly is a mystery,' James said. 'The scene up at the house came as a real shocker. So, prepare yourselves.'

'We'll check this one first and then go there,' Coppell said. 'Did you manage to draw any conclusions from what you saw?'

James told him what to expect and what he believed had happened.

'But I could be wrong. And I have no idea who was attacked first or exactly when it all happened, although I suspect it was on Christmas Eve.'

He told them about Nigel taking part in the Santa Claus parade and said he thought it was likely he was murdered while walking home from the village square.

'Any chance he might have been caught on a CCTV camera?' Coppell asked.

James nodded. 'Possibly. Several were installed in and around the centre of the village about eighteen months ago. I expect there'll be footage of him from Christmas Eve. But there aren't any this far out.'

Dr Flint pursed her lips and gave a slow nod. 'Best we get straight down to business then. Let's see if Nigel's body can offer up any clues.'

'And while you do that my team will start a sweep of the area,' Coppell said.

James decided it was time to alert his boss as to what was going down. Superintendent Jeff Tanner was based at headquarters in Penrith, but would almost certainly be off with his family on Boxing Day.

James tugged out his phone and got a surprise when it started buzzing as soon as he opened it.

His wife was calling him and he answered instinctively.

'Hi Annie. I can't talk right now. Is everything okay?'

'Yes, but I thought you should know that two of our neighbours have been here asking if I know what's going on up at Maple Lane. I told them I didn't, but I gather that the news of a body being found is spreading like a wildfire through the village.'

'That doesn't surprise me, love. The lane is filled with coppers and people in white suits.'

'Oh, no. Please tell me it isn't Nigel.'

James hesitated for a moment before responding. 'What I'm about to reveal you have to keep to yourself, Annie. At least for now.'

'That goes without saying. You know that I never share what you tell me. So, come on, what is it?'

After a pause, he said, 'I'm afraid it is Nigel's body. But that's not all. Elizabeth is also dead. It's now officially a double murder investigation.'

Annie gasped into the phone and James instantly regretted telling her.

'This is dreadful,' she said, her voice dropping to a whisper. 'I want to ask more questions, but I don't think I can. Not right now. I need to …'

'I understand, love,' James said, sensing she was struggling to deal with the shock. 'It's not what you expected to hear. But look. I'm in the lane right now and will soon have to go and break the news to their son. We can talk later. But in the meantime, if someone tells you something that you think I should know then I want you to send me a text. Okay?'

'Okay. You just take care and don't worry about me.'

CHAPTER EIGHT
ANNIE

When Annie came off the phone, she felt a flash of heat spread through her body.

What James had told her had come as a huge shock. Her throat tightened and for a few moments she struggled to get the air into her lungs.

Thankfully Theo was asleep in his cot and Bella was engrossed in a game on her tablet. It meant she could sit down on the sofa and try to process the awful news.

Nigel and Elizabeth Booth were among the villagers she had got to know since her return to Kirkby Abbey after spending thirteen years living and working in London. The pair had been friends of her late parents and had both attended their funerals.

Annie had also befriended their daughter-in-law, Colleen, who had started taking her own daughter, Rosie, to the same mother and toddler group where Annie took Theo. Colleen's husband, Liam, was a delivery driver and on the few occasions she'd met him he had come across as friendly and likeable.

What this was going to do to the couple just didn't bear thinking about. The impact the murders would have on the village itself was also going to be severe.

She had already got a sense of what was to come from the two neighbours who had dropped by a short time ago, alarmed by the news that a body had been found in Maple Lane. It wasn't the first time her friends had come knocking to ask her what she knew about a major crime that had been committed in the area.

To them, James was something of a local celebrity, having solved so many horrendous cases, and they assumed he shared information with her, which he did to a degree even though he wasn't supposed to.

This case was going to arouse far more interest than usual because it was so close to home. And when the full details were out there, concern would mount inexorably and there would no doubt be a degree of panic in the village.

Fevered speculation would be rife and the murders would dominate conversations. People would understandably wonder if the couple had been killed by someone they knew. Someone who lived in the village. Someone who may well strike again.

After all, it might not become clear for some time if Nigel and Elizabeth were victims of random or targeted attacks. They had both had long police careers. They'd made lots of arrests between them and so there would presumably be lots of suspects.

Annie recalled how she and everyone else in the village were traumatised by the actions of the serial killer who struck in Kirkby Abbey in the run up to Christmas four years ago.

Now something similar had occurred. Something that would be another wretched blow to the community.

Every nerve in her body was suddenly buzzing and sweat was

forming on her brow. She stood up and crossed the room to the window. After opening it a fraction, she breathed in the cold air to revive her senses.

And that was when she saw that a group of five people had gathered on the pavement across the road. They included the two neighbours who had called on her earlier.

She didn't need to be told what they were talking about. That was obvious from the way they kept shaking their heads and pointing in the direction of Maple Lane.

This was just the start, Annie realised. Before long people would be gathering in groups across the village to express their concerns and fears to each other.

Then the newspaper hounds and TV crews would descend on Kirkby Abbey and it would become the centre of yet another unedifying media frenzy.

The grim prospect filled Annie with dread and made her think of James and the enormous amount of pressure he was now going to be under as he sought to find out why Nigel and Elizabeth were murdered. And who murdered them.

'What are you looking at, Mummy?'

Bella's voice made her jump and she turned to see that her daughter had left the sofa and was standing behind her, clutching her tablet.

'Oh, it's nothing, darling,' Annie said. 'Just some friends across the road.'

'When will Daddy be back to take us out?'

Annie felt a wave of heat spread through her body as she suddenly realised that yet again the kids wouldn't be seeing much of their father for days or possibly weeks. It was hard not to feel sorry for them and for James.

'He's had to go to work,' she said, stroking her daughter's head.

'So, we probably won't be going anywhere today. But don't worry because we can play lots of games together.'

Bella seemed satisfied with that. She beamed a smile, turned abruptly, and crossed the room to throw herself back on the sofa.

Annie just stood there watching her for a full minute as a ball of anxiety grew in her chest and tears pressed against her eyes. She had a bad feeling about what lay ahead and yet again it made her wonder if they should have moved back to London when they had the chance.

CHAPTER NINE

After coming off the phone to Annie, James spent a couple of minutes scribbling notes in his pad. Questions that needed to be answered. Tasks that would have to be carried out. People he'd want to interview.

His mind was reeling under a jumble of thoughts and with so much going on around him he was finding it difficult to concentrate.

Top of his to-do list was letting his boss know what was going on.

He put the pad back in his pocket and took out his phone to make the call. Superintendent Jeff Tanner didn't sound surprised to hear from him.

'Control alerted me a few minutes ago,' he explained. 'I was told that you were at the scene, so I knew you'd be in touch.'

'Are you at home, guv?' James asked.

'No. We're with the in-laws in Hexham. Been here since Christmas Eve, which I gather is when Elizabeth and Nigel were killed.'

'That's what we think. It's a real jaw-dropper and I still can't believe it. How much do you know?'

'Only that they both have knife wounds and that Elizabeth was found dead in their home while Nigel's body was next to the lane leading up to it.'

James told him about the bread knife that might have been the murder weapon and that there was no evidence of a break-in at the house.

'Pam and Tony are here now and so we should know more soon,' he went on. 'We're lucky that the weather has calmed down.'

'What about next of kin?' Tanner asked.

'There's a son who resides here in the village with his wife and daughter. I aim to visit them soon. Elizabeth's brother lives in Lancaster. We'll get the locals there to deliver the news to him before the media mob gets wind of it.'

'Well, it sounds like you have things under control, James. I know you were off-duty like me, so thanks for responding. It's not going to be easy dealing with something like this right on your doorstep, especially as the victims are people you knew.'

'It can't be helped. But look, I think we ought to set up a temporary base here in the village, just as we did four years ago during that other spate of killings.'

'Good point. You have my blessing. And, for your information, we're leaving here early in the morning. I'll drop the family off at home first, then pop into the office. If the case is still ongoing, which I expect it will be, I'll head down south to you. If there are any developments in the meantime call me, and leave it to me to liaise with the Constabulary press office.'

'Will do, guv. And make them aware that this is going to attract a lot of attention as well as a high level of disquiet in the community here. Some of the villagers already know that at least one body has been found. And my wife just told me that a couple of our neighbours actually turned up at our house to ask if she knew anything about it.'

'It'll freak 'em out for sure when they know the full story,' Tanner said. 'I'll warn the press office that it's something we'll all have to take into account and manage. Just as we did four years ago.'

As James hung up he reflected on what Tanner had said, his mind carrying him back to when his team had turned the small village hall into a makeshift incident room before.

Tables were used as desks and the wall-mounted display panel became the evidence board. It worked well and helped them save a great deal of time and energy during the investigation. But not in his wildest dreams did he expect that they would ever have to go down that road again.

He pulled up his coat collar to protect against the chill breeze and checked his watch. It was half twelve, so he'd already been here for about an hour. And two hours had passed since Stewart Farrell had found Nigel's body.

Dr Flint was now kneeling on the ground next to it and James watched as she closely examined his chest wound.

At the same time Tony Coppell was busy photographing the scene while his team scoured the area for clues buried beneath the snow.

The conditions presented them with a real challenge, and they all knew that when the snow melted vital clues could be washed away. But it was something they were all used to, and James was confident that if there was anything to be found then they would find it.

'I've got some updates for you, guv,' Abbott said, breaking into his thoughts as she stepped up behind him. 'Liam Booth lives in Chapel Road. I assume you know it.'

James nodded. 'I do. It's not that far from here. Just off the main road.'

'I also have an address and phone number for Elizabeth's brother. Officers are on standby in Lancaster to go and break the news to him as soon as you give the go ahead.'

'Then I suggest you do that right away and ensure they tell him that we'll want to talk to him as soon as possible.'

'I've already done that. I also managed to get through to DI Stevens and DC Foley. They'll soon be making their way here.'

'And I've spoken to the Super,' James said. 'He agrees with me that it makes sense to set up a base here in the village hall just like we did four years ago. That's assuming we don't crack the case between now and tomorrow morning, which I reckon is highly unlikely.'

'What do we do now then, guv?' Abbott asked.

'You and I will go to Liam Booth's house. It's only a short walk from here but I think we should go by car. Can you go and arrange it while I have a quick word with Pam?'

Abbott darted off and James stepped over to where Dr Flint was now standing over Nigel's body while dictating notes into her phone. When she saw him, she pocketed the phone and said, 'My initial assessment is that you're almost certainly right in respect of the time of death. He was killed at some point on Christmas Eve. I'm sure of it. And I can confirm that there are stab wounds to his chest and the right side of his stomach. Both potentially fatal. And there's been extensive bleeding.'

'What about the weapon used?'

'The edges of the wounds are torn and shredded which most

likely indicates a serrated blade. So, it could well have been a kitchen knife. I'll know more once I get him to the lab. And it's worth noting that I haven't spotted any defensive wounds, but they could be hidden under the costume he's wearing.'

'So, what next?' James asked her.

'I'll go up to the house and examine Elizabeth. Then I'll arrange for both bodies to be taken to the morgue. I'll have to schedule the post-mortems for first thing tomorrow because there's no way I can fit them in this afternoon with the workload we've already got on.'

'Thanks, Pam.'

'What's your next step?'

James felt his stomach twist in an anxious knot. 'I have the unenviable task of telling a young man that both his parents have been murdered.'

CHAPTER TEN

Abbott was waiting for James at the entrance to the lane. She was standing next to a patrol car and holding the rear door open for him.

The scene was very different from when he'd arrived earlier. There was now a line of patrol cars parked along the near side of the road while on the other side a small crowd had turned up, eager to find out what was going on.

'You really can't blame them,' Abbott commented. 'I'm sure that in their situation I'd be just as curious.'

James didn't respond, but he knew she was right, and it raised concerns about preserving the integrity of the two crime scenes. When he was in the back seat of the car, he phoned DC Sharma.

'You need to ensure there are plenty of uniforms in the woods on all sides, Ahmed,' he said. 'They provide easy access for those who want to get close to the action, including news hacks who will be on our backs soon enough.'

'I'll see to it right away, boss,' Sharma replied. 'Meanwhile, we still haven't come across the missing knife in the house.'

'That doesn't entirely surprise me,' James said. 'The killer probably took it with them.'

'And so far there's no other potential evidence to suggest what went down here. But the two mobile phones that were in the living room are on their way to the lab. We tried to get into them but they're locked.'

'That's great. Dr Flint will be with you soon. She's just finishing up in the lane. Jess and I are on our way to speak to the son, and we'll have a debrief when we get back.'

'Okay.'

'And one other thing. Get someone to check the CCTV and door cameras in and around the village. We need to round up footage from Christmas Eve.'

James felt the muscles knotting in his stomach as they headed towards Chapel Road. In a few minutes he would have to break the news to Liam Booth that both his parents had been murdered. It was going to come as such a shocking blow to him and his wife that their lives were never going to be the same again.

And as if that wouldn't be upsetting enough, the couple would also quickly realise that they were being treated, at least initially, as suspects. This was something that couldn't be helped and was due to the fact that most murders were committed by people known to the victims, with a large proportion being family members. James didn't think that was likely here, but at this early stage he had to keep an open mind.

Chapel Road was on the western edge of the village, close to the Catholic church. It had a row of ten old terraced houses on one side and detached properties on the other, beyond which lay open fields.

There was no one about and no cars parked in front of number five, the home of Liam Booth and his family.

James's whole body was tight with tension as he climbed out of the patrol car and rang the bell. But for the second time that day there was no response and a wave of unease swelled in his chest.

'Let's check next door,' he said, and this time Abbott pressed her finger on the button.

A woman who looked to be in her late sixties answered within seconds. She had a full head of silver-grey hair and was wearing a kitchen apron with pictures of Christmas trees on the front.

As soon as she saw James her face fisted into a frown. 'I know who you are. You're the detective who lives here in the village. I've seen you around and I've met your wife.'

James smiled at her. 'That's right. I'm Detective Chief Inspector Walker and my colleague here is Detective Sergeant Abbott. And you are?'

'Kate. Kate Mason. Miss.' Her eyes moved beyond James to the patrol car at the kerb and alarm flickered across her face. 'What's this about? Have I done something wrong?'

James shook his head. 'No, of course not. We came here to speak to your neighbours, Liam and Colleen Booth. But they don't appear to be in.'

'That's because they went to stay with Colleen's parents for Christmas. They live in Shap.'

'When are they due back?'

'Not until tomorrow. I've got the address if you want it. They left it with me, along with their numbers, in case I needed to get in touch.'

'That would be really helpful,' James said.

'Come in then. It's all written down.'

On the inside the house was dark and drab and filled with the aroma of something cooking.

They followed Miss Mason into the kitchen where she picked up a sheet of paper from the worktop.

'Here it is,' she said, handing it to James, who used his phone to snap a photo of the contact details.

'Why do you want to speak to them?' Miss Mason asked. 'I'm assuming it's not to deliver good news.'

There was no way James could tell her before speaking to Liam and his wife, so he said, 'I'm not able to share that information with you at this stage, I'm afraid. But can you tell me when the family left for Shap?'

She nodded. 'On Christmas Eve. About five o'clock as I recall. It was a last-minute thing. They had been planning to spend yesterday with Liam's mum and dad who, as you must know, live here in the village. But then decided not to.'

'Have you any idea why?'

'Well, Colleen let it slip to me the day before Christmas Eve that Liam had fallen out with his parents again. They'd had another big row apparently.'

James and Abbott exchanged glances before he said, 'Do you know what it was over?'

'Colleen didn't tell me, but I assume it was because Nigel and Elizabeth are selling their house and plan to buy a villa in Spain. Liam doesn't want them to go and it's become an issue. He's been pleading with them to downsize instead and stay here in Cumbria. And he wants them to let him have some of the spare cash so that he and Colleen can buy a place of their own. They're both in their thirties and are anxious to get on the housing ladder. But his parents have said no.'

'Do they not own the house next door then?' James asked.

A shake of the head. 'No, they rent it. They've told me they're desperate to buy but can't afford it. And from various

50

conversations I've had with Colleen I get the impression that they're not well off financially.'

'I take it Colleen isn't working right now as their daughter is so young?'

'No, she's too busy looking after Rosie. But Liam is a delivery driver. He's out on the road most days. But I'm sure he can't earn much.'

'And can you tell us how long they've lived here in the village?' This from Abbott.

'About a year. They came back after living down south for many years. Both he and Colleen were brought up in Cumbria, but they met while working in Manchester and got married three years ago. They returned here after she fell pregnant with Rosie.'

James didn't want to carry the conversation on for fear of giving too much away, so he said, 'Well, you've been most helpful, Miss Mason. We'll see ourselves out. And there's no need to let Mr and Mrs Booth know about our visit. We'll be heading for Shap very soon.'

'I just hope and pray that whatever you're going to tell them will not spoil their Christmas,' she said. 'They're a lovely couple and they have such a sweet daughter.'

CHAPTER ELEVEN

When they returned to the car James told the driver to take them straight back to Maple Lane.

Turning to Abbott, he said, 'I need to check some things before we head for Shap. But what's your take on what we were just told?'

'Well, it's clear that the relationship between Liam and his parents is strained,' she replied. 'But as we both know, fewer couples are prepared to downsize these days in order to help their kids onto the property ladder. They'd rather bolster their retirement savings and enjoy a more comfortable and financially secure lifestyle. And that often leads to family rifts.'

'It's an issue we'll have to raise with Liam and one we'll need to follow up. For now, he's a person of interest. We both know it's not unknown for parents to be murdered by their sons and daughters. I investigated one such case in London where a man shot and killed his mother and father, who were in their seventies, so that he could get his hands on his inheritance.'

Abbot's expression was sceptical. 'From what we already know about Liam Booth it's hard to believe he would have murdered his parents to stop them selling up and moving abroad.'

'You're right, but even people who come across as nice and loving can have demons lurking on the inside.'

Abbott nodded. 'I suppose that's true enough.'

A few more villagers were lining the pavement across the road from Maple Lane when they got back there. James was pleased to see that the number of uniforms at the scene had also increased.

DC Sharma was issuing instructions to some of them when James and Abbott walked up to the spot where Nigel's body lay. He broke away from the group to inform James that Dr Flint and Tony Coppell were now up at the house.

'I'll leave Jess to tell you what we've learned, Ahmed, while I go and speak to them,' he said. 'But I'll be quick about it because we need to get to Shap as soon as possible.'

A forensics van was now parked on the driveway and before entering the house, James donned a white suit and shoe covers.

SOCOs were already at work inside processing the scene. They were moving from room to room taking photographs and making notes.

Dr Flint and Coppell were both in the kitchen standing either side of Elizabeth's body.

Seeing it again was just as heart-wrenching for James as the first time. He had to swallow hard to dislodge the lump in his throat.

'So, what have you got for me?' he said, addressing himself to Dr Flint.

She lowered her face mask and wet her lips.

'Well, for starters, I'm as certain as I can be that she was killed on the same day as her husband, that being Christmas Eve,' she said. 'And even at this early stage I'm willing to bet that the same knife was used on both of them. The blade entered the throat at an upward angle, which would indicate that her attacker was either shorter than her or she was lunging forward, perhaps in an attempt to disarm them, when penetration occurred.

'As for the head wound, that's consistent with falling backwards onto the edge of the breakfast bar. Also, although there's a lot of blood beneath the head that spilled from the throat wound, there's only a small amount of spatter on the floor around the body and on the cupboard doors. It suggests to me that there wasn't much of a struggle. I suspect it would have been short but fierce and probably lasted just a matter of seconds.'

'I would concur with that,' Coppell said. 'The mess in here is limited to the stool having been knocked over and the broken mug on the floor. It could mean that the killer entered the kitchen and took Elizabeth by surprise, or she let them in and was engaging with them before the attack took place.'

'I take it you haven't found the bread knife that's missing from the block on the worktop?' James said.

Coppell shook his head. 'Not yet. And you were right about there being no sign of forced entry into the house. I checked myself.'

James looked again at Elizabeth's body and felt a stirring inside, a quickening of his heart.

He was still finding it difficult to accept what had happened to her and Nigel, and a memory of the last time he saw them together flashed through his mind. It was just over a week ago, when he went into the village convenience store to buy a paper and a bottle of wine.

They were there stocking up on groceries and were clearly pleased to see him. They asked about Theo and Bella and told him that several couples had expressed an interest in buying their house.

'As soon as it's sold, we're going to rent a place on the Costa Blanca while we search for our own dream villa,' Elizabeth said to him. 'And when we've got it, we'll expect you, Annie and the kids to come and visit.'

They were the last words his former colleague and good friend spoke to him, and thinking about them now sent a shiver across his skin.

CHAPTER TWELVE

James left the house and returned to the lane. It had got even busier during the last few minutes and among the new arrivals were DI Phil Stevens and DC Caroline Foley. They were being briefed by Abbott and Sharma.

James found it reassuring that the four detectives who he rated most highly were already getting to grips with the situation. This was a case that was personal to all of them. They had known and liked both victims and were not going to rest until the killer was behind bars.

'I'm glad you got here so quickly,' he said to Stevens and Foley. 'I take it you've been brought up to speed.'

'We have, guv,' Stevens replied.

James nodded. 'Well, this is going to be a tough one for all of us. So be prepared to give it your all.'

'We will,' Stevens replied. 'You can count on that.'

Phil Stevens, at forty-one, was one of the team's most experienced officers. He'd moved up the ladder to replace James as Detective Inspector and had proved himself to be a loyal and committed lieutenant. It was rare for him to show any signs of emotion, but James could see the glint of it in his eyes now.

'It's not just the team who are struggling with this,' Foley said. 'The murders have sent shockwaves through the entire Constabulary. Elizabeth and Nigel were popular and they made lots of friends over the years. I gather calls have been coming into headquarters at a rate of knots.'

James could tell from Foley's scratchy voice and tight features that she was also finding it hard to grapple with. But that didn't surprise him. She was the youngest member of the team at thirty and when she joined just over eighteen months ago, Elizabeth had acted as her mentor. As a result, they had formed a strong friendship.

Time to crack on with business, James told himself, and took the pad from his pocket. But before going through the to-do list he'd scribbled down, he told them what was going on up at the house.

'The forensic evidence is so far leading us to believe that the two murders were carried out within minutes or hours of each other on Christmas Eve,' he said. 'The working assumption at this stage is that we're looking for a single perpetrator and that the same weapon, most likely the missing bread knife, was used on both victims.'

He then assigned Sharma the task of coordinating the search for it in and around the lane and at the house.

'And continue working with uniform to stop people coming here through the woods,' he said. 'If you think we need more help, then request it.'

He then told them he wanted to get house-to-house inquiries underway, starting with streets closest to Maple Lane.

As he was speaking, Abbott's phone rang and she moved away from the group to answer it.

'We also need to make sure that we can use the village hall,' he went on. 'Can you check on that, Phil? I think we should maintain a round-the-clock presence here from the start. A pop-up police station in effect. Hopefully it will afford villagers a degree of comfort and be a place they can go if they have something to tell us. A few desks and laptops linked to headquarters, plus a meeting room, should suffice. Just as it was four years ago.'

He moved on to other matters, including checking CCTV cameras, keeping tabs on what, if anything, the techies found on the mobile phones taken from the house, and drawing up a list of all of Nigel and Elizabeth's closest friends and relatives.

'I'll go to Shap now to break the news to the son and when I get back, we'll meet up again. Then we'll—'

He was interrupted by Abbott, who hurried up to them holding out her phone.

'That was the office,' she said excitedly. 'They wanted to bring to our attention two things that could prove significant.'

'We're listening,' James said.

'Well, a call was logged on Christmas Eve morning from a woman living close to here. She spotted a man in her neighbour's back garden. She was concerned because she knew that the neighbour was attending the Santa Claus parade in the village centre and the house was empty.'

'Was it followed up?' James asked.

'A patrol car was dispatched, but the guy fled when the woman called out to him. By the time the patrol got there he was nowhere in sight. They did a quick recce of the area but saw nothing suspicious. But then, just half an hour ago, another call was received, this time from a man living in another street but also close to this location. He and his wife just returned from spending Christmas Eve and Christmas Day with friends only to find they'd been burgled. Whoever it was broke a window to gain access and apparently left quite a mess.'

James felt his heart take a leap. 'Let's get on it right away. It could be someone who was targeting homes he thought were empty due to the parade and such. Then he came here and messed things up. You've got the details, Jess, so go and check it out. Get a couple of uniforms to accompany you and try to find out if any other homes have been broken into.'

He then turned to Foley. 'You come with me to Shap, Caroline. And we need to get there sharpish. I don't want the family to hear what's happened from someone else.'

CHAPTER THIRTEEN

It took James and Foley just over forty minutes to get to Shap in the rear seat of a patrol car. Road conditions weren't too bad considering the amount of snow that had fallen on Christmas Day, likely because the gritters had been out in force.

The village was fifteen miles north of Kendal and just off the M6 at junction 39.

They'd been given the address of Colleen's parents, whose names were Norma and Dominic Vine, and it was just after 2 p.m. when they arrived at the Vines' residence.

Their home turned out to be a small semi-detached house in a quiet street. The woman who answered the door looked to be in her late fifties, early sixties. She had a fleshy, nondescript face framed by thick brown hair that was streaked with grey.

'Are you Mrs Vine?' James asked her.

She narrowed her eyes at him. 'That's me. What can I do for you?'

James whipped out his warrant card and held it up. 'I'm with Cumbria Police. Detective Chief Inspector Walker. My colleague is Detective Constable Foley. We understand that your daughter Colleen and son-in-law Liam are here, and we need to speak to them.'

Her face registered alarm as her eyes darted between them.

'Yes, they're here along with their daughter,' she responded. 'But why do you want to see them?'

James started to reply, but held back when a familiar face suddenly stepped into view behind her.

It was Liam, and his eyebrows shifted upwards dramatically when he saw James. 'Detective Walker! I just spotted the police car outside. What the hell are you doing here?'

James drew in a lungful of air. 'There's some news we need to pass on to you, Liam. It's about your parents.'

'What about them?'

'I think it would be best if we came inside.'

Liam threw his shoulders back and the muscles flexed in his jaw. 'Why can't you tell me here? Has something happened to them?'

'I'm afraid so, but I don't think—'

'No. Just come out with it, for heaven's sake. Are they all right or should I be worried?'

James cleared his throat. 'They're both dead, Liam. And it appears they have been since Christmas Eve. I'm so very sorry.'

It took a moment for this to sink in and when it did Liam's hands flew to his mouth and a cry erupted from his throat.

'That c-can't be true,' he stammered, shaking his head. 'It's not possible. They were fine when I last saw them.'

'I'll explain what's happened,' James said. 'But I really think it should be inside.'

Liam started to respond, but the words stuck in his throat.

His mother-in-law drew in a tremulous breath and instinctively put an arm around his waist.

'Come on, son,' she said to him. 'Let's hear what they have to say.'

Liam didn't resist, and as Norma began to steer him back along the hall, his wife came down the stairs, oblivious to what was going on.

'I've put Rosie down for a nap and now—' She stopped abruptly when she saw the two detectives and the distraught look on her husband's face. 'My God, what's happened? I've only been gone a few minutes.'

'It's my mum and dad,' Liam told her. 'These detectives have come here to tell us they're both dead.'

Liam's father Dominic wasn't at home. He was employed as a chef at a restaurant in Penrith and was working the Boxing Day shift. So, it was just Liam, Colleen and Norma who sat side by side on the sofa in the living room as James, sitting on an armchair facing them, revealed that Nigel and Elizabeth had been murdered.

They each reacted differently. Norma's bottom lip quivered and tears pooled in her eyes. Colleen broke down and buried her face in her hands. And Liam just shook his head and stared at the floor, as though he simply couldn't accept what he'd been told.

James struggled with his own emotions as he went on to tell them how Nigel and Elizabeth had died and where their bodies were found.

Colleen managed to regain her composure enough to ask why it was believed the murders had taken place on Christmas Eve. James explained that Nigel was wearing his Santa Claus suit and in all likelihood was returning from the village parade early that afternoon when he was attacked.

'But that makes no sense,' she said, as more tears spilled from her eyes. 'They were a warm, loving couple. Why would someone want to kill them?'

James shrugged. 'The motive is a mystery at this stage. And we don't know if the perpetrator was known to them or a complete stranger.'

'But surely you must have some idea,' Liam said, lifting his gaze from the floor. 'Could it have been because they used to be coppers? Someone who had a grudge against one or both of them? I know that over the years they were threatened lots of times. It's one of the reasons I never wanted to follow in their footsteps.'

'It is quite possible,' James said. 'And it's a line of inquiry we'll follow up. But as you would expect at this early stage there are lots of unanswered questions. You see, we've found no signs of a break-in at their house, and we haven't established who was killed first. It's therefore not yet possible for us to determine exactly what took place and why. But a major investigation is underway, and I promise we will do all we can to track down whoever was responsible.'

Colleen stood up suddenly and rushed towards the door, saying she was going to be sick. James gestured for Foley to go with her and then turned his attention back to Liam.

The news appeared to have sucked the life out of him. He was a tall, broad-shouldered man with sharp features and a full head of brown hair. But it was as though he had suddenly diminished in size while at the same time the blood had retreated from his face.

'I know this is going to be difficult, but I do need to ask you some questions,' James said.

Liam closed his eyes and his breathing started coming in a

series of violent gasps. His mother-in-law placed one hand on his shoulder and another on his knee.

'Must you do it now?' she asked. 'He's in a state of shock. I'm not sure that whatever he tells you will make any sense.'

Liam's eyes snapped open. 'No, it's okay, Norma. I want to help. I have to.'

James took out his notebook and pen and said, 'Let's start with the last time you saw or spoke to your parents.'

Liam didn't have to think about it. 'I talked to Mum on the phone on Monday, the day before Christmas Eve. But it's been over a week since we last got together.'

'Is that unusual? After all, your homes are within walking distance of each other.'

Liam hesitated for a moment before responding. 'Well, the truth is I had a falling out with Mum and Dad that's been carrying on for weeks. It got so bad that I decided we shouldn't spend Christmas Day with them and came here instead. And now we'll never get to make up and I'll live with the guilt for the rest of my life.'

'What was it over? The falling out?'

Liam sighed. 'They were selling their house and moving abroad. I didn't want them to go and I made my feelings clear. I wish now that I'd kept my mouth shut.'

'Why didn't you want them to go?'

He shrugged. 'I moved here to be near to them. It came as an unwelcome surprise when they said they were moving to Spain. I tried to persuade them not to, but it fell on deaf ears.'

His wife came back into the room then, followed by Foley. Colleen's eyes were dull with shock and her arms were wrapped around her upper body. She was a tall, athletic woman, with a smooth face and lustrous fair hair. He'd never seen her looking so gaunt and fragile.

'I'm sorry about that,' she said, as she returned to the sofa. 'This is all too much.'

'I was just asking Liam some questions,' James said. 'He's told me that he last spoke to Elizabeth the day before Christmas Eve. Had you spoken to her since then?'

She shook her head. 'I tried ringing them yesterday to wish them a Merry Christmas, but they didn't answer their phones. So, I sent them a message and attached a photo of Rosie to it. The last time I saw Elizabeth was on the Thursday. We bumped into each other in the village and had a chat. She said she was feeling really down and was so sad that their retirement plans had caused so much fuss. You see, they were—'

'I've told them about the fallout,' Liam said.

Colleen drew a breath. 'It's been really hard for us all.'

After a short pause, James said, 'We've spoken to your neighbour who told us you left your home at about five o'clock on Christmas Eve to come here. Can you tell us where you spent the day leading up to that point?'

It was Liam who answered first. 'I had no parcel deliveries so I went for a hike, which I often do on my days off. I was out between about eleven and two. It's something I do at least once a week and the route I take starts just across the road from our place.'

'Does it go anywhere near Maple Lane?'

He frowned. 'No, it doesn't. It's in the opposite direction.'

'And did you go by yourself?'

'I always do.'

'And what about you, Colleen? Did you go out?'

'No, I didn't. I stayed in until we drove here. I had a lot to do sorting things out for us and the baby.'

Liam leaned towards James. 'Why do we have to account for

our movements? Do you seriously suspect that we might have killed my parents and that's why you want to know if we have alibis?'

'Absolutely not,' James responded, and felt a stab of guilt for lying to them. 'They're routine questions that have to be asked during an investigation of this kind.'

Liam appeared to accept that as a reasonable answer and leaned back on the sofa.

'It surprised me that your parents' house doesn't have a door-cam or any internal cameras,' James said. 'Did they not think it was necessary?'

Liam released a shaky breath. 'They did have a security system for ages, but a couple of years ago it started to develop problems and then stopped working. They uninstalled it and decided that since they'd never had a break-in and felt perfectly safe in the house, there was no need to replace it.'

James asked a few more questions and then told them that the Constabulary press office would soon be issuing a statement if they hadn't done so already.

'Once the news is out the media will try to speak to you,' he said. 'I'll arrange for a family liaison officer to be on hand to help you keep them at bay. Do you intend to stay here or return home?'

'We'll go home, but not until tomorrow,' Liam said.

James nodded. 'I think that's sensible. There's a lot going on in Kirkby Abbey right now and your fellow villagers are desperate to know what has happened.'

'So, they're still in the dark?'

'They should be. I wanted to break the news to you before word spread.'

James put his notebook in his pocket and got to his feet.

66

'We'll go now, but I'll see you again when you're back home so that I can update you on the investigation. There will also need to be a formal identification process.'

Liam nodded. 'It will give me a chance to say goodbye.'

James gave Liam his card. Before he and Foley left the house, he expressed his condolences again and reiterated his promise to bring the killer to justice.

CHAPTER FOURTEEN

On the way out of Shap, James got the driver to stop at a convenience store and he dashed inside to buy drinks and sandwiches for all three of them. It was the middle of the afternoon and they'd gone without lunch, so Foley and the driver were immensely grateful.

They tucked in during the drive back to Kirkby Abbey and between mouthfuls James told Foley what Liam had said to him while she was out of the room.

'He was open about falling out with his parents,' he said. 'He told me he tried to persuade them not to sell up and move abroad, but they weren't prepared to.'

'Then I reckon he'll be consumed with guilt,' Foley said.

James shrugged. 'Who knows? I assume he'll get to inherit the house and whatever savings they had since he doesn't have any siblings. It'll mean he'll be able to move in there or sell it and buy a place of his own.'

'Do you seriously think he's a credible suspect, guv? He looked genuinely upset to me.'

'It could have been an act, so we can't rule him out as a person of interest. As you know, financial gain is one of the most common motives for murder, especially when it involves family.'

'So how do we play it?'

James gave it some thought. 'We start by finding out how bad things actually were between Liam and his parents. Is it at all possible that he got so wound up with their intransigence that it became more than a simple domestic dispute and he snapped?'

'I suppose that would depend on how desperate he was to get his hands on their money,' Foley responded.

'Exactly. So, can I task you with looking into it? Firstly, arrange for a family liaison officer to contact him. Then see what you can find out about him. Does he have a criminal record? Is there a history of violence? Check his finances and dig out the details of Elizabeth and Nigel's will. Also, put a call in to his employers. I know he's a delivery driver, but I'm not sure who he works for.'

'We can put some of these questions to him tomorrow when he's back in the village.'

'We will. And if he says anything to set off alarm bells, we'll interview him under caution.'

'I think we should also have a word with his wife when he's not in the same room,' Foley said. 'I thought it was rather telling that she took the trouble to try to contact Elizabeth and Nigel on Christmas Day and then sent them a text with a baby picture when she couldn't get an answer.'

'That's a good point. I got the impression from what she said that she was fond of them. And I'd like to know if she also fell out with them or if she wasn't happy with the pressure her husband was putting on them. She may well have told him to forget about the house and the money and let them go off and enjoy a comfortable retirement.'

They were still talking about Liam when James received a call from his boss.

'I thought you should know that the Chief Constable is about to release a statement confirming that a married couple have been found dead at separate locations in Kirkby Abbey and a murder investigation has been launched,' Superintendent Tanner said. 'He will also name Nigel and Elizabeth as the victims and point out that they were both retired police officers.'

'Is it necessary to provide so many details this early on?' James asked him.

'He feels he has no choice. The rumour mill is spinning out of control and their identities are already circulating in the village apparently. I'm told the story is also circulating online and I know that the press office has taken calls from local and national media outlets.'

'It was inevitable, I suppose.'

'Do family members know yet?'

'I've just broken the news to their son, Liam. He's been spending Christmas with the in-laws in Shap. I'm not sure if we've managed to contact Elizabeth's brother yet, though.'

'Where are you off to now?'

'Back to Kirkby Abbey,' James said. 'We should be there in about twenty minutes.'

'Have you any updates for me?'

James relayed the conversation he'd had with Liam and mentioned that they'd learned that a house near the Booths' home was burgled, possibly on Christmas Eve.

'Plus, a man was also seen acting suspiciously in the garden of another house on that morning. We believe this would have been around the time the murders were committed. It means there's a chance, albeit a slim one, that the same guy then moved on to Maple Lane.'

'It's worth following up, for sure,' Tanner said. 'Keep in touch if anything else comes up.'

James hung up and returned to sipping his coffee and munching on his sandwich while discussing the case with his DC.

CHAPTER FIFTEEN
ANNIE

Annie was sitting on the sofa with her hands cupped around a mug of coffee. There was a dull thudding in her chest and her pulse was roaring in her ears.

She had never known a day like this. She'd stayed at home but her phone hadn't stopped ringing and after lunch two more of her friends had dropped by to see if she could confirm that a double murder had been committed in Maple Lane.

But it was clear that they already knew almost as much as she did. A rumour that Elizabeth and Nigel Booth were the victims had begun circulating and a police car had been seen outside the home of their son Liam and his wife.

That was the thing about living in such a close-knit community. Everyone knew, or wanted to know, everyone else's business. And when something bad happened it was virtually impossible to keep a lid on it.

Since Annie had been told about the killings, she'd found it hard to contain her emotions. There was a ball of sadness in her chest and it was weighing her down.

The kids had provided some distraction, but she felt guilty for not being able to embrace the Christmas spirit with them. Luckily Bella had kept herself busy with the TV and her tablet, and Theo had been content to crawl around the floor and nap for long periods in his cot.

Annie couldn't wait for James to come home, but she didn't think it would be any time soon.

Meanwhile, the questions were building up in her head. Was he making progress? Would it be an easy case to solve? Had Colleen and Liam been given the devastating news yet?

The more her mind wrestled with what had taken place, the harder it was to come to terms with it. And she felt sorry for James because Elizabeth had worked with him from the day that he joined the team in Kendal up to her retirement. He had often applauded her sense of humour and praised her work ethic. Annie had herself been struck by what a nice person she was. Warm and amiable, with a tough, no-nonsense approach to the job.

Her face kept pushing itself into Annie's thoughts and she didn't want to imagine how James must have felt when he saw Elizabeth lying dead on her kitchen floor.

It all served to remind her how fragile life was, especially coming at the end of a year when her own uncle Bill had died and James's sister Fiona had been diagnosed with breast cancer.

It seemed like only yesterday when they had moved here from London and she'd begun teaching at the village school. They'd managed to settle in quickly and she'd found it such a relief to be so far away from the crime-infested capital.

But then, less than two months into their new life, a serial killer went on the rampage in the village and it made her realise yet again that murderous monsters don't just confine themselves to large towns and cities.

'I'm hungry, Mummy.'

Bella's screechy voice wrenched Annie out of the pit of despair that she was slowly sinking into.

She turned to her daughter, who was sitting on the armchair, tablet on her lap, her eyes not moving from the small screen.

'I'll go and make you some dinner, sweetheart,' Annie said, getting to her feet.

She'd already decided to cook some chicken nuggets for Bella and when she got to the kitchen, she headed for the fridge. But just then the doorbell rang, so she changed direction and stepped into the hall.

When she opened the door, she was surprised to see her best friend, Janet Dyer, standing there.

'I wasn't expecting you,' she said.

'I know,' Janet replied. 'I've left the boys with my mum and I came here because the police have just confirmed on the news that it was indeed Elizabeth and Nigel who were murdered this morning.'

Janet lived with her twin sons only a short walk away and worked as a carer for elderly folk who lived in the village and the surrounding area. It wasn't often that Annie saw her looking so flustered.

'I didn't realise they'd gone public with it,' Annie said.

'Well, they have, and I need to talk to James about it, assuming he's here.'

'He isn't, but come in out of the cold and tell me what's so important.'

She steered her into the kitchen where Janet removed her anorak and planted herself on a chair at the table.

'So where are the kids?' Janet asked.

'Theo's asleep upstairs and Bella is playing on her tablet in the living room,' Annie said. 'And just so you know, James was called out as soon as they found the bodies this morning.'

Janet nodded and Annie sat down opposite her.

'So, come on,' Annie said. 'Get it off your chest. Why do you want to talk to him?'

Janet gave a little shrug. 'It's just that after I heard that it was Elizabeth and Nigel who'd been killed, I recalled something that I witnessed at the weekend. It was an incident right here in the village and I think the police should be told about it because it might well have something to do with what's happened. I was hoping to speak to James in person so I could tell him what I saw, but you can pass it on to him.'

Annie felt a flush of heat in her chest as she leaned forward, resting her elbows on the table.

'I'm listening, Janet,' she said. 'Tell me what it is that's got you so worked up.'

CHAPTER SIXTEEN

It was almost dark by the time the patrol car arrived back in Kirkby Abbey. By then James's eyes felt dry and heavy and his head was crowded with so many thoughts and questions.

First stop was Maple Lane, which was still a hive of activity. The crowd of onlookers across the street had grown and the lane itself was ablaze with various sources of forensic lighting.

James also noted the presence of a BBC News satellite truck and spotted a reporter doing a piece to camera on the pavement.

'I see the vultures have started to descend,' Foley remarked. 'I dread to think how many will be here by tomorrow morning. It'll be another bloody media circus.'

James didn't doubt that for a single second. This case was going to make headlines nationally as well as locally. For the news hounds there were so many enticing elements to it. The murder victims were not only a married couple, they were also former police officers. And the husband was dressed as Santa Claus when he was attacked. Plus, the murders had taken place on Christmas Eve in the same Cumbrian village where a serial killer had struck four years ago.

'Let's just hope that we can secure a quick result,' James said. 'The longer it goes on the more the pressure will build, and not just on us. Villagers will have to face the uncomfortable truth that the killer could be in their midst, and that's sure to lead to a rising sense of panic.'

James pushed the thought from his mind as he got out of the car and strode up the lane with Foley by his side.

The SOCOs were still searching for the murder weapon and other potential evidence around the spot where Nigel's body had been found.

DC Sharma was on hand to inform them that more uniforms had been drafted in to search the surrounding woods and to ensure that no individuals could gain unauthorised access to the lane or to the Booths' house.

'Dr Flint has finished up and the bodies are about to be transferred to the morgue,' Sharma said. 'I've also sent a team of officers to visit homes nearest to here to see if anyone saw anything on Christmas Eve. But I've already been told that quite a few are empty because the owners are either away for Christmas or they're second homes that are unoccupied for weeks or months at a time.'

'Have you heard back from the others?' James asked.

Sharma nodded. 'DS Abbott has spoken to the couple whose house was burgled while they were away and the woman who reported the guy lurking in a neighbour's garden. She's now checking on other nearby homes. Meanwhile, DI Stevens is at the village hall sorting things out.'

'In that case do me a favour, Ahmed, and get back in touch with them and with any other members of the team who are here. Have them meet me for a briefing in the village hall in, let's say … half an hour. And I want Tony there, too. Where is he?'

'Up at the house with Dr Flint.'

'Then I'll go and tell him myself. As soon as I'm back, you, me and Caroline will head to the village hall together.'

There was still a lot going on at the house, but the update from Tony Coppell wasn't very encouraging.

'We've carried out a thorough search of the house and garden, but we haven't come across the knife that's missing or any other objects that could have been used as a weapon,' he said. 'But my team won't be calling it a day for some time. There will be people working here through the night.'

'Can you come along to the village hall?' James asked. 'I'm staging an impromptu briefing there in half an hour.'

'Of course.'

'Do you need me there, too?' Dr Flint asked as she came out of the kitchen into the hall.

'Not unless you can tell us something that we don't already know,' James replied.

'No, I can't. And I'd rather stay here until the transfer of the bodies is complete.'

'No problem. Are you still hoping to carry out the PMs tomorrow? If so, I'll make sure that one of my team attends.'

'Indeed, I am. I'm so sorry I won't be able to fit them in today. And I'll get back to you with the results as soon as possible. I don't anticipate there will be any surprises, though.'

James was walking back along the lane when his phone beeped with an incoming text message. It was from Annie, saying she wanted him to call her. Fearing that something was wrong, he rang her straight away.

'Is everything all right?' he asked when she answered.

'All fine,' she said, much to his relief. 'Except that Janet has dropped by with some information that she wants me to pass on to you. She thinks it might have a bearing on your investigation.'

'In what way?'

'Well, she was in the King's Head last Saturday afternoon when she saw Nigel and Elizabeth involved in an altercation with another couple she didn't recognise. The couple were yelling and swearing at them, and she heard the guy accuse Nigel of being responsible for his son's death. She said their behaviour towards Nigel in particular was quite threatening. And the woman told Elizabeth that she should be ashamed of herself. Anyway, the owners, Luke and Martha, ordered them to leave and they had to be virtually pushed out of the door.'

'That's interesting,' James said. 'Is Janet still with you?'

'She's in the loo. Do you want me to put her on when she comes out?'

'I'd rather talk to her face-to-face. Can you ask her if she's able to go along to the village hall? I'm on my way there now to brief the team. We can take down the details and follow it up straight away. If she can't make it let me know.'

'It shouldn't be a problem. She lives just around the corner from the hall, after all.'

'Great.'

'And should I assume that you'll be home late?'

'You most definitely should. Give the kids a goodnight kiss from me and I'll be back as soon as I can.'

CHAPTER SEVENTEEN

The hall was just behind the village square and the brick façade was adorned with Christmas lights and decorations.

A patrol car was parked in front and two uniformed officers were standing outside the entrance. They were being bombarded with questions by about a dozen villagers grouped on the pavement.

As James walked towards the hall with Sharma and Foley, he immediately became the focus of the villagers' attention.

'Detective Walker, have you found out yet who killed Nigel and Elizabeth?' This from a woman who James knew as one of the teachers at the village school.

'The investigation is ongoing,' he said, as the group closed in around him. 'And I promise to keep everyone informed of the progress we make.'

'Is it true that they were both stabbed to death, Nigel in the lane and Elizabeth in their home?' asked a man named Frank, one of the local plumbers.

'I'm afraid I can't disclose details of the case at this stage, Frank,' James said. 'I'm sure you can understand.'

A short, elderly woman tapped his arm and said, 'But we need to know how worried we should be. Is the killer still in the village? Are we all in danger? And will it be safe for me to walk home from here?'

The questions came thick and fast and James tried to allay fears by telling the group that there was a strong police presence in and around the village, and there was no reason to believe that the killer would strike again. But he held back from saying that he believed the offender had left the village because that would have been an outright lie.

'More information on what has happened will be forthcoming,' he said to them as he stepped closer to the entrance. 'I do appreciate how shocked you all are after hearing that two of your friends and neighbours were the victims of such appalling criminal acts. But rest assured that we will do all we can to find out who was responsible. And please, if you have any information that you believe would be of help to us, then don't hesitate to come forward.

'We're in the process of setting up a temporary base here in the village hall and from tomorrow we aim to provide advice and information. But right now, my colleagues and I need to have an urgent discussion.'

The group parted to let him through and when he reached the entrance, he noticed a sign had been stuck to the door which read: 'POLICE NOTICE: TEMPORARILY CLOSED TO THE PUBLIC'. He recalled that the same sign had been put up when they took over the hall four years ago.

He told the uniformed officers that a Miss Janet Dyer was due to arrive shortly for a meeting with him.

'Please could one of you bring her straight inside?' he said. 'And if things get out of hand here then don't hesitate to call for backup.'

The hall normally hosted bingo sessions, boot fairs and quiz nights. But now it was occupied by a bunch of coppers investigating a double murder.

There was a small stage and plenty of tables and chairs. Doors led to a kitchen, a separate meeting room and the toilets.

In addition to Foley and Sharma, there was DI Stevens and DS Abbott, plus three uniforms.

James went and stood in front of the stage and just as he did so Tony Coppell made an entrance. He'd discarded his forensic suit and was now wrapped up in a long black overcoat.

'I think that's all of us so I'll get cracking,' James said.

He began by reminding them that this was the second time the hall had been used as a makeshift incident room.

'It will likely be disturbingly familiar to those of you who were here four years ago when we were chasing down a serial killer,' he said. 'We'll use this place when it's convenient to do so, but some activities will still have to be carried out back at headquarters, including interviews under caution.'

He felt it was also necessary to remind them that he himself lived here in the village and would therefore be a useful source of local information.

'But you don't need me to tell you how hard the villagers are taking it, and justifiably so,' he said. 'This case is personal to them and us, and so it's important that we maintain their confidence and keep them on side.'

He then started the ball rolling by telling them about the visit to Shap and that DC Foley would be looking into what they had learned.

'Caroline will find out what she can about Liam Booth and just how bad the fallout was with his parents. She'll look into his finances and check to see if he's on any of the databases. She'll also be talking to his employers and gaining access to his parents' will. He'll be back here tomorrow and we'll talk to him again.'

'What's your impression of the man, guv?' Abbott asked.

James shrugged. 'I've met him before and he always came across as pretty normal. And he appeared genuinely upset when we broke the news to him. But, as I said to Caroline, it could have been an act. His parents have probably left the house to him as he's an only child. So, it means he'll get his wish to jump onto the housing ladder and clear any debts he might have. And as we all know, people have murdered their friends and family members for a lot less.'

DI Stevens jumped in at this point to let it be known that he had just spoken to Elizabeth's lawyer brother, Darren Hanson.

'Officers with Lancaster Police broke the news to him a short time ago,' he said. 'But it was over the phone because he's been spending Christmas in France with friends. He wanted to speak to one of us and was put through to me.'

'How did he take it?'

'Badly. I didn't get to talk to him for long because he was going somewhere and wanted to sort out a flight back to the UK. He's hoping to be here tomorrow. But what he did tell me was revealing. He said that Elizabeth rang him in France on Christmas Eve morning to say that she hoped he'd enjoy his festive break. But during the conversation she told him she'd had another big row with Liam on Monday, and her son had told her he wasn't going to join her and Nigel for lunch on Christmas Day. She was really upset and Nigel was livid apparently. Unfortunately, Mr Hanson was in the car and the signal was bad so he couldn't say much more. I told him to contact me as soon as he's back in the UK.'

'Liam did tell us that he spoke to his mum on Monday, but

he didn't say that they argued, and that reinforces my belief that he should be considered a person of interest for the time being.'

James asked DS Abbott to tell them about the burglary that took place over Christmas while the homeowners were away. But as she began reading from her notes the briefing was interrupted by the arrival of Janet Dyer. She entered the hall accompanied by one of the uniforms who'd been stationed outside.

James told the team that the meeting was being put on hold while he carried out a brief interview with a villager who had some potentially useful information to impart.

CHAPTER EIGHTEEN

James knew Janet Dyer pretty well given her closeness with Annie.

He'd last seen her on Christmas Eve when she'd popped round with her sons and they'd exchanged gifts and cards. She was someone he liked and respected, and she had been a good friend to Annie. She'd also supported his wife when she'd struggled to cope with the pressure that his job all too often placed on her.

He thanked her for coming, then got her to join him and DC Foley in the small meeting room. When they were seated around one of the tables, she said, 'I'm sorry it took me so long to get here. I had to go home on the way from your house to let my mum know what was happening. She's looking after the twins.'

'That's not a problem,' James said. 'Annie told me what you saw and heard in the King's Head on Saturday, but it's important that I hear it from you. So, can you start at the beginning? Detective Foley will be making notes.'

Janet shifted uneasily on her chair and her eyes misted over suddenly.

'This is really difficult for me because it was the last time that I saw Nigel and Elizabeth,' she said. 'I had some free time on Saturday afternoon because my ex had the boys. So, I went to the King's Head for drinks with Mum, who had come here that day to spend Christmas with us. We were joined by Tina, who's a fellow carer.

'Nigel and Elizabeth arrived shortly after we did and sat down at the other end of the saloon bar. We said hello to each other and then about half an hour later this couple came into the pub. I was facing the door so I watched them look around and as soon as they spotted Nigel and Elizabeth they went straight to their table and started yelling at them.'

'And you have no idea who they are?'

She shook her head. 'I'd never seen them before. My guess is they were in their late forties or fifties. They were both wearing heavy outdoor coats and the man had a beard.'

'So, what followed?'

'Well, I heard the man accuse Nigel of being responsible for his son's death. And he called him a piece of police scum. Then the woman, who might or might not have been his wife, jabbed a finger at Elizabeth's face and said that she was no different and ought to be ashamed of herself.

'I watched as Nigel jumped to his feet and told them both to calm down, but the man then took a step towards him and said that he intended to make him pay for what he'd done. Then he lowered his voice and some things were said that I didn't hear.

'That was when Luke Grooms and his barman Ted rushed over and told the couple to leave the pub. They were having none of it and pushed them towards the door and outside.'

'What happened next?' James asked.

'Well, I was one of several people who got up and went over

to their table to see if the Booths were all right. They said they were, but it was obvious that they were shocked and shaken. Luke asked them if he should call the police, but Nigel said no. He told Luke that he knew the couple and that it was just a stupid misunderstanding. But he didn't hang around to elaborate. Instead, he took his wife's hand and they made a speedy exit from the pub.'

'Did you see the other couple again?'

'No. I can only assume they walked away, but I'm pretty sure they don't live here in the village. So, they probably had a car parked nearby.'

James felt his pulse escalate and turned to Foley. 'We'll finish up with the briefing and go straight to the King's Head. I know they've got security cameras there so hopefully the incident will have been recorded. Identifying this couple is a priority.'

He thanked Janet again and told her that at some point she might be expected to make a formal statement.

'I'll be happy to,' she replied. 'But do you think this couple, whoever they are, could have carried out the murders?'

James blew out a breath between clenched teeth. 'We won't know for sure until we've talked to them. But it's clear they had a score to settle with Nigel and Elizabeth. We need to find out what it was over.'

CHAPTER NINETEEN

It was just after 5 p.m. when the briefing resumed in the hall, some seven hours since Nigel's body had been found in Maple Lane.

In that time, several potential lines of enquiry had emerged, so at least they were making some progress. But as far as James was concerned it wasn't enough. They needed to move more quickly and come up with more leads before they were put under severe pressure from above.

He told the team what Janet had witnessed and said that whoever was checking CCTV cameras should look out for the mystery couple.

'I'll go along to the King's Head with Caroline from here and if there's security camera footage of them, we'll get an image circulated,' he said. 'But look, the guy was heard accusing Nigel of being responsible for their son's death. That's pretty serious. So, let's trawl through the system for recent deaths that could in any way be linked to Nigel. It's a long shot, I know, but worth a try.'

He then went back to the point where he had cut short the briefing in order to interview Janet.

'You were going to tell us about the couple who discovered this morning that their house had been broken into,' he said to Abbott.

The DS consulted her notes. 'The house is on Driscoll Street, which is only a few hundred yards from the entrance to Maple Lane,' she said. 'A Mr and Mrs Tyler live there. They went to Blackpool the day before Christmas Eve and left the house empty. But they returned to find a back window had been broken and forced open. And the place had been ransacked. It was all small stuff that was taken, mostly cash and jewellery. I've got a list. We can't be sure if it took place on Christmas Eve or yesterday, though. Or even last night.'

'Can we get forensics along there?' James asked, feeling frustrated at not having more information.

Abbott nodded. 'I've sorted it, guv.'

'Good. Now what about the woman who saw someone in a neighbour's garden?'

'Her name is Tricia Jones. She lives in Oak Lane, which is next to Driscoll Street. At about ten in the morning on Christmas Eve she spotted a guy acting suspiciously in the house next door's back garden. She knew it was unoccupied so she went outside when she saw the bloke peering through the kitchen window. When she called out to him, he looked at her briefly and then hurried out of the garden onto the path at the back.'

'Did she give you a description?'

'Only that he was of average height and wearing a hooded jacket. She was too far away to see his face, except that she's sure he was white.'

James nodded. 'So, it could be that he was the same person

who broke into the house in Driscoll Street. If he was, then who's to say that he didn't head up to Maple Lane from there?'

'I've got uniforms checking other nearby houses to see if anyone else saw him,' Abbott said. 'And homes that look empty will be checked over for signs of a break-in.'

James stroked the stubble on his chin and turned to Coppell.

'So, what's the situation with forensics, Tony?' he asked.

Coppell shrugged. 'My lot are doing all they can to secure and preserve potential evidence at both crime scenes. But so far there's very little of it. I've assigned a crew to work through the night and what we've already bagged up will be analysed thoroughly back at the lab.

'The scene on the lane is naturally proving the most challenging because of the contamination and damage caused by the snow. And we're having to move fast because the forecast is for more snow tonight.'

That wasn't what James wanted to hear. He made a thoughtful noise in his throat and stole a look at his watch.

'At this point we have four persons of interest,' he said. 'Liam Booth, the couple who confronted our victims in the pub days before the murders, and the hooded bloke spotted in the garden on Oak Lane on Christmas Eve. It's not that bad a start.'

Which was true, but he still felt they ought to be doing better, given the amount of publicity the case was already attracting.

He then asked Stevens to speak to headquarters and arrange for a team to work the night shift.

'DCs Hall and Isaac are already on their way here, guv,' Stevens told him. 'And plenty of uniforms will be on duty. Plus, a couple of civilian staff are coming down to set up the base here. That won't take long though.'

James nodded. 'Sounds good. I reckon that for now we work

on the presumption that Nigel and Elizabeth knew who attacked them. It would help to establish a sequence of events. If, as we suspect, the bread knife missing from the kitchen was indeed the murder weapon in both cases, then that would suggest that Elizabeth was killed first. The killer may then have fled the house with the knife and bumped into Nigel on the lane as he returned from the Santa parade. It could be that the killer expected them both to be out when they turned up there. Of course, it's nothing more than a working hypothesis at this stage, but at least it's something we can press ahead with.

'We'll go to the King's Head now, and come straight back here after we've spoken to the owners and checked the security cameras,' he said. 'Then we'll decide what needs to be done before we call it a day. So, stay put and use your phones to make any urgent checks and enquiries.'

CHAPTER TWENTY

James and DC Foley faced an even larger group of villagers when they stepped outside the hall.

More questions were fired at them and one woman broke down in tears after telling them that Elizabeth Booth had been a close friend.

James felt obliged to respond and said, 'Elizabeth was my friend, too, as well as being a colleague. So, I completely understand how you feel. Everyone in the Cumbria Constabulary is deeply shocked, and we're not going to rest until the killer is brought to justice.'

'How do you know that there's only one killer?' someone behind him called out.

James turned, but he wasn't sure who had asked the question.

'We're not positive, but it's what we believe,' he said. 'The investigation has only just begun and right now there are many aspects of the case we can't be sure of. However, we will be keeping you all posted as things progress. But right now, we need to leave here to follow up a line of inquiry. So, I'm sorry that I'm not able to answer more of your questions.'

No one complained as he and Foley stepped off the pavement and hurried across the road.

'We'd better brace ourselves for a similar reception at the pub,' Foley said. 'I'm sure there will be quite a few people there.'

'That's true,' James responded. 'I hadn't thought of that.'

'Well, we might as well seize it as an opportunity then. While you speak to the owners and view the security camera footage, I'll ask customers if they were around on Christmas Eve and saw anything suspicious, such as a guy in a hood or an angry-looking couple.'

'That's a good idea, Caroline. And see if any of them saw or maybe spoke to Nigel and Elizabeth on that day.'

As they traversed the village square, James was reminded that it was there on Christmas Eve that he last saw Nigel. It had been quite crowded, and everyone was in a jubilant mood. Now it was empty, and the festive spirit had evaporated despite the decorations and bright flashing lights on the tall Christmas tree.

By contrast, the King's Head was quite busy and when they walked through the door conversations were halted.

He was a regular there himself and knew most of those present, so several of them didn't hesitate to approach him to ask what was going on.

He decided that it'd be easier to address them all at once so he raised his voice and explained that he and his colleague were going through the village asking people when they last saw Nigel and Elizabeth.

'Detective Constable Foley will speak to you while I chat to Luke and Martha,' he said. 'But please do appreciate that we're restricted in what we can say about the investigation that's been launched into the murders.'

Luke and Martha were both behind the bar and Luke signalled for James to head towards the door marked 'staff.'

As he did so it struck him how sombre the atmosphere was. the King's Head was the liveliest of the two pubs in the village, partly because it rented out rooms so there were always new faces, and it was James's favourite. There was an open fire, a low, oak-beamed ceiling, and soft leather sofas. And it was usually very noisy. But not now.

As he approached the staff door, he looked up at the security camera above it and hoped that it had been recording last Saturday.

Luke and Martha greeted him warmly. They were a popular couple in their sixties and were always very friendly.

Luke was heavy set with broad-shoulders and a shiny bald head. His wife was a large woman with wrinkles carved into a face framed by shapeless grey hair.

She spoke first, in that deep, crusty voice of hers.

'It's impossible for me to imagine how hard this must be for you, James,' she said. 'I know that you and Elizabeth were very fond of each other. She once told me how glad she was that you'd come up from London. She said you'd brought some much-needed experience to the team in Kendal.'

'She was a lovely lady and a good police officer,' James said. 'And Nigel was a great character too, although I didn't know him that well because we never worked together.'

'Have you any idea who did it to them?' Luke asked.

'Not yet, but it's early days.'

'So, how can we help?'

'Janet Dyer has told me about an incident that took place here last Saturday,' James said. 'Nigel and Elizabeth were having drinks when they were approached by a couple who said some nasty things to them.'

94

Luke nodded. 'That's right. I'd forgotten all about that. It was horrible, a clear case of harassment. Ted and I shoved them out as quickly as we could. I wanted to call the police and report them, but Nigel said there was no need.'

'Well look, I know you have cameras here so I'm hoping it was recorded.'

The couple exchanged looks and Luke nodded again. 'It must have been. And nothing gets wiped for at least two months.'

'Are those two suspects then?' Martha said. 'I suppose they could be given the way they behaved.'

'Janet told me she didn't recognise them. Did you?'

They both shook their heads. 'Never seen them before,' Luke said.

'Then perhaps they came here that day with the sole purpose of confronting the Booths,' James said. 'Which is why I need to see the footage. Can you show me?'

The pub's two internal cameras were linked to a computer in the small office behind the kitchen. It was a straightforward set-up and it took Luke just minutes to rewind the recorded footage from Saturday.

'The camera isn't fitted with a microphone because they're more trouble than they're worth from a data protection perspective,' Luke explained.

The table occupied by Nigel and Elizabeth was at the furthest point away from the camera and James thought it unlikely that their conversation would have been picked up anyway. However, the picture quality wasn't bad and he watched Nigel and Elizabeth sharing a bottle of white wine and chatting to each other with smiles on their faces.

And then the mystery couple entered the pub and James felt

his breathing stall. The middle-aged pair were bundled up in bulky coats and James got Luke to pause the footage and zoom in so that he could get a good look at their faces.

The man was of average height with a beard and swept back dark hair. The woman was wearing a black bobble hat and had a narrow face with sharp features.

James was sure he hadn't seen them before. He took a photo of the screen with his phone and asked Luke to continue playing the clip.

Then he saw the couple stride towards Nigel and Elizabeth's table and the man started pointing and yelling at them.

They had their backs to the camera at this point and so their faces weren't visible.

'How much did you hear of what they were saying?' James asked.

It was Martha who responded. 'I was closest and it was the man who was the most vocal. He said Nigel was to blame for his son's death and promised to make him pay in some way. And he called him police scum. He didn't seem to care that other people were listening. When Nigel got to his feet and squared up to him, his voice dropped, but he kept on talking. I couldn't hear what he was saying after that.'

'What did the woman say?'

'Not as much, but she did tell Elizabeth that she should be ashamed of herself.'

James nodded. What he was hearing tallied with what Janet had told him.

On the screen, Luke and his barman Ted Fuller were seen rushing towards the table where they stepped between the couples. Luke grabbed the man's arm and pointed towards the door.

'I couldn't let it carry on,' he said. 'They were out of order and I feared a fight would break out. So, I told the couple to fuck off or I'd call the police. I nudged the guy towards the door and expected him to have a go at me, but he just shut up and signalled for the woman to follow him out.'

As Luke spoke, James watched the pair do just that, and after they'd gone Nigel sat back down and put an arm around his wife, who was clearly upset.

Janet Dyer and several other customers appeared on screen then and started speaking to them. Luke joined them and Nigel could be seen shaking his head. Minutes later Nigel and Elizabeth got up and exited the pub.

'Nigel insisted that there was no need to call the police, so I didn't,' Luke said. 'I wish now that I had. It was all so confusing because neither he nor Elizabeth would tell us what it had all been about.'

James asked Luke if he could send the clip to him or make a copy. Luke obliged by producing a USB stick from the desk drawer and plugging it into the computer.

'You can take it with you, once it's copied,' he said.

James thanked him and explained that they would circulate an image of the couple in a bid to identify them.

'That will be step one,' he said. 'Step two will be to find out what the hell the guy meant when he said he'd make Nigel pay for what he did.'

CHAPTER TWENTY-ONE

Back in the bar, Foley was sitting at a table with a man James recognised. He was a local car mechanic named Chris Quentin and Foley had just learned that he was one of those who had taken part in the Santa Claus parade with Nigel on Christmas Eve.

As James sat down with them, Foley said, 'Chris says Nigel was a bit subdued that day and when the parade ended, he didn't hang around for the carol singing.'

Chris picked it up then, saying, 'I asked him if he wanted to go for a drink with me and some of the other guys. But he told me he was going home to Elizabeth because she was preparing some lunch for him, and they were hoping to go out later.'

'Did you see him leave the square?' James asked.

He shook his head. 'He disappeared into the crowd. It must have been almost noon by then.'

Chris rolled out his bottom lip and rubbed a knuckle under his nose. 'This is all so fucking horrible, Detective Walker. I really liked Nigel. I've seen quite a lot of him since he retired from the police. He was sociable and funny and we're all going to miss him and his wife.'

James was fully aware that it was a sentiment shared by all those in the village who had known them. And it made him all the more determined to catch the Booths' killer.

He took out his phone and showed Chris the photo he'd taken of the couple on the security footage.

'Do you happen to recognise these two?' he asked.

Chris squinted as he stared at the screen. 'I've never seen them before. Have they got something to do with it?'

James shrugged. 'We don't know yet.'

He then got up and walked around the bar, showing the photo to the other customers. But none of them recognised the couple.

Before leaving the pub, James attached the photo to an email and sent it to headquarters. He tapped out a message saying they were persons of interest in the double murder in Kirkby Abbey and he wanted the image circulated to all stations in the county. He was hoping that with any luck someone would recognise them.

It had begun to snow outside and the temperature had dropped noticeably. It was undoubtedly a factor in why there was no longer a crowd in front of the village hall when James and Foley returned there.

Inside, the team of detectives had grown and now included DCs Dawn Isaac and Kevin Hall, who would be on duty throughout the night.

James briefed everyone on what he had learned at the King's Head and showed them the image from the CCTV. But again, no one recognised the couple.

'It should already be in circulation,' James said. 'So hopefully we'll know who they are soon enough. But the threat the guy made to Nigel has to be taken seriously. We need to establish why he believed that Nigel was responsible for the death of his son.'

DI Stevens lived in Kendal and would be heading back there soon, so James asked him to hand the USB stick over to the technical team.

'I'd also like you to attend the post-mortems, which are due to take place in the morning,' he said.

They continued to discuss the case and what investigative routes to go down. James assigned more tasks and had to break away twice to take calls.

The first was from Superintendent Tanner, who wanted an update. The second was from Gordon Carver, a reporter with the *Cumbria Gazette* who wanted to know if James could add to the information that he was getting from the Constabulary press office.

Carver was the only journalist who had James's number. He'd given it to him because he'd proved helpful during previous investigations.

'All I can say, Gordon, is that at this stage we don't have a lot to go on. So, there's not much that I can tell you. But this is a very distressing case and you can quote me as saying that we're pulling out all the stops to solve it. We're already following up several leads, but I can't share the details at this stage.'

'Are there any firm suspects?' Carver asked.

'Not yet. But as soon as there's a development, you'll be among the first to know.'

It was clear that Carver wanted to prolong the conversation, but James said he had things to do and abruptly ended it.

That was when he looked at his watch and saw that it was ten o'clock already.

'Time to call a halt to the meeting,' he said. 'I want those of you who've been on all day to go straight home so that you're fresh and ready to go in the morning. And don't go to headquarters. Be here by eight o'clock. We'll decide then how the day should pan out. It'll depend, of course, on whether anything develops overnight.'

CHAPTER TWENTY-TWO
ANNIE

It was after ten o'clock and tiredness was tugging at Annie's bones, but she wasn't yet ready to go to bed.

Too many thoughts were swimming through her head and she knew that she'd find it hard to sleep.

She wanted to be up and awake when James arrived home because she was desperate to know if he and his team were closing in on the killer.

Throughout the afternoon and evening she'd struggled to process what she had seen and heard. Two more friends had phoned her to ask if she had information on the murders that wasn't yet in the public domain.

And the story had dominated the TV news bulletins, including the one she had just tuned into. It was on the BBC and Annie's heart lurched as she listened to what the presenter had to say.

'We return now to our main story – the murders of a married couple in a quiet Cumbrian village.

'Nigel and Elizabeth Booth were both retired police officers and their bodies were discovered this morning. Mrs Booth had been stabbed to death in her home and her husband, who also suffered stab wounds, was found in bushes next to the lane leading to their secluded property. He was wearing a Santa Claus suit because he had just taken part in a festive parade.

'Police believe they were killed on Christmas Eve, but they're baffled as to the motive behind the murders, which have shocked the small village of Kirkby Abbey.

'We can go live there now to our reporter Dan Goodison.'

The reporter was standing across the road from the entrance to Maple Lane. He described how it was closed off as police searched for evidence while a small group of villagers looked on.

Then he mentioned the Booths and Annie's eyeballs tingled when a photo of the couple appeared on the screen. It prompted her to think about Liam and Colleen, and she wondered for the umpteenth time that day how they were handling the news.

The reporter went on to say that Detective Chief Inspector James Walker was the senior investigating officer on the case.

'Detective Walker was also in charge of the investigation four years ago into a series of murders that took place in the same village. He and his team, who are based in the market town of Kendal, have been here since this morning and I've been told that a number of officers will remain throughout the night.'

There followed short clips of interviews with villagers.

Several described the Booths as solid, well-loved members of the community who were going to be sorely missed. Others expressed their concerns that the killer might be someone who resided in the village.

Annie was so absorbed in what was on the TV that she didn't hear the front door open along the hall. So, when James walked into the living room, she was taken completely by surprise.

'Flipping hell, you gave me a scare,' she said, as she shot to her feet.

'I'm sorry, love,' James said. 'I didn't think you'd still be awake.'

'I wanted to wait up for you. And with all that's going on I knew I wouldn't be able to sleep anyway.'

As she stepped towards him, she saw how tired he looked. His face was pallid and drawn, and there were shadows beneath his eyes. She also noticed the snowflakes coating his hair and shoulders.

'I didn't realise it had started snowing again,' she said. 'I haven't looked out of the window since putting the kids to bed.'

They gave each other a hug and Annie offered to make him something to eat and drink.

'Just a cup of tea to warm me up and some biscuits,' he said. 'It'll give us a chance to have a brief chat. And then it'll be off to bed because I'm bloody knackered and I have an early start in the morning.'

But it wasn't a quick chat and James didn't stick to a cup of tea. They talked for almost an hour and he poured himself two neat whiskies in that time. Annie could tell that he needed them to help him unwind.

It was a long time since she had seen him looking so stressed. The case was already having an impact on him and that concerned her. Usually, he was able to remain detached, but it was clear that this investigation was already starting to get inside his head and fill it with angst.

There were times when he followed protocol and refrained from sharing with her details of a case he was working on. But this wasn't one of them because he knew how much she'd want to know what was going on, and he also needed to ask her some questions.

Was she aware of the rift between Liam and his parents over their plan to sell up and move abroad?

No, she wasn't.

Had Colleen ever mentioned to her that they were desperate to get onto the property ladder?

No, she hadn't.

And had Colleen ever given any indication that her husband had a short temper and a violent streak?

No, she hadn't.

But Annie had to remind him that she wasn't close to the woman and usually only chatted with her at the mother and toddler club.

He told her about his conversation with Janet and what had been captured on CCTV at the King's Head. And he described how Liam and Colleen had reacted when they were given the news.

'My heart is breaking for them,' Annie said as tears pressed against her eyelids. 'I just can't get my head around what's happened, and I don't suppose I ever will.'

When they eventually crawled into bed, they both struggled to go to sleep. Annie was glad that James dropped off first, and when he started snoring, she put an arm around him and rested her head against his shoulder.

CHAPTER TWENTY-THREE

James had set the alarm for seven in the morning, but he awoke at six to discover that Annie was already up.

Before slipping on his dressing gown, he checked his phone and was relieved to see that he hadn't received any messages during the night.

Then he went downstairs to the kitchen where he found Annie sitting at the table drinking coffee.

'How long have you been up?' he asked her.

'About half an hour. I heard Theo crying so I went to settle him down and decided there was no point going back to bed.'

'Then I suppose we both had a bad night.'

She nodded. 'I just couldn't stop thinking about what's happened. It's worse than any nightmare I've ever had.'

He crossed the room and kissed her forehead. 'I know exactly what you mean.'

'There's water in the kettle,' she said. 'I'll make you some breakfast before you go out.'

He poured himself a coffee and sat down next to her. She pushed the TV remote control across the table towards him.

'I expect you'll want to see the news,' she said. 'I didn't turn it on in case I disturbed you.'

The rolling news channels were still leading with the murders even though there hadn't been any major developments overnight. They'd gathered more background information on the victims and spoken to many more villagers.

Sky News had used a drone camera to secure aerial footage of Maple Lane and the Booths' house. Although it was dark there was plenty to see thanks to all the lighting generated by police vehicles and scene of crime teams.

The Chief Constable had issued a statement saying how the murders of the two former officers had devastated the Constabulary. And the constituency MP, who had known both Nigel and Elizabeth personally, paid tribute to them.

A parish councillor who was interviewed let it be known that villagers were already organising a candlelit vigil in honour of the couple, which would take place at five that very evening.

'I'd like to go along to that,' Annie said. 'I'll try to get someone to take care of the kids. If I can't, I'll take them with me.'

It came as no surprise to James that a vigil was going to be held so soon given the tsunami of shock and grief that had overwhelmed the community.

He'd have to ensure that his officers were there and also go along himself to pay his own respects. And there was always the outside chance that he'd see or hear something that would assist the investigation.

'I'd better get showered,' he said. 'I'll head to the village hall first. I'm not sure if I'll be going to headquarters today.'

'So do you want a full English or something else for breakfast?' Annie asked him.

He stood up and gave her another kiss. 'I actually fancy a bacon sandwich. Toasted. Is that okay?'

'It'll be ready and waiting when you come back down.'

Before he stepped in the shower, he looked out of the bedroom window and noted that it was no longer snowing, although quite a bit had fallen during the night.

When he checked the weather forecast on his phone, he was pleased to see that the day ahead was going to be calm, cold and dry.

Once he was showered and dressed, he called headquarters to tell them that he would soon be on his way to the village hall. And he instructed the support officer who answered to let all members of his team know that he'd be setting up an online video briefing from there.

Bella and Theo were still asleep in their rooms so he didn't pop his head in for fear of waking them. But he couldn't help feeling guilty because he and Annie had planned to round off the Christmas break with a visit to a festive kids' fair being staged in Kendal.

When he was back downstairs, Annie told him there was no way she was taking them by herself.

'It'll be another stay-at-home day for us,' she said as she placed his bacon sandwich on the table in front of him.

As he stepped out of the house after eating it, the first decision he made was to leave the car on the driveway and walk to the village hall. It would only take him a few minutes to get there and the exercise would help him to get his thoughts together.

It was almost twenty-four hours since Stewart Farrell had

stumbled upon Nigel Booth's body in the lane and still no one had been arrested. That would no doubt be of concern to the Constabulary's top brass. As with all high-profile cases they were desperate for it to be wrapped up quickly, especially because the longer it went on the less likely it was that there would be a favourable outcome. The next twenty-four hours were going to be crucial and so his team needed to make the right decisions and come up with an effective strategy for taking things forward.

It was still dark as he strode through the narrow streets of Kirkby Abbey and his breath escaped in thick vapour clouds.

There were a few people about and he spotted four uniformed officers on foot and a patrol car driving around. It made him wonder how they'd be able to maintain such a heavy presence in the village if the investigation dragged on for days or even weeks.

By now it was common knowledge that the police were using the hall as a base, so he wasn't at all surprised to see a news satellite truck outside when he got there.

A reporter was on the pavement speaking into a camera, no doubt providing a live update for his channel's early morning viewers.

James breathed a sigh of relief when he managed to slip into the building unnoticed. And when he entered the hall itself, he was taken aback.

There were at least a dozen people present – including detectives, uniforms and civilian support staff. Tables were being used as desks with TVs and laptops on them, and an evidence board had been set up on a stand. Photos of Nigel and Elizabeth had already been pinned to it, along with pictures of the crime scenes with their bodies in situ.

'It didn't take us as long as we thought it would to get everything in place,' DC Isaac said as she approached him.

James smiled at her. 'You've made a good job of it.'

'Thanks, boss. Headquarters just got in touch to tell us that you're planning to hold a briefing soon.'

'That's right.'

'Well, before we get started, we can update you on a few things.'

'Good. And as soon as you've done that, I want you and DC Hall to go home and get some sleep. You've had a long night and I expect that you'll need to come back here this evening.'

CHAPTER TWENTY-FOUR

James scheduled the briefing for 8 a.m., by which time Detectives Abbott, Sharma and Foley would hopefully be at the hall. Other team members, including DI Stevens, would join via video link.

But first he sat down with Isaac and Hall, who both looked extremely tired. There was only so much they'd been able to do during the night, but they were nevertheless kept busy.

'We spent some of the time going door-to-door with uniform,' Isaac said. 'But not much came of it. I can tell you, though, that there are a lot of nervous people in the village. Several were even reluctant to open their doors to us. What's happened has really got them worried.'

'I don't suppose that will change until we collar whoever carried out the murders,' James said.

DC Hall then explained that he had spoken to the family liaison officer who had been assigned to Liam and Colleen.

'She visited them in Shap and spoke to them for about an hour,' he said. 'They plan to return to their home here in the village between nine and ten this morning. The coroner's office has informed us that a formal identification of the bodies can take place this afternoon after the post-mortems have been carried out. We can arrange for Liam to get a lift there. And I know that you've already asked DI Stevens to attend on your behalf, guv.'

Then it was back to Isaac who said that SOCOs were still at work in Maple Lane, but the murder weapon had still not been recovered.

'However, they have found a copy of Nigel and Elizabeth's will at the house,' she said. 'As we suspected, they've left everything to their son. The house, the car, all their belongings, plus their savings. Someone up at HQ gained access to their joint bank account and there's a total of forty thousand pounds in it. They also took out a funeral insurance package several years ago, so Liam won't have to pay for those.'

'Any idea how much the house is worth?' James asked.

Isaac nodded. 'It was easy to check. The estate agent is local and it's on the company website. The place is on the market for eight hundred thousand.'

James whistled through his teeth. 'That's a fair amount.'

'It certainly is. And it means that Liam and his family will now be comfortably well off.'

'Indeed, it does,' James said. 'But as tempting as it is, we shouldn't jump to the conclusion that he murdered his parents in order to claim it.'

At just after eight o'clock, when the briefing got underway, James's brain was already aching with the effort of thinking.

He began by passing on what Isaac and Hall had told him regarding the contents of Elizabeth and Nigel's will, the value of their house, and the amount of money in their bank account.

This prompted several of the team to express the views that Liam Booth should be elevated to a prime suspect from a person of interest.

DC Foley followed this by saying that she had run some checks and could confirm that Liam did not have a criminal record and there was nothing in the public domain to indicate a history of violence.

'One thing we need to establish is how bad things were between him and his parents,' James said. 'I'm hoping Elizabeth's brother can shed some light on that when he arrives from France later today. He's already told DI Stevens that Elizabeth revealed to him that she had a big row with Liam on Monday and that was when he decided not to join his parents on Christmas Day.'

James moved on to the couple who confronted the Booths in the King's Head on Saturday.

After that it was DS Abbott's turn to inform the team that there had been no developments in the case of the burglary that took place at some point over Christmas on Driscoll Street.

'But we do know that on Christmas Eve a woman in nearby Oak Lane reported seeing a man wearing a hood in her neighbour's back garden,' she said. 'The house was empty and so he aroused her suspicion. When she called out to him, he hurried off. At the moment there's no evidence to link those incidents to the murders, but it has to be a serious consideration.'

Over the next half an hour the team discussed various other potential lines of inquiry and listed questions that they needed to find the answers to.

Was Elizabeth the first to be murdered by someone she allowed into her home?

Was that person a friend or acquaintance, or a complete stranger?

Was the missing bread knife used as the murder weapon?

Did the killer flee the scene after stabbing Elizabeth and then encounter Nigel in the lane?

Or was that not how events unfolded?

'Various factors are going to make this case particularly challenging,' James said. 'There's the lack of forensic evidence, the fact that there are two crime scenes, and the pressure we're going to be under from deeply concerned villagers who fear that this might be the start of another killing spree in Kirkby Abbey.'

He went on to assign more tasks to individual officers and began to pull together a plan for the day ahead.

It was coming up to nine o'clock when a member of the digital forensics team joined the meeting from Kendal. She announced that the mobile phones taken from the Booths' home had been unlocked and the data extracted.

'The phones belonged to Mr and Mrs Booth and we've accessed a number of recent WhatsApp exchanges between them and their son, Liam,' she said. 'I wanted to bring the last exchange to your attention immediately because some of the content is quite disturbing. I've copied it onto a document that I'm about to circulate. Plus, I've added several messages from Liam's wife to her parents-in-law.'

James called a temporary halt to proceedings and they all waited with bated breath for the document to come through.

CHAPTER TWENTY-FIVE

The document was attached to a group email and it stretched to three pages. The digital forensics team had provided a log of phone calls from the past two months between Liam and each of his parents.

The last one, from him to his mother, was on Monday, the day before Christmas Eve, and it had lasted four minutes.

But it was the WhatsApp exchange which took place an hour later that raised eyebrows within the team. It was on a chat group entitled FAMILY in which Liam, Nigel and Elizabeth were the only members.

Liam: *I want you to know that I won't change my mind about Christmas Day. We're not coming over and I don't want you to come here. Instead, we're going to Colleen's parents. Unlike you, they give a toss about us and would help us out if they could afford to.*

Nigel: *Don't be so nasty, son. We've done a lot for you. We don't have a money tree in the garden and it's not our fault that you've squandered what we've given you.*

Liam: *Bollocks. If you cared about us, you wouldn't keep spending my inheritance on holidays abroad. And now you're planning to fuck off to Spain to live a life of luxury while I struggle to keep a roof over our heads. You should both be ashamed of yourselves.*

Nigel: *But you know that it's always been a dream of ours to move to sunnier climes after we retired. Don't you think we deserve it?*

Liam: *As far as I'm concerned, you're a pair of selfish shits who deserve to rot in hell.*

Elizabeth: *Liam, please stop. You're upsetting us again. We've been over this so many times and it's got to the point where we can't talk to you anymore.*

Liam: *Well don't worry because we won't be having any more conversations and I'm going to make sure that you never see your granddaughter again.*

The exchange ended there and the digital forensics team noted that Liam immediately took himself out of the WhatsApp group. After that Liam didn't call either of his parents again and they didn't try to call him.

However, there was a message sent from his wife to her parents-in-law on Christmas Day. Colleen wasn't part of the family chat group so had contacted them without sharing the message with her husband.

> **Colleen:** *Hi Nigel/Elizabeth. I'm so very sorry that we're not with you today. I know that he lost his temper with you and said some horrible things. I've told him he shouldn't have, but he'd been drinking again and worked himself up. Please find it in your hearts to forgive him. Meanwhile, merry Christmas from me. And here's a picture of Rosie after she woke this morning. I hope it cheers you up xxx*

The attached photo showed seven-month-old Rosie lying on a carpet clutching a small, cuddly teddy bear.

Neither Nigel nor Elizabeth had responded to the message. Unsurprising, given that the evidence suggested they were both dead when it landed on their phones.

The document offered James a graphic insight into relations between Liam Booth and his parents. That last WhatsApp exchange was a real eye-opener, but several other exchanges posted before then were also listed. In each one Liam aimed abusive remarks at his parents and they responded by trying to placate him.

It provided confirmation that he had developed a serious grudge against them over their determination to use all the money from the sale of their house to fund their move to Spain. And it appeared that his drinking may well have helped fuel the fire that burned in his head.

'This is a significant development,' James said when the briefing resumed. 'It certainly shines a new and unpleasant light on Liam Booth. The language he used in that final exchange is indeed disturbing and we need to confront him about it.'

James consulted his watch and saw that it was almost nine already.

'Caroline, you'll be going with me to interview Liam. I need you to check with the FLO to see if he's back home yet,' he said. 'If so, we'll head straight to his house.'

His phone chose that moment to start buzzing. When he saw that the caller was Superintendent Tanner, he said, 'Discuss it between yourselves while I talk to the boss. I think he may well be on his way here.'

CHAPTER TWENTY-SIX

'I'm in the office after dropping my family off at home,' Tanner said. 'I hope to be in Kirkby Abbey in about an hour and I'll come straight to the village hall.'

'I might not be here when you arrive, guv,' James said.

'That won't be a problem. Just make sure that there's someone around to brief me on any new developments that have come to light. Also, I've just spoken to the Chief Constable and he wants me to hold a press briefing there at some point today. The interest in this case is off the scale and it's time we faced the media. The press office will organise it.'

'Are you aware that there's going to be a vigil in the village at five o'clock?'

'Yes, I am. And I think it's important that I attend. I take it you'll be there?'

'Of course.'

'Good. Now, what's the latest? How close are we to unmasking our killer?'

'We've still got a way to go, but there's been a development in respect of the son, Liam.'

James told him about the WhatsApp chat with his parents that had just come to light.

'Are you seriously suggesting that this could be a case of double parricide?' Tanner responded.

The phrase – which meant the murdering of both parents by a son or daughter – was one that James had rarely heard mentioned during all his years with the police.

'It has to be considered given the level of anger he directed at them,' he said. 'And in that last WhatsApp exchange he even wrote that he was going to make sure that they never saw their granddaughter again.'

'Then shouldn't you bring him in?'

'I'm about to go and have another conversation with him. But we have to bear in mind that it's very rare for offspring to kill one of their parents, let alone two.'

'I know that, James, but it's also a fact that increasing numbers of young adults rely heavily on the bank of mum and dad to get by. When the door is closed on them it can cause fierce arguments and simmering resentments.

'I'll never forget the case of a bloke named Stephen Seddon, who was jailed in 2013 for shooting dead both his parents in Greater Manchester, where I was working at the time. He did it to get himself out of debt. He was the sole beneficiary of their estate, which was worth over two hundred grand. Nigel and Elizabeth have left a lot more than that to their son.'

'That's a fair point,' James said. 'And if he is the one who stabbed them both to death then I just hope we can prove it.'

'I look forward to hearing what you think after you've spoken to him again. Meanwhile, I've got a few things to sort here before I set off.'

James confirmed to the team that Tanner would soon be joining them.

'He's going to stage a media briefing here, so I want us to be in a position to provide him with a full update before then.' He nodded at Sharma. 'There's a good chance he'll arrive here before I return from speaking to Liam. So, can you sort that for me, Ahmed?'

He then told Abbott to continue pursuing the burglar and man in the hood who was seen in the garden of a house in Oak Lane on Christmas Eve.

As he was speaking, DI Stevens, who was taking part from his desk at Kendal HQ, announced that he'd received a message from Dr Flint telling him she would soon be starting on the post-mortems.

'Get going then,' James said. 'And let us know if she finds anything that we're not expecting.'

James turned back to DC Sharma and asked him to gather information on the vigil that was due to take place.

'Find out who is organising it and what it'll involve,' he said. 'And make sure we have a fair number of uniforms there.'

They carried on discussing all the other tasks that needed to be carried out and only stopped when Foley received a message informing her that Liam Booth and his wife had arrived home.

As James was slipping on his coat, his attention was drawn to the evidence board on a stand to his right. For several long moments his eyes lingered on the images of the crime scenes that showed the bodies of Nigel and Elizabeth.

He felt his chest tighten and the blood storm through his veins. And he didn't turn away until Foley touched his shoulder and asked him if he wanted to walk to Liam's house or go by car.

'We'll walk,' he said. 'It's only a few streets from here.'

CHAPTER TWENTY-SEVEN

They managed to avoid the media mob who remained out front by leaving through a fire exit at the rear of the building.

The village was still under a layer of snow, but up above the clouds were gradually parting to reveal patches of pale blue sky.

On the short walk to Chapel Road James and Foley discussed how they should approach the interview. It was a tricky one because James was hoping that Liam had not committed the murders and was guilty only of shameful behaviour towards his parents. If that was the case then he would obviously be consumed by grief and regret, so to be questioned as a suspect was therefore going to exacerbate his pain and most likely trigger an angry response.

By now more people had emerged from their homes, encouraged no doubt by the improved weather and the fact that the police were actively patrolling the streets.

But it wasn't like any normal Friday morning. Despite the cheerful Christmas decorations all over the shop fronts, the atmosphere was heavy with dread and despondency.

Chapel Road was busier than James expected it to be. Two uniformed officers were standing on the pavement in front of Liam's house and across the road a group of five or six people were immersed in conversation.

James noticed that one of them was *Cumbria Gazette* reporter Gordon Carver, who was busy making notes while listening to what was being said to him.

As the detectives approached the house, all heads turned towards them and Carver reacted instantly by sprinting across the road. He got to them before they reached their destination and they stopped walking.

'I might have known that you'd turn up,' James said.

Carver smiled at him. 'I came to see if the son of the murdered couple would say anything on the record. But he doesn't want to so I'm getting some quotes from the neighbours.'

Carver was in his early thirties, with sharp features and cropped reddish hair. James actually had a lot of respect for the man and a constructive quid pro quo arrangement had developed between them.

'Have they told you anything that they might not have told us?' James asked him.

A shake of the head. 'I don't think so. The quotes I've got allude to how shocked and fearful they all are and how popular the Booths were. Listening to them took me back four years to when I covered the serial killings here in the village and met you for the first time.'

James nodded. 'As I recall, you lived here in Kirkby Abbey back then.'

'That's right. I moved to Kendal two years ago.'

'Then I'm sure you can appreciate how everyone feels.'

'Indeed, I can. So, would I be right in thinking that there's no point in me trying to elicit some on-the-record quotes from you at this point?'

James grinned. 'You would. I'm about to speak to Liam and his wife and I haven't got the time. But, as always, I'll be sure to keep you in the loop as the investigation progresses.'

Carver shoved his notebook into his pocket. 'Well, I'll be around all day, Detective Walker. I'll be covering the media briefing that's being arranged and the vigil. So, if you feel inclined to impart any information, give me a call.'

CHAPTER TWENTY-EIGHT

It was the family liaison officer who opened the front door to them.

'I told Mr and Mrs Booth that you were coming,' she said. 'They've just put their daughter down for a nap and are waiting for you in the living room.'

Samantha Cooper was a highly dependable and compassionate FLO and had worked with James on numerous cases.

'How are they both?' he asked as he and Foley stepped inside.

'Not good, obviously,' she responded. 'Several neighbours have turned up hoping to pass on their condolences, but they couldn't bring themselves to speak to them. And there was a reporter I had to turn away as well. The guy from the *Cumbria Gazette*.'

It was a small, nondescript living room with a three-piece suite and a TV on a stand. Liam and Colleen were sitting side by side on the sofa, pain etched on their faces.

Liam acknowledged the two detectives with a sharp nod and gestured towards the armchairs.

When they were seated, he said, 'Do you know when I'll be able to see my parents, Inspector?'

James leaned forward, elbows on knees. 'It should be possible this afternoon after the post-mortems have been carried out. Officer Cooper will be informed and she'll then make arrangements for you to visit the morgue.'

'Have you any idea yet who killed them?' he asked. 'On the news they're giving the impression that you haven't got a clue.'

'There are several lines of inquiry that we're pursuing, but it's true to say that we don't yet know who was responsible.'

'But do you think it could have been someone they knew and someone we know?' Colleen said as she stared at James, her eyes swollen and moist, her bottom lip trembling.

'That is possible, and I know it's a horrible thought,' he responded, 'but I remain confident that we'll bring to justice whoever was responsible. Have you been told about the vigil that is going to be held later?'

Liam nodded. 'It's being organised by one of Mum and Dad's friends. He called us last night to ask if we were okay with it. I told him we were, and we'll be making a point of going along ourselves.'

Before bringing up the WhatsApp exchange, James decided to raise another issue.

'Something has come to our notice that I need to ask you about,' he said. 'Are you aware that your parents were subjected to a bout of verbal abuse during a visit to the King's Head pub last Saturday afternoon?'

They looked at each other, clearly confused, and it was Liam who said that it was news to them.

James took out his phone and showed them the image of the couple.

'These two entered the pub and went straight over to Nigel

and Elizabeth's table,' he said. 'They were caught on the security camera and other patrons in the pub heard the man accuse your father of being responsible for his son's death. Have you any idea what he meant and who the couple are?'

They both shook their heads, frowns deepening.

'I've never laid eyes on them before,' Colleen replied.

'Me neither,' Liam said as he continued to stare at the photo. 'Do you think it could have had something to do with a case that Dad once worked on?'

'That's a possibility. We've circulated the image and I'm hoping that we'll soon know who they are and what it was all about.'

James lowered his phone and sat back. He left it a few moments before he announced that they had accessed the data on Nigel and Elizabeth's phones.

To Liam, he said, 'You told us that you spoke to your mum over the phone on Monday. Angry words were obviously exchanged over their retirement plans, and then a short time later you provoked a bitter exchange with both parents on WhatsApp. What you said to them was extremely unpleasant and even quite vicious.'

Liam stiffened and his expression was suddenly wary. 'What has that got to do with anything?' he snapped. 'I made no secret of the fact that I fell out with them over their decision to move abroad.'

James nodded. 'That you did, Liam. But it wasn't clear to us how angry you were over the issue until we saw what you wrote.'

Liam clenched his jaw and his voice became more strident.

'When you came to Shap you asked me where I was on Christmas Eve and it felt like you suspected me of killing my own parents. And now it feels like that again. This is fucking outrageous.'

Colleen reached over and put an arm around him. 'Don't let it upset you, love. I'm sure that's not what they're getting at.'

Turning back to James, she said, 'Please tell us you're not seriously suggesting that words expressed in a WhatsApp chat group have cast suspicion on my husband.'

'Of course, that's not what I'm suggesting,' James said. 'But his choice of words has raised concerns with us.'

Colleen shook her head and a spurt of irritation flashed in her eyes.

'Then what did he write that was so bad? I'm assuming it was in the family group? I'm not in it, so I don't know.'

Liam shrugged his shoulders. 'Go ahead and tell her. I don't care. I can't even remember what I wrote.'

James pulled up the relevant document on his phone and read from it.

'You told them that they should be ashamed of themselves for deciding to move to Spain,' he said. 'Then your father said that you had squandered so much of the money they'd given to you. You reacted by calling them a pair of selfish shits and said they deserved to rot in hell. You also said that you would make sure that they would never see their granddaughter again.'

Liam started shaking his head, his eyes shining with emotion.

'I didn't mean to write that stuff and I'd forgotten that I did,' he said contritely. 'It was because I was upset and had been drinking. I got carried away. It's yet another thing I'll never be able to forgive myself for.'

He dropped his face into his hands suddenly, prompting Colleen to lean towards him. But as she started to say something, he shot to his feet and declared, 'I need to go out back and have a fag. I'm sorry, but if I don't, my head will fucking explode.'

As he headed for the door, James signalled for Foley to go with him.

Colleen remained on the sofa and James was glad. This was the chance he'd been hoping for to speak to her without her husband being present.

CHAPTER TWENTY-NINE

As Colleen watched her husband leave the room, tears filled her eyes and she started blinking rapidly.

'I'm sorry about that,' she said. 'Please don't read anything into it. He's really struggling.'

'I can see that,' James said. 'How are you coping?'

'Not very well. I just can't come to terms with it. Nigel and Elizabeth were good, honest people. It beggars belief that someone, anyone, would want to kill them.'

'Did you get on with them?'

She pressed the heels of her hands against her eyes and took a deep breath. 'I couldn't have wished for better in-laws. They were nice to me from the first day I met them almost four years ago. Liam and I had been together for several months by then and as you know we were living and working in Manchester even though we were both born and bred in Cumbria. He brought me here to Kirkby Abbey to introduce me to them and we hit it off straight away.'

'But you remained in Manchester until about a year ago. Is that right?'

She nodded. 'It was after I became pregnant with Rosie that we decided to move back. We thought it would be good for her if she lived close to both sets of grandparents.'

'And when did things start to go wrong between Liam and his parents?'

She scrunched her face up as though in pain. 'It was about five months ago when Nigel and Elizabeth returned from a holiday in Spain and told us that they had decided to move there. Liam took it badly and since then has tried to talk them out of going.'

'And that's because he wanted them to stay here and downsize so that they could free up money that they would then give to him?'

'That's correct, but to be fair they did tell him years ago that that was what they intended to do when they retired. Instead, they changed their minds and said they were going to live out the rest of their lives in a Spanish villa overlooking the sea. And it'd mean he'd have to wait until they'd died to get any of his inheritance.'

'But surely that wasn't unreasonable of them,' James said.

'That was what I told him. It really upset me when he started arguing with them over it.'

'So, it was all about Liam wanting them to give him money to put towards a house that you and him could buy.'

The muscles around her eyes tightened and she shook her head. 'There was more to it than that. You see, since we've been married Nigel and Elizabeth have given us quite a lot of money from their savings. They paid for our wedding, bought Liam's van for him, and helped us out when we needed it. But that didn't stop the debts from piling up and it became a problem.'

'Is that what Nigel was alluding to in the WhatsApp exchange when he accused Liam of squandering some of the money that they had given him?'

Another nod. 'My husband would be the first to admit that when it comes to handling money, he's not very good. His dad accused him more than once of being financially reckless. Too often he buys things we don't need and he also likes to gamble, which I didn't become aware of until a year into our marriage.'

'So how are your finances right now?'

A shrug. 'Not good. We're maxed out on our credit cards and Liam's job barely covers our outgoings. But we get by.'

James told her that he'd seen the WhatsApp message that she sent to her in-laws on Christmas Day.

'You said you were sorry that Liam had lost his temper and suggested it was because he'd been drinking "again". Has he got a problem with alcohol?'

'No, he hasn't, but whenever he's really stressed out, he either goes on a hike or downs a few whiskies.'

'And does he often lose his temper?'

A flash of panic passed over her face. 'No, he doesn't. And I don't want you to get the wrong impression from what I'm telling you and from those awful things he wrote in that WhatsApp chat. That was him trying to express his feelings and doing a rotten job of it. Liam is a good man. A kind man. And he loved his parents dearly even though he got upset with them over their decision to move away. But before then they'd always got on and I'm sure that eventually he would have come to accept it and things would have got back to normal. And if you think he could possibly have been the person who killed them, then you couldn't be more wrong. I was here when he returned from his hike on Christmas Eve. He was tired but he didn't say or do anything to make me think that he'd done something bad. And trust me, if he had I would have known.'

A sob left her throat then and James could see that she was fighting back tears.

'I didn't mean to upset you or Liam, Colleen,' he said. 'But Nigel and Elizabeth were murdered for a reason and it could well be related to something that's been going on in their lives in recent weeks or months. So, it's important we find out where they've been, what they've done and what interactions they've had with friends and family.'

She opened her mouth to speak, but stopped herself when Liam came back into the room, followed by Foley.

'My apologies,' he said to James before noticing the expression on his wife's face. 'What's wrong, Colleen? You look as though you're about to cry.'

She sucked air between her teeth and stretched her face into an unconvincing smile. 'Detective Walker has been asking me about Nigel and Elizabeth and I'm finding it hard to talk about them.'

Liam sat back on the sofa and wrapped an arm around her shoulders.

'We won't keep you much longer,' James said. 'There are just a couple more questions that I need to ask.'

Liam turned to him and when he spoke his voice was glacially cold.

'Well, get on with it, Inspector. And then please go because I'm scared that I might say something to convince you that I'm an evil bastard who murdered his own mother and father.'

James felt his chest tighten and knew that he would have to choose his words carefully.

'First, can you tell me if you're aware that your parents left everything to you in their will?' he said.

Liam stared at James with undisguised hostility. 'Of course

I bloody well know that and I was told years ago that nothing would go to my uncle. I don't have any brothers or sisters. And before you ask, I also know how much the house is worth. But I don't know how much money is in their bank account. Even if I'd suspected they'd had millions stashed away, I still wouldn't have killed them to get my hands on it. They were my parents and I loved them with all my heart.'

He was shaking now and there was a light sheen of sweat on his forehead.

James left it a few seconds before asking his final question.

'You've told us that on Christmas Eve you didn't leave for Shap until five o'clock in the evening,' he said. 'Before that you went for a hike while Colleen stayed at home with Rosie. Can I ask why you didn't attend the Santa Claus parade in the village square?'

Liam's features softened slightly and his eyes misted over.

'We had been planning to go before I had words with Mum over the phone the day before. She told me that there was a potential buyer for the house,' he said. 'It upset me and I lost it. I told her I didn't want to see her and Dad over Christmas and that we'd be spending it with Colleen's parents instead. For that reason, I decided it would be a bad idea to come face to face with Dad in the square because things might well have turned nasty. But now I know that it was just another of the many bad decisions I've made that will haunt me forever.'

He started crying then and as Colleen pulled him close to her chest, James and Foley got up and exited the room.

135

CHAPTER THIRTY

Officer Cooper followed the two detectives back onto the street where James told her to stay in close contact with the couple and arrange for Liam to visit the morgue for the identification process.

'The guy remains a person of interest for obvious reasons,' he said. 'It's clearly possible that he killed his parents and is now playing the part of the grief-stricken son. But I don't feel we have enough to haul him up to Kendal HQ for a formal interview under caution. If we do and get it wrong, then it might backfire on us.'

'Leave it with me, sir,' Cooper said.

The group of neighbours who had gathered across the road earlier had dispersed and there was no sign of Gordon Carver or any other journalists and photographers.

'So, what's your take on what Liam said to us?' James asked Foley as they started walking towards the village hall.

'I agree with you, guv,' she replied. 'It's certainly too early to rule him out. He's clearly in an emotional state, but I'm not sure if that's down to guilt or grief.'

'Well, if he did take a detour to Maple Lane during his hike on Christmas Day, he's done a good job of fooling his wife,' he said. 'She's convinced he didn't do it. After you left the room, she opened up about him. He's a drinker and a gambler, apparently, and has got them into debt. His parents have helped them out quite a bit.'

'It's what a lot of parents do,' Foley said. 'My own mum has let me live with her rent free since I broke up with my girlfriend well over a year ago. It's meant I've been able to build up my savings.'

'Good for you, Caroline. But in Liam's case it sounds very much like he abused their generosity and harboured a strong sense of entitlement. The question is – did he flip out when he learned that the bank of mum and dad was about to close the doors on him?'

James and Foley entered the village hall through the back way to avoid being confronted by the hacks out front. Most of the team were still there and Superintendent Tanner had just arrived.

Tanner was a thick-set man approaching fifty and he had done a lot to help James settle in after the move from the Met to the Cumbria Constabulary. He was an experienced, well-respected officer who'd been in his current position for just under two years. He was smartly dressed in a dark blue suit, the same one he usually wore whenever he appeared before the cameras.

'DC Sharma was about to update me,' he said to James. 'But if you're going to brief the troops, I'll listen in. I'm meeting the press outside in about half an hour, so we need to decide what I can and can't tell them.'

Before James cracked on with the briefing, he received an update from DC Sharma on Elizabeth Booth's brother, Darren Hanson. The lawyer had arrived already at Manchester airport from France and was making his way to his home in Lancaster. From there a patrol car would pick him up and bring him to Kirkby Abbey.

'Let me know as soon as he arrives,' James said, before calling the team together. He began by telling them what they had got from Liam Booth.

'DC Foley is going to find out what more she can about him,' he said. 'I've asked her to obtain a warrant to search his house and gain access to his digital devices. Plus, I want to know the state of his finances. But we have to tread carefully because there's still no firm evidence linking him to the killings.

'He claims he went hiking between about eleven and two on Christmas Eve and the route took him in the opposite direction to Maple Lane, so it will be a result for us if he turns up on CCTV or door-cam footage somewhere he wasn't meant to be.'

'We're still trawling through it, guv,' Sharma said. 'But so far nothing of interest has come up. And the image from the security camera of the couple who confronted the Booths in the pub has still not struck a chord with anyone yet.'

'If that's still the case by this time tomorrow let's go public with it,' James said. 'It's just a shame that there aren't more cameras in and around the village.'

The briefing continued for another fifteen minutes before they were informed that the media had gathered outside and were waiting for Tanner to appear.

'I want you by my side,' the Super said to James. 'There are sure to be a lot of questions that you'll need to answer.'

CHAPTER THIRTY-ONE

James could feel the adrenaline flowing through his system as he stepped outside.

Addressing the media was one of his pet hates and it always made him uncomfortable. But he knew it couldn't be avoided. The police needed to work in tandem with the news services on high-profile cases such as this one.

A group of about twenty had come along, including reporters, photographers and TV camera operators. They'd been allowed to set up position in the small car park just to the right of the building.

Among them were a few faces that were familiar to James, including Gordon Carver and a prominent BBC regional presenter named Grace Dean.

Reporters were clutching notebooks and microphones, and cameras were set up on tripods.

Tanner kicked things off by introducing himself and then explaining for those who didn't know that James was the senior investigating officer on the case.

'This is like no other investigation that DCI Walker and myself have ever had to deal with,' he said. 'We both knew the victims who worked closely with us before they retired from the force. They were dedicated police officers who served the county of Cumbria for many years. They were also decent, much-loved members of this community. And I want everyone to know that we will not rest until the creature who so brutally murdered them is behind bars.'

Tanner then read from his hastily prepared notes and gave a brief account of what had happened in Maple Lane on Christmas Eve.

'A number of active lines of inquiry are now ongoing,' he went on. 'Dozens of officers have been drafted in from all over the county to assist and we've set up a temporary base here in the village hall. We want anyone who believes they might have information that could be helpful to the investigation to come here and talk to us.'

He then invited questions and James felt a clutch of apprehension when the verbal baton was passed to him.

The first question came from a reporter representing the *Daily Mail* who asked if detectives had established a motive for the killings.

'I'm afraid we haven't,' James answered. 'But we're fairly certain that it wasn't robbery as there was no sign of a break-in at the Booths' home and it doesn't appear that anything was stolen.'

The same reporter followed up with, 'Do you believe that the killer was known to her and she allowed them into the house?'

James nodded. 'That is possible.'

'Then does it follow, Detective Walker, that the killer could be living here in the village?' This from Gordon Carver.

James had no choice but to acknowledge that it was indeed

possible, but at the same time he wanted to strike a note of confidence so as not to fuel fear among residents.

'I want to stress that we have no reason to believe that anyone else in the village is in danger,' he said. 'No evidence has come to light that would suggest this was the work of a serial killer who is likely to strike again.'

His answer prompted someone else to bring up the subject of the murders that took place in Kirkby Abbey four years ago.

'I worked on that investigation and I can assure you that the circumstances surrounding these killings were markedly different,' he said.

More questions followed. Were there any suspects yet? Had police discovered the murder weapon? Who discovered the bodies? Was it likely the Booths were murdered because they used to be police officers?

Off the back of that last question the BBC's Grace Dean asked if the police were aware of the vile comments that were circulating on social media.

James and Tanner exchanged baffled looks and the Superintendent responded.

'We have no idea what you're referring to,' he said. 'Would you care to elaborate?'

'Of course, but I don't know much because it's only just been brought to my attention by the newsroom.' Then, reading from her phone, she continued. 'Comments have appeared on various sites. Some are saying that Mr and Mrs Booth deserved to die simply because they were former detectives. Others are congratulating the killer on behalf of people who over the years have been treated badly by what they describe as "a corrupt and repellent police force". And unsurprisingly the most vocal are the followers of groups that stir up hatred against all police officers.'

James felt the anger stir inside him and decided that it was best to let Tanner respond. He condemned what he described as appalling behaviour, and he expressed deep concern that the BBC had seen fit to draw attention to it. But it got the rest of the pack excited and they clearly saw it as an angle worth pursuing.

From then on, the questions focused on the careers of both Nigel and Elizabeth and whether they might have fallen victim to an unhinged individual who had developed a hatred for all coppers. Or perhaps it was somebody who one of both of them had made an enemy of during their time on the force.

Tanner confirmed that the team were seriously considering both theories, but he stressed that the Booths had always been honest, hard-working officers with untarnished reputations.

'And I don't think we should equate what has happened to them with anti-police sentiment,' he said before drawing things to a close.

CHAPTER THIRTY-TWO

When they were back inside the hall Tanner didn't try to conceal his anger and disappointment.

'I wish we had known about those fucking online rants before we got into that,' he said. 'I would have pulled together a more constructive response.'

'You did well, guv,' James told him. 'It's just a shame that the woman from the BBC had to bring it up.'

Tanner shook his head. 'I just find it so extraordinary that there are people out there who reckon the cold-blooded murders of a retired couple can be justified purely on the grounds that they used to be police officers.'

'It feeds into the narrative that all coppers are bad,' James said. 'And we both know that it's a view which is sadly gaining traction in this country.'

It was well known that public trust in the police had sunk to an all-time low. It stemmed from perceived abuses of power and unedifying instances of misconduct and criminality, such as the murder of Sarah Everard by a serving police officer.

Internet trolls were continually whipping up hatred by highlighting cases of corruption, racism, misogyny and unwarranted acts of violence against innocent people. *Kill The Cops* and *All Police Are Scum* were the titles of just two of the many websites that had sprung up in the past year alone. It was little wonder therefore that attacks on the police had increased dramatically. But thankfully it was still extremely rare for those who had left or retired from the force to be targeted solely because they'd been coppers.

And that was one of the reasons why James suspected that the motive behind the murders of Nigel and Elizabeth Booth was not so straightforward.

The team talked about the media briefing for a short while and a civilian support officer was tasked with monitoring all the online comments and discussions relating to the case.

Tanner then announced that he was going up to Maple Lane to familiarise himself with the crime scenes. James was intending to accompany him until he was told that Elizabeth's brother, Darren Hanson, had arrived.

'I need to talk to him, guv, so get DC Sharma to go with you. He's spent quite a bit of time up there already.'

James told Foley to wait in the small meeting room while he went to greet Hanson.

Elizabeth's younger brother arrived wearing a dark green waxed jacket and carrying a rucksack.

He was a sinewy man in his early fifties with chiselled features and a strong jaw. His face was pitted with stubble and there were tired shadows beneath his eyes.

'Thank you for arranging for a car to bring me here,' he said. 'It's been a mad rush. And would you be able to get someone to take me back later, after the vigil that I've been told is going to take place around five?'

'Of course. That won't be a problem. And please allow me to say how sorry I am for your loss. In addition to being one of my closest colleagues, Elizabeth was also a good friend.'

'Thanks, Detective Walker. She often mentioned you and I know you got on like a house on fire.'

He took Hanson to the meeting room and introduced him to Foley, who offered to get him a coffee.

'I'll have one after this,' he said as he took a seat at the table. 'I'm desperate to hear what you have to tell me. I've heard all the stuff on the news, but I want to know if you're holding anything back. I also want to know if my nephew Liam is a suspect.'

'Do you think he should be?' James asked.

'I most certainly do. When I spoke by phone to Detective Stevens, I told him about the row Liam had on Monday with his mum. It really upset her and when she called me, she was in tears. There was more I wanted to say to your man, but the signal was bad. Now I can tell you what a bastard Liam is and that I think he might have killed his parents to get his hands on their house and money.'

The words were rasping in his throat now and his eyes glistened with repressed anger.

'We have spoken to Liam about the fallout with his parents,' James said. 'And we're eager to hear what you have to say. But first I think I should bring you up to date on a few things.'

He began by confirming that Nigel and Elizabeth had died from stab wounds and post-mortems were now being carried out on their bodies.

'Liam will be going along to formally identify them in a short while,' James said. 'But I'm happy to arrange for you to see your sister at a later date if you want to.'

145

He took out his phone and brought up the image of the couple who confronted Nigel and Elizabeth in the King's Head pub on Saturday.

'I want you to tell me if you recognise this couple.'

As Hanson stared at the photo, James explained why he was showing it to him.

'I definitely have no idea who they are,' Hanson said after a few seconds. 'And I can't think what Elizabeth and Nigel could possibly have done to upset them.'

James made a point of telling him that he wouldn't be able to visit their house on Maple Lane.

'It's still being examined by forensic officers and will be out of bounds to everyone else for at least another day or two.'

Before moving onto Liam, James asked Hanson if his sister had mentioned anyone else who she and Nigel were having problems with.

'No, she didn't,' he replied. 'We were close but I usually only spoke to her about once a fortnight, although it's been more often since Liam started to make her life a misery. And the last time I came here to see her was about three months ago.'

By now his face was raw with grief and he was struggling to keep his voice steady.

James paused to allow him to compose himself before asking him about Liam.

'I know he was the sole beneficiary of his parents' will. The problem was he didn't want to have to wait for them to die to get it,' he said. 'He's useless with money and has built up a lot of debt. Sis always took pity on him, especially after he married Colleen, who is a gem by the way, and I don't know how she puts up with him.

'He drinks too much and has a foul temper. I don't suppose he told you that he's on anti-depressants? In fact, he's like a lot of the men I've represented over the years as a lawyer. He's volatile, full of self-pity and struggles to suppress his emotions. That's why I believe you shouldn't dismiss him as a suspect just because he was their son.'

'How do you get on with him?' James asked.

'I don't now, but before he got married and took on financial responsibilities, he was okay. I only found out how much he was poncing off his mum and dad after my sister started to confide in me. It wasn't nice. He was putting so much pressure on them to give him handouts. When they decided to sell the house and buy a villa in Spain, he went ballistic and told them that it wasn't fair on him, Colleen and Rosie.

'I know from what Elizabeth told me that during one argument with Nigel, Liam smashed his fist against a wall and called them a pair of selfish bastards. I told them not to give into his pathetic demands and to fulfil their dream. The last I heard that's exactly what they were planning to do.'

Hanson fell silent suddenly, the expression on his face mutinous.

'Is there anything more that you wanted to say?' James asked.

Hanson shook his head as he slowly let the air out of his lungs. 'I reckon I've said enough. But I hope you can see things from my point of view now, Detective Walker. Liam may well have loved his parents, but I don't believe it would have stopped him from killing them to get himself out of debt and bring in enough money to reboot his life.'

CHAPTER THIRTY-THREE

Hanson opted not to have a coffee and instead said he was going to the White Hart to have lunch. He was also hoping to meet up with one or two of his sister's friends there.

James went back into the hall and passed on what he had learned to those of the team who were still there.

'Elizabeth's brother painted quite an unpleasant picture of his nephew,' he said. 'And he seriously believes that Liam Booth could be the killer.'

'It's now pretty clear that Liam gave his parents a lot of grief,' Foley responded. 'All they wanted to do was make the most of their retirement by moving to the Med and buying a villa there. But he turned their dream into a nightmare. It doesn't surprise me that Mr Hanson is pointing the finger at him.'

'There's still a lack of hard evidence, though,' James said, concerned that his team would focus too much on one suspect. 'Sure, Liam had motive and opportunity, but that's nowhere near enough to build a case against him that's beyond reasonable doubt.

'We still need to identify the couple who launched a verbal assault against Nigel and Elizabeth in the King's Head. They obviously don't live in the village, so they probably came here with the sole purpose of confronting them. But why? And what the hell did the guy mean when he accused Nigel of being responsible for his – or their – son's death?'

'Although the image from the pub CCTV has been circulated, the Christmas break means that quite a few people in the Constabulary haven't yet seen it because they're still off,' DS Abbott pointed out.

'And what about the burglary in Driscoll Street?' James asked. 'Any update on that?'

Abbott shook her head. 'Unfortunately not. And the same applies to the man in the hood seen on Christmas Eve in that garden in Oak Lane. We still can't be sure if he's the burglar or if any other homes have been broken into, and no more reports have come in.'

Like a lot of towns and villages across Cumbria, Kirkby Abbey contained a large number of second homes and holiday lets. It was a controversial issue because over the years it had resulted in rocketing housing costs for locals and dwindling footfall for local businesses. In addition, it had led to a huge increase in the number of burglaries across the county due to the fact that empty properties provided easy pickings for thieves.

As they continued discussing the case a catering van turned up outside to deliver snacks and drinks. It had been arranged by headquarters and would be providing a regular service while the hall was being used as a base.

James helped himself to a coffee and a cheese sandwich, and just as he started eating it word came through that the post-mortems on Nigel and Elizabeth's bodies had been completed.

Minutes later, Dr Flint phoned James to tell him that she would be writing a full report but that it wouldn't contain any surprises.

'There's no question they died from stab wounds that I'm certain were inflicted by the same weapon, the bread knife' she said. 'The blade is thin and flexible with a serrated edge that leaves a distinctive pattern upon entry. And it's usually extremely effective when thrust into someone's chest or throat. It's my firm belief that the couple died within minutes of each other on Christmas Eve, but I can't be more precise in respect of the time. It's also likely that Nigel put up a bit of a struggle, which is why he was stabbed twice – in the chest and stomach.'

She went on to say that she was now preparing the corpses for the formal identification by Liam.

After ending the call, James checked the time. Almost three o'clock. He could barely believe that nine hours had passed since he'd climbed out of bed and they were almost through day two of the investigation.

The morning had flown by and yet he was already feeling drained and tired. He was also experiencing a growing sense of frustration that the investigation was moving at an unnervingly slow pace. He just wished there'd be a breakthrough that would at least confirm that the thoughts and theories they were exploring were not wide of the mark.

He only had to wait another half an hour before his wish was granted.

'I've just received a call from uniform, guv,' Foley told him. 'They've found what they believe to be the murder weapon.'

CHAPTER THIRTY-FOUR

Once again James decided to walk to the location, which was at the northern end of the village, and he took Foley with him.

It was a strange feeling not having to drive everywhere. James simply wasn't used to it, and neither were his colleagues. Usually during an investigation, they spent a lot of time on the road, travelling between towns and villages and remote spots in the countryside where crimes had been committed.

Flitting around his own small village on foot was taking a bit of getting used to. But he believed it made sense given that there was never far to go.

The weapon had been found in a skip on the driveway of a property on Ruskin Street. That, and the fact that it was a bread knife, was all he'd been told.

There was a lot going on by the time they got there and a surprising number of people were already on the scene along with a forensics van. As well as uniformed officers and suited SOCOs there was Superintendent Tanner, DC Sharma and Chief Forensic Officer Tony Coppell.

Their presence was quickly explained by Tanner, who said, 'Ahmed and I were talking to Tony up on Maple Lane when he received a call from uniform telling him to come straight here.'

The property itself was a detached house that was undergoing major renovation, hence the skip, which was filled with bricks, planks and broken masonry. The house was unoccupied and the building team working on it were presumably still on their Christmas break.

There were five other detached houses on the street, each about fifty yards apart and set back behind hedges and trees. The street came off the perimeter road close to Maple Lane and wound through the village, ending just before the square.

'It was Constable Walsh who found the knife wrapped in a tea towel,' Coppell said. 'He was one of the officers searching the bins and hedges in this area and decided to take a peek inside the skip. He spotted the towel, which had been dropped on top of the debris and was half covered with snow. Luckily for us he checked it out.'

There was a plastic sheet on the ground next to the skip and the knife was resting on top of it beside the tea towel.

James knelt down over the sheet. The knife had no marks on its serrated blade, but the tea towel was stained with what was almost certainly blood.

'I've checked back on the photos I took up at the Booths' house,' Coppell said. 'The knife is most definitely the one that's missing from there. Plus, the tea towel matches several others in the kitchen. It looks clear that the killer wrapped the knife in it when leaving the house and then used it to wipe the blood from the blade. But I very much doubt that we'll be able to lift any prints or DNA deposits because of the snow.'

'At least it backs up our theory about the bread knife being the murder weapon,' Sharma said. 'And this would suggest the killer got rid of it while fleeing the scene.'

'It also potentially gives us good reason to believe that the killer is local and headed into the village after committing the murders,' James said. 'It's a pity this street is so quiet. There's no CCTV and if any of the houses have cameras, I doubt they'll reach down beyond the driveways.'

Nevertheless, James saw it as a breakthrough of sorts and said as much to Tanner.

'But if the killer hasn't left a mark on either the towel or the knife then it's unlikely to take us very far forward,' the Super said.

'I'll whisk them straight back to the lab for analysis,' Coppell said. 'There's always the possibility we'll get lucky. Meanwhile, there's something else that you need to see. One of my team came across it in the house and I was going to bring it to your attention just before I got the call to come straight here. I'll go and get it.'

Coppell stepped over to the forensics van. The back doors were open and the inside was stacked with the various bits of kit needed to process crime scenes. From a box he took out a large, clear evidence bag and brought it back to show James and the other detectives.

'It's a Christmas card for Nigel and Elizabeth,' he said. 'One of fifteen we found in the house. I got someone to read through them all this morning and this one stood out.'

He was wearing latex gloves so he removed the card from the bag and said, 'The card itself is nothing special, but what's written inside will doubtless arouse your suspicion.'

He then proceeded to read the words out loud. 'Merry Christmas, Elizabeth. I really believe that it's time to put the past behind us. To that end, would it be okay for me to come and see you on Christmas Eve? I really feel that it's time we stopped

153

avoiding each other and it would mean so much to me if we could become friends again. If you don't want me to drop by then send me a text and I won't. But if I don't hear from you, I'll come along in the morning. All my love and my regards also to Nigel. Zelda.'

Tanner was the first to respond. 'That was a good spot, Colin. Does anyone know who this Zelda character is?'

'The name rings a bell,' James said. 'I'm sure I've heard it mentioned more than once.'

'Then that probably means she lives here in the village.' This from Foley.

James nodded. 'It's a stand-out name and so it shouldn't take us long to trace her. In fact, there's a good chance that my wife can help. She's more clued up than I am on who lives here. Let me call her.'

When Annie answered the phone, she told him she'd arranged for one of their neighbours to come and look after the kids while she attended the vigil later.

'That's good to hear,' James said. 'But I'm calling to ask if you know someone named Zelda who lives here in Kirkby Abbey.'

'Of course. Zelda Macklin. She runs the charity shop off the square. A nice, friendly lady. My mum knew her well.'

'Well, we've just discovered that she might have visited Nigel and Elizabeth on Christmas Eve.'

'Really? That's interesting because I know for a fact that she and Elizabeth weren't on speaking terms.'

'Do you know why?'

'It's a right old saga apparently. It started years ago when Nigel ended a short relationship with Zelda to hook up with Elizabeth, who he went on to marry. Zelda took it hard and called time on their friendship. I gather they did make up for a while after Zelda herself got married to a guy named Graham. He was running the charity shop back then. But they fell out again after Graham vandalised someone's car and Elizabeth was forced to arrest him.'

James was unaware of the incident, so when Annie said it took place about eight years ago, he wasn't surprised.

'Can you tell me anything more about the car thing?' he asked.

'All I know from what I've been told is that Graham had been involved in a long-running dispute with his neighbour over access to a shared driveway. One day it got out of hand and Graham smashed the other guy's windscreen with a hammer. The neighbour called the police. At that time Elizabeth was on her way home from Kendal HQ so she was contacted and told to go there. When she saw what had happened and after speaking to both parties, she felt she had to arrest Graham and naturally Zelda was none too happy.'

'Did it go to court?'

'It did, and he received a fine.'

'Have you got their address?'

'Her house is in Badgers Lane, but I don't know the number. She lives alone, by the way. Graham died not long before you and I moved here four years ago.'

'Are you going to tell me what's going on?' Annie asked.

'I'll fill you in later, love,' James said. 'I have to go, but you've been really helpful. I'll see you at the vigil no doubt, or possibly before then if I can find time to pop home beforehand.'

CHAPTER THIRTY-FIVE

When James came off the phone, he gave Zelda Macklin's name to one of the uniforms and asked him to radio control and get her full address.

He then relayed to the others what Annie had told him, adding, 'So it looks like we have another person of interest. Caroline and I will go straight to Badgers Lane. Ahmed, will you get someone to double check Elizabeth's phone records? Make sure that she didn't message Zelda to tell her not to turn up at the house on Christmas Eve. I suppose there's a chance it wasn't spotted if she did.'

This was another unexpected development and James felt a nudge of excitement. He got Coppell to hold up the Christmas card so that he could take a photo of what Zelda had written.

Then he and Foley set off after he declined the offer of a lift in a patrol car.

Yet again their destination was only a short walk away and if they arrived on foot, it was less likely they'd draw attention to themselves.

Zelda's full address came through on James's phone just before they got there. It was a small detached house and there was only one car on the driveway that it shared with the neighbouring property.

James vaguely recognised the woman who answered the door and he assumed it was because he'd seen her out and about in the village.

She was in her fifties, with loose grey hair falling about her shoulders. Her face was pale and listless, and James got the impression that she was not in good health.

'It's Mrs Macklin, isn't it?' he said and she reacted by flashing an uncertain smile. 'I'm Detective Chief Insp—'

'I'm well aware of who you are,' she interrupted him. 'Everyone in the village is. And I've even met your wife a few times. Her name's Annie, isn't it?'

James nodded. 'That's correct. I'm here with my colleague, Detective Foley, and we'd like to speak to you about your visit to the home of Elizabeth and Nigel Booth on Christmas Eve.'

Zelda stared at him for a long moment, as if she was working out in her mind how best to answer.

Then a frown gathered on her brow and she said, 'What makes you think I went there?'

'We found the Christmas card you sent to Elizabeth telling her that you wanted to,' James said. 'We're checking her phone to see if she replied with a message asking you not to. But I'm guessing she didn't.'

Zelda exhaled with an audible sigh and stepped back from the door, leaving it open.

'You'd better come in then,' she said. 'I'll explain why I went there and why after I heard about what happened to them, I decided not to tell anyone.'

They followed Zelda into the living room where she waved them towards the sofa. 'Sit yourselves down, detectives. And before you start asking your questions, there are two things that I want you to know. Firstly, I swear I did not kill Elizabeth and Nigel. And secondly, I accept that it was stupid of me not to have let you know about my visit to their house on the same day they were murdered there.'

Her voice was surprisingly measured and calm, but James could see that her body was shaking beneath the shapeless trousers and thick red jumper she was wearing. And when she sat in the armchair facing them, he also noticed that tears were sprouting from the corners of her rheumy blue eyes.

'I haven't been able to leave the house since I heard about it yesterday afternoon,' she said. 'I can't stop crying. It's so devastating, especially as it happened after I met up with Elizabeth for the first time in years.'

'I take it from what you wrote in the card that you and she were once friends, but that something happened that caused you to stop talking to one another,' James said.

She met his gaze and held it. 'That's right, I'm afraid. Our on-off relationship has been the subject of gossip in the village for years and it's not something I'm proud of because I was to blame.'

She paused there to take a tissue from her pocket and used it to dab at her eyes.

James thought about making her aware of what Annie had told him, but decided to let her tell her own story.

In a voice that was weak and croaky she explained that when she was in her early twenties, she started a relationship with Nigel and fell in love with him. But then he suddenly ended it and started seeing Elizabeth, who at the time was one of her closest friends.

'I felt hurt and betrayed, so I refused to have anything more to do with either of them,' she said. 'But eventually I came to realise that I was being childish and unfair, and I asked Elizabeth to forgive me. She did and we were reconciled.'

She then moved on to the incident involving the neighbour's car.

'Once again I behaved badly and took it out on her,' she said. 'Since then, we've avoided each other and even when my husband died, and she asked to come to the funeral, I told her that she wouldn't be welcome.'

'What prompted you to send her the Christmas card then?' Foley asked.

Zelda rubbed her temples with her fingers while at the same time crushing tears with her eyelids.

'I posted it on impulse a week ago because I received some bad news that made me want to tell her how sorry I was for the way I'd treated her,' she replied. 'I fully expected her to send me a message telling me that she didn't want to see me. And I wouldn't have blamed her if she had. But there was no message and I was chuffed to bits.'

James frowned. 'The bad news you received that encouraged you to want to visit Elizabeth. What was it?'

She took her time responding, and when she did tears started to roll down her cheeks.

'Three weeks ago, I was diagnosed with lung cancer,' she said. 'It's terminal and I've been given between one and two years. After it sank in, I decided to put right the things that I'd got wrong in my life. And that included reconnecting with Elizabeth before it was too late.'

Zelda closed her eyes and squeezed the wet tissue in her fist.

James felt compassion swell up inside him because he was

reminded of the day his own sister broke the news that she had breast cancer. The shock of that had made him reassess his outlook towards so many things.

'We're really sorry to hear that, Mrs Macklin,' Foley said. 'That's a terrible thing to have to deal with.'

Zelda opened her eyes and gave a small nod. 'Indeed, it is, but it's my own fault for failing to give up smoking. My late husband warned me that if I didn't stop, I'd eventually cause harm to myself, and he was right.'

'Is your condition public knowledge?' James asked.

She shook her head. 'I only told Elizabeth and Nigel and they were really sympathetic. Elizabeth gave me a hug and she even had a cry.'

James cleared his throat. 'I'm glad you've confided in us about your condition, Mrs Macklin. But we do still need to ask you about Christmas Eve, starting with what time you arrived at the house and how long you were there.'

'I arrived just before nine in the morning,' she answered. 'I was only there for an hour, but I got to see Nigel in his Santa Claus suit for the parade. Elizabeth had decided not to go with him because she wanted to do some things around the house.'

'Do you know if she was expecting any other visitors that day?' James asked.

'I don't think so. She actually asked me if I wanted to stay with her for a while longer, but I couldn't because I had things to do at home.'

'So they were both alive when you left their house?' Foley said.

'They were.'

'And did they seem concerned about anything?'

'Not at all. They were both in high spirits and Elizabeth seemed really pleased to see me. We agreed to meet up again after Christmas and she even said that she would help support me when I started to receive treatment.'

'And how did you get to and from Maple Lane?' James asked.

'I walked.'

'On the way there and back did you pass anyone? Or did you see anyone acting suspiciously?'

Another shake of the head. 'No one at all. It was very quiet and Maple Lane was deserted.'

James was finding it hard not to believe what she was telling them. Her account of what happened on Christmas Eve sounded plausible and she was coming across as sincere. But over the years he'd fallen for a good few sob stories that had turned out to be entirely fake.

'I can tell from your faces that you're not convinced,' Zelda said. 'Well, feel free to search the house and subject my clothes to all that forensic stuff that I've seen them do in films. If you want to confirm what I said about the cancer then just get in touch with Dr West here in the village. He knows all about it.'

'We will have to carry out those checks simply because you were at the house on Christmas Eve,' James said. 'However, right now I have no reason to believe that what you've told us isn't the truth. I'm just confused as to why you didn't come to us after you heard that Nigel and Elizabeth had been murdered.'

She gulped in some air and the edges of her mouth turned downwards.

'I just panicked,' she said. 'I feared that if I told the police you would jump to the wrong conclusion because of what happened between me and Elizabeth in the past. Plus, there was nothing I could tell you anyway about what happened to them after I left there. And it didn't occur to me that you'd read the Christmas card.'

James concluded the interview then, but before leaving the house, he told her to expect a visit from uniformed and forensic officers. Finally, he asked if she was going to attend the vigil in the square.

'I've already thought about that and decided not to,' she answered. 'Most of the villagers know about my behaviour towards Elizabeth, so I don't think I'll be welcome there.'

She closed her eyes then and more tears were squeezed out.

As James got to his feet, he found it hard not to feel sorry for her, even though he wasn't prepared to rule her out as a suspect just yet.

CHAPTER THIRTY-SIX
ANNIE

It was twenty to five and Annie was ready to leave the house. Karen from two doors down had arrived to babysit the kids and she was keeping them occupied in the living room.

Annie had already given them an early dinner and planned to be back well in time to put them to bed.

Karen was only eighteen and lived with her parents who were also going along to the vigil. She had babysat for Annie and James several times when Janet hadn't been able to and had proved herself to be reliable and trustworthy. And, most importantly, the kids liked her.

Annie's mind was all over the place as she pulled on her coat. It had been another difficult day trying to keep Bella and Theo happy while there was so much going on to distract her.

The two friends who had come over before had dropped by again to seek reassurance that James was closing in on the killer. Then she saw him on the TV news answering questions from reporters outside the village hall. That was followed by him phoning her to ask about the woman who ran the charity shop.

Did it mean that Zelda Macklin was a suspect in the murders? Surely that was about as likely as a heatwave hitting Cumbria in the coming days.

But it was definitely odd that Zelda had gone to the Booths' house on Christmas Eve. Everyone knew that the pair had avoided each other for a long time. Was it possible that they had agreed to make up and Elizabeth had invited Zelda there for a chat? Or had Zelda turned up unexpectedly because there was something she wanted to get off her chest and things turned nasty?

The more Annie thought about it the more confused she became. But she supposed that was hardly surprising given the level of trauma that had been inflicted on the community by the murders of Elizabeth and Nigel.

All those she had spoken to were also struggling to get their heads around what had happened. Their quiet, comfortable existence had been shattered for the second time and they'd been left to wonder if they were safe or if there would be more killings. And right now, it seemed that there was nobody, not even James, who could put their minds at rest.

Before leaving the house, Annie phoned James to check if he was going to stop in on his way to the vigil. But he told her that he couldn't because he had to return to the village hall for a quick debrief with his team.

'I'll catch up with you there, love,' he said.

After kissing the kids, Annie stepped out into a late afternoon that was dark and bitterly cold. But she was comfortable enough with a beanie hat on her head and a scarf around her neck.

164

The streets were quite busy with people like her heading towards the square to pay their respects. This was a village in mourning and Annie wondered if it would ever fully recover from what had taken place.

Within minutes she was turning the corner into the square and the sight that greeted her snatched her breath away.

Scores of people had gathered to honour Nigel and Elizabeth, and many of them were holding lit candles.

Bunches of flowers had been placed on the ground around the brightly lit Christmas tree and people were blowing their noses and shedding tears.

There were also a large number of police officers in high visibility jackets present, and Annie was sure that they, too, would be feeling emotional.

Her heart was beating uncomfortably hard as she joined the crowd and she immediately cast her eyes around for James, but he was nowhere to be seen.

She did spot Liam and Colleen, though. Two police officers were escorting them towards the front and people were standing back to let them through.

Minutes later the ceremony got underway with a short speech from the village priest who spoke movingly about the couple and said how the community would have to find the strength to recover from such a terrible loss. He rounded off with a couple of prayers and then handed over to Superintendent Jeff Tanner, who Annie hadn't seen in quite a while.

'I've been asked to say a few words as someone who worked on the force with both Nigel and Elizabeth,' he said, his voice solemn. 'I'll start by saying that every police officer's worst nightmare is to attend an event such as this in order to eulogise a colleague or colleagues who have been cruelly murdered. The deaths of

165

this wonderful couple have left the Cumbria Constabulary badly shaken.'

He went on to promise that he and his colleagues would not rest until the person responsible had been apprehended.

People in the crowd were then invited to step forward to share their memories of Nigel and Elizabeth, and some of them did. Annie had to close her eyes briefly as she listened, hot tears forming behind the lids.

The ceremony itself was over in about twenty minutes, but the crowd remained in the square and talked among themselves. Some of them approached Liam and Colleen to offer their condolences and Annie also chose to do so.

As she drew close, she could see that Colleen's face was swollen from crying and it was being left to Liam to respond as best he could.

Annie was within touching distance of the couple when she was roughly shoved out of the way by a man who seemed to appear out of nowhere.

His loud, angry voice rose above the chatter as he rushed forward to confront Liam, who spun round to face him.

'I know that you murdered my sister, you bastard,' the man yelled. 'You wanted their money and it was the only way you could get your hands on it. All they wanted was to sell up and move to Spain and you weren't going to let them.'

Before Liam could say or do anything, the man lunged forward, grabbed his coat, and pushed him backwards.

'Only a greedy, vile creature would kill his own parents and that's what you are, Liam Booth,' the man screamed. 'You won't get away with it, and if the police don't charge you right away then I'll keep on at them until they do.'

There were loud gasps all around as the police officers

moved in to seize him. But as Annie watched in stunned silence, she got another shock when hands were placed on both her shoulders.

Her body froze and panic squeezed the breath from her lungs. But it was over in the blink of an eye when James's voice suddenly sent a wave of relief sweeping through her.

CHAPTER THIRTY-SEVEN

'It's only me,' James said. 'I saw him push you out of the way. Are you okay?'

Annie turned towards him and he could tell from her expression that he had given her a scare.

She started to respond, but held back when Darren Hanson started shouting again.

'I need to take care of this,' he said, keeping his voice low. 'It's best you go straight home.'

'Is that Elizabeth's brother?'

'Yes, and he's convinced that Liam killed her and Nigel.'

'My God.'

James pulled away from her and moved towards Hanson. He was sandwiched between two officers who were holding on to his arms.

'You need to calm down, Mr Hanson,' James told him. 'This is out of order. These people came here to pay their respects, not to listen to you hurling abuse.'

Hanson thrust his chin towards Liam and continued his rant.

'No way was I gonna pass up the chance to let people know that he's the one who did it. His tears are fake. Surely you can see that.'

Liam stared back at him, his expression one of shock and outrage. He had his arm around his wife, who was covering her face with her hands.

'I know you're upset, Uncle Darren, but you're being ridiculous,' he said, loud enough for people to hear. 'I would never have done anything to hurt my mum and dad. I can't believe you think that. They meant the world to me.'

James stepped between them before Hanson had time to respond and ordered the uniforms to take him round to the village hall.

'Are you arresting me?' Hanson snapped 'Because if you are—'

'If you don't calm down, I'll have to,' James interrupted him. 'Now please go with the officers and I'll come and speak to you in a minute.'

As Hanson was ushered away, James turned to Liam. He was standing by himself now and Colleen was behind him being consoled by Samantha Cooper.

'I suggest you go straight home, Liam. I'll make sure he doesn't bother you again.'

He shook his head, his anxiety tangible. 'But he had no right to say that, especially in front of all these people. Christ only knows what they're thinking.'

James was only too aware that the crowd around them had grown.

'I'm sure that no one will take him seriously, Liam. I'll ask him to retract his accusation.'

'I shouldn't bother because I guarantee that he won't.'

'Then are you going to consider pressing charges? He did lay his hands on you, after all.'

'There's no point. We both know that. He's just lost his sister and wants someone to blame. And that someone is me. If I try to take it further, it will almost certainly prove to be a waste of time.'

James cast a look at Colleen. She was becoming increasingly distressed as more people came to join those gathered around them, eager to know what was going on. They included at least one newspaper photographer whose camera was flashing repeatedly.

'You need to get your wife away from here,' James said. 'Go with Officer Cooper and I'll call in on you as soon as I can.'

Much to James's relief, Liam did so and ignored the questions that were thrown at him by onlookers.

By now Detectives Abbott and Foley had turned up and were telling people to move on. No objections were raised and the crowd quickly dispersed, but they continued to talk among themselves and James could see that what Hanson had said had jolted and confused them.

He knew there was no way of stopping it from spreading all over the village. It would be an added complication in respect of the investigation and put enormous pressure on Liam. For as long as the case remained unsolved, he was going to have to deny that he had murdered his parents, and it was highly unlikely that everyone would believe him.

The issue he'd had with them over their retirement plans was now out there and that alone would be enough to convince some people of his guilt.

And it wouldn't be long before those same people started asking why, in the absence of any other credible suspects, the man hadn't been arrested.

James avoided eye contact with people as he moved through the crowd and off the square. When he reached the village hall, he wrenched off his coat and puffed out his cheeks. The full weight of the day's events had hit him and his head was full of noise.

He saw Elizabeth's brother as soon as he entered the hall. He was sitting at one of the tables while being watched over by the two officers who had brought him in.

As James approached him, he looked up, anger shaping his features.

'So, what happens now, Inspector?' he asked. 'Are you going to arrest me?'

'Luckily for you, your nephew doesn't want to press charges even though you effectively assaulted him,' James said. 'And I'm prepared to leave it at that so long as you go straight home and allow me and my team to find out who killed your sister. Just because you believe it was Liam doesn't mean that it was. You'll end up in deep trouble if you carry on accusing him. And you'll also make our job much harder.'

'But he did it,' Hanson replied gruffly. 'He must have. Nobody else would have wanted to kill them.'

'You can't be sure of that, Mr Hanson. And neither can we. We need more than just a motive to charge someone. We need hard evidence, and right now we don't have any.'

Hanson remained silent for a moment and then huffed out a breath. 'I'll drop it for now then. But I won't let it go. And for what it's worth, I'm sorry I spoiled the vigil for everyone else. It was good of them all to attend.'

His words prompted a burst of tears and he lowered his head.

'A car will be waiting outside to take you back home to Lancaster,' James said. 'I think you should stay away from Kirkby Abbey for the time being but I'll arrange for one of my officers to keep you updated on the investigation. At some point you will probably have to engage with Liam over funeral arrangements. Or perhaps get someone to do it on your behalf.'

As Hanson was being escorted out of the hall, Superintendent Tanner and the other detectives entered it.

'That was all very unfortunate,' Tanner said. 'I'm glad you managed to calm him down.'

'He's in a right old state, but then Liam and his wife must be too,' James said. 'After we're done here, I'll go and see them.'

Tanner nodded. 'You should know that I was cornered by a couple of reporters in the square. I told them that they shouldn't read too much into what was said because emotions are running high among family members.'

'That might be enough to encourage the hacks to believe there was no truth in it,' James said. 'But I fear that at least some of Liam's friends and neighbours might need more convincing.'

CHAPTER THIRTY-EIGHT

James didn't leave the village hall for another half an hour. He wanted to make sure that everyone knew what the plan was for tomorrow.

It also gave him a chance to update Detectives Isaac and Hall who had turned up for their second night shift in Kirkby Abbey.

He told them about Zelda Macklin visiting the Booths' house on Christmas Eve morning and what they had learned about Liam. He also asked them to let Lancaster police know what Elizabeth's brother did at the vigil and that he had been advised to stay away from the village for the time being.

Superintendent Tanner announced that he'd be returning to Penrith and would be updating the Chief Constable in the morning.

'Keep me informed of any developments and leave it to me and the press office to fend off the media mob,' he said. 'This case is causing mass hysteria in newsrooms and that's never a good thing from our point of view. It always leads to wild speculation and distortion of the facts. So, we need to resolve it before things get out of hand.'

Tanner had raised a valid point. In James's experience the highest profile cases were always the most difficult to investigate because you had to respond to excessive scrutiny and the increased risk of leaks.

'I want you to report back here first thing in the morning unless you hear from me in the meantime with instructions to go elsewhere,' he said to his team. 'And let's hope that we can start making meaningful progress.'

James could feel the pressure forming behind his eyes as he headed towards Liam's house. Lots of conflicting thoughts were tumbling through his mind and it was becoming harder to focus.

He didn't want to believe that Liam Booth had murdered his parents, but he was beginning to suspect that the rest of the team did. And that was understandable in view of the appalling way the guy had behaved towards them.

The case against him was made all the more compelling by the debts he'd built up and the fact that he often turned to drink when he was stressed out. He also had a weak alibi and was one of the people who would have been granted access to the house on Maple Lane.

But without concrete forensic evidence, or a witness who could put him there on Christmas Eve, what they had didn't really amount to much. And it certainly wouldn't be enough to make a double murder charge stick.

James fully expected to see one or two newshounds outside the house when he got there, but much to his relief the street was empty.

Officer Cooper opened the door to him and when he stepped inside, she told him that she would soon be off home, but had given the couple the number of another FLO who'd be on call throughout the night.

'Their daughter is asleep upstairs and the babysitter just left,' she added.

Once again, Liam and Colleen were sitting next to each other on the sofa and looking as miserable as sin.

Rivers of mascara ran down Colleen's cheeks and when she spoke, her voice was laced with despair.

'Darren had no right to do that,' she sobbed. 'It's hard enough trying to deal with what's happened without Liam being forced to defend himself.'

'I've spoken to Mr Hanson,' James told her. 'He's now being taken back to Lancaster and has been told not to return here any time soon.'

'But the damage has been done,' Liam said, and James could see the tension hardening the lines around his eyes. 'How the fuck will I convince people that he was lying?'

James offered him a reassuring smile. 'Try not to let it get to you, Liam. I'm certain that what was said won't have been taken in by most of those who heard it.'

Liam pushed out a heavy sigh. 'I don't believe that and I'm sure you don't either.'

James thought it best not to respond to that and told them both that he was sorry the vigil had ended the way it did.

Colleen's eyes flared with emotion. 'I wish now that it hadn't taken place. It was far too soon. We should never have agreed to it.'

James's heart went out to her and he could fully appreciate why she felt that way. The pain of losing her in-laws was bad enough, but it had been compounded by the suspicion surrounding her husband.

He decided there was nothing to be gained by staying any longer and told them he would talk to them again tomorrow.

'Are you sure you're going to be okay?' he asked.

They nodded in unison and Liam reached for his wife's hand. 'All we can do is look out for each other and hope to God that you get the bastard who ruined our lives,' he said.

CHAPTER THIRTY-NINE

James felt mentally fried by the time he got home. His eyes were dry and tiredness was infusing his bones.

Annie had a ready meal waiting for him in the oven and as soon as he removed his coat, she handed him a glass of white wine.

'Get that down you,' she said. 'After the day you've had I'm sure you could do with it.'

He fired a large measure down in one gulp and felt it bite into the back of his throat. After that he couldn't be bothered to shower and so changed out of his suit into his pyjamas and dressing gown. Before going back downstairs he peeked in on the kids and saw that they were both sleeping soundly.

It was approaching nine o'clock when he sat at the table to tuck into his dinner. Annie had already eaten hers. He chugged back more wine as he ate and it soon felt as though his senses had been restored.

Annie was keen to know what had happened after she'd left the square.

'Liam and Colleen were still in shock when I called in on them,' he said. 'And they're naturally fearful of what it will mean for Liam if people start pointing the finger at him.'

'What Elizabeth's brother said has already got villagers talking,' Annie replied. 'Soon after I got back here Janet dropped in to ask me if I'd witnessed the commotion. She'd been told about it by someone else.'

James shook his head. 'It doesn't look good for him or for us.'

'I take it an arrest isn't imminent then?'

'I wish it were, but exactly what happened in Maple Lane three days ago remains a mystery. And the pressure is building on me and the team to get a result.'

'Are you going to tell me about Zelda? You gave me the impression that she's a suspect.'

Once again James departed from protocol and gave her a detailed account of what Zelda Macklin had told him. Annie sat there, white-faced and aghast, as he revealed the woman's claim that she had lung cancer.

'I don't disbelieve her,' he said. 'But we are checking it out with her doctor.'

'And do you seriously think she could have carried out the murders?'

'I just don't know, and it's far too early to give her the all-clear. She hadn't been on speaking terms with the couple for a long time and then suddenly turned up on Christmas Eve to tell them about her cancer. It seems odd to me. And suspicious.'

When he finished his meal, they retreated to the living room where James switched from wine to whisky and Annie helped herself to a gin and tonic.

James was eager to see if the murders would feature in the ten o'clock news bulletins, but before they began a weather forecast painted a gloomy picture for Saturday. Heavy snow alerts were being issued for parts of the north, including Cumbria.

When BBC News came on the murders were relegated to the third story in the running order and the report began with footage of the vigil. It came as a huge relief to James that Darren Hanson's outburst hadn't been caught on camera and didn't even get a mention. The segment ended with the reporter telling viewers that the police still hadn't made any arrests in connection with the murders.

They managed to watch the coverage on Sky and ITV as well and neither of them mentioned the drama at the end of the vigil.

At just before eleven James was following Annie upstairs to bed when his phone rang. The caller turned out to be DC Isaac.

'My apologies for ringing you so late, boss,' she said. 'But there's been a development and I assumed you'd want to know about it immediately.'

'What is it, Dawn?' he replied.

'It's to do with the photograph we circulated of the couple who were caught on CCTV having a go at the Booths in the pub last Saturday.'

'Have we managed to identify them?'

'Indeed, we have. An officer in Penrith just saw the picture and recognised them immediately because he'd met them before. He said they've changed their appearance since then, so I'm assuming that's why they weren't familiar to more of us. The guy had grown the beard and the woman, his wife, had changed her hair colour. They live in Milnthorpe and a patrol is on its way to their address as we speak.'

179

'Do we know yet what their connection was to Nigel and Elizabeth and why they came to Kirkby Abbey that day to confront them?'

'We do. And we also know why they held Nigel responsible for their son's death.'

CHAPTER FORTY

James woke up at six on Saturday morning and could not get back to sleep. There was just too much racing around in his head.

It had been like it for most of the night. After that first call from Dawn Isaac just before he climbed into bed, his mind had resolutely refused to switch off. The DC had called again half an hour later with an update, after which James felt a kernel of excitement take root in his chest.

Sensing that Annie was also awake, he whispered to her that he was going to get up.

'You stay put and I'll be as quiet as I can. Hopefully you'll be able to drop off again.'

He managed to get showered and dressed in under twenty minutes and gave Annie a kiss before stepping out of the bedroom. Once downstairs, he called Isaac to see if she had any more updates on the couple from the CCTV footage who had finally been identified. But she hadn't.

'Put everything that we've got down on paper so that I can read from it when I brief the team,' James said. 'And that includes a few newspaper cuttings from the time so I can put myself fully in the picture.'

He again elected to walk to the village hall, his breath fogging in the cold air, and he arrived at their makeshift incident room in next to no time.

Detectives Isaac and Hall were both there waiting for him along with a bunch of tired-looking PCs.

It had been a long and quiet night during which nothing of significance had happened except for establishing the identities of the couple who had accosted Nigel and Elizabeth.

'They still haven't returned to their home in Milnthorpe,' Isaac said. 'According to their nearest neighbour they drove away on Christmas Eve morning and haven't been back since. We've been trying to trace relatives but so far without success. There's now a patrol car parked up outside their house.'

'What about their phones?' James asked.

'No joy there either. We've managed to establish that they changed their phones and numbers some time ago. Their service provider hasn't yet reassigned the old numbers and it appears they didn't share their new numbers with neighbours.'

James's head was spinning with questions as he prepared to share the information on the couple with the rest of the team. But before they were all together for the morning briefing, he called Superintendent Tanner to update him in advance of his own meeting with the Chief Constable.

'It sounds promising, James,' he said. 'I can well remember the case. It was just before you arrived here in Cumbria.'

'I recall it too. It was quite high-profile for obvious reasons.'

'How many of you recall the name Gabriel Pope?' James asked the team when he began the briefing.

Three of the detectives raised their hands, including DI Stevens.

'He was the guy convicted of raping a young woman at a hotel in Ambleside just over four years ago,' Stevens said. 'She was the bride-to-be on her hen night and he was staying in the same hotel on a friend's stag night. He claimed they had consensual sex, but she said he forced himself into her room and had his way with her. She kept it to herself for a couple of days but then told her husband-to-be who made her go to the police.'

'That about sums it up,' James said. 'The jury believed her and he was sentenced to nine years. He's been serving his sentence in Wakefield prison where three weeks ago he committed suicide by slashing both his wrists with a knife in his cell.'

'I remember hearing about that,' DC Foley said.

James nodded. 'It was brought to my attention as well.'

'I think I know where you're going with this, guv,' DS Abbott piped up. 'It was one of the cases that Nigel headed up. In fact, I seem to remember him standing outside the court after the sentencing and describing Pope as a despicable pervert who had got what he deserved.'

'That's right. And the couple who berated him and Elizabeth in the pub a week ago today are the guy's parents, Sarah and Malcolm Pope. They always insisted their son was innocent and condemned the police, and Nigel in particular, for believing the woman who accused him of rape. And it seems that after their son killed himself, they decided to blame that on Nigel, too.'

'The couple left their home in Milnthorpe on Christmas Eve and their current whereabouts are unknown. There's a patrol car outside their house and we're trying to track them down. Their home number is in our files, but they've replaced their mobiles, and it seems they haven't given out their new numbers.'

James reminded the team what the couple said to the Booths in the pub and replayed the CCTV clip on the TV monitor that had been brought to the hall.

'So are the pair now at the top of our list of suspects?' Sharma asked.

'Yes, along with Liam Booth. He remains a strong contender for the time being and not just because his uncle is convinced that he's the killer. I know that some of you think so, too, and I can see why. He has a strong motive and his behaviour towards his parents in the run up to Christmas Eve was close to threatening.' James nodded towards Foley. 'Actually, I think it's time we put him under surveillance. Maybe we should have done so yesterday. Will you sort that out, Caroline? Bring in a plain clothes officer to watch the house, but tell them to keep a discreet distance.'

'No problem, boss,' Foley said.

'Meanwhile, have you come up with anything else on him?'

'I have, in fact. With the help of the civilian support staff, I've established that he actually has several accounts with different banks and they're all overdrawn. And get this. A few months ago, he downloaded a survey that was carried out by an investment platform into the financial affairs of millennials. It found that two in five young people fear that their parents are frittering away their inheritance on things they don't need, such as holidays. Some twenty per cent of those interviewed also admitted to arguing about their future finances with their parents. And, incredibly, almost half also said they shouldn't have to wait until their parents die to receive the money.'

'And how do we know he downloaded it?' James asked. 'We haven't yet gained access to his devices.'

'Because he forwarded the document to his dad and told him to read it. We came across it on Nigel's emails.'

'I'm sure that went down well with Nigel and Elizabeth,' someone said.

'We're still waiting on the warrant to carry out a search of Liam's home,' Foley continued.

'We need to take a cautious approach from now on where he's concerned,' James said. 'After what happened at the vigil last night, I reckon he's now guilty in the eyes of more than a few villagers. And that's likely to cause problems for him and us. He might well require a degree of protection if this drags on and a growing number of people come to believe he's the killer.'

'I have to admit that I'm now one of them, boss,' DI Stevens spoke up. 'He had motive and opportunity, and it's clear from those WhatsApp exchanges with his parents that he felt they were shafting him by moving to Spain. He comes across to me as a nasty, entitled bastard who we now know has a drink problem and a foul temper.'

James nodded. 'I understand where you're coming from, Phil. But what we need is hard evidence and we don't have it.'

'Then maybe it's time to bring him in and subject him to some pressure,' Stevens said. 'I'm not convinced our priority should be to protect the guy.'

One of the things James liked most about Stevens was that he always spoke his mind. His views on aspects of a case were often at odds with what James believed, but that never stopped him expressing them.

'I take your point, Phil, and I agree it's something we should give consideration to,' he said.

'Several PCs were approached during the night by villagers asking when Liam was going to be arrested. To them it seems like an open-and-shut case,' DC Hall pointed out. 'But I reckon that's mainly down to what happened at the vigil.'

The conversation soon moved on to other lines of inquiry.

'Foley, I'd like you to return to Zelda Macklin's house to have another chat with her,' he said. 'She's given us the go ahead to search the place so take a couple of uniforms with you and see if there's anything to be found there. I doubt that there will be, but since she was at the house in Maple Lane on Christmas Eve, we need to treat her as a serious person of interest. And you also need to confirm with her doctor that she does have cancer. I don't doubt that it's true, though.'

After the briefing, the rest of the morning progressed slowly. They heard from forensics that no fingerprints or DNA deposits had been found on the murder weapon retrieved from the skip. And only Elizabeth's prints had been found on the broken mug in the Booths' kitchen.

'What about the hooded guy seen lurking in the garden on Oak Lane on Christmas Eve?' James asked Abbott.

Abbott shrugged. 'He hasn't shown up on any CCTV footage and no one else has reported being burgled. But some people still haven't returned home from their Christmas breaks.'

James thought about this and said, 'We need to check all homes in the village that have door-cams. If the properties are empty for whatever reason, then we contact the owners to find out when they'll be back. Once they are we can obtain any recorded footage from Christmas Eve.'

They had to wait until eleven o'clock before they received some positive news. It was Sharma who took the call.

'Sarah and Malcolm Pope have at last arrived back at their house in Milnthorpe,' he said. 'They've been approached by officers who told them that we want to ask them about their visit to Kirkby Abbey last Saturday and why they confronted Nigel and Elizabeth Booth.'

'And what was their reaction?' James asked.

'They said that if we send someone over now, they'll be happy to talk to us.'

'And do we know where they've been since Christmas Eve?'

'They claim they were staying with friends in Liverpool until early this morning.'

CHAPTER FORTY-ONE

Milnthorpe was a thriving market village on the banks of the River Bela in Southern Cumbria. It was just under thirty miles from Kirkby Abbey along the A684 and down a stretch of the M6 motorway.

James and Stevens travelled there as passengers in a patrol car. It snowed for part of the way, but not hard enough to cause problems on the roads.

Sarah and Malcom Pope lived in a detached bungalow on the outskirts of the village. It was on a generous plot of land with views of the river to the front and fields to the rear.

The officers who had been there earlier had already left and so there was only one car, a white Ford Fiesta, on the driveway.

The patrol car pulled up behind it and the two detectives climbed out and went straight up to the front door, which was pulled open just as they reached it by the bearded man from the pub CCTV footage.

'You must be Malcolm Pope,' James said.

The guy nodded. 'That I am. And you are?'

'Detective Chief Inspector Walker, Cumbria Police. My colleague is Detective Inspector Stevens. We'd like to thank you for agreeing to see us.'

Malcolm blew out a frustrated breath. 'We were given the impression that we didn't really have a choice. It was either let you come here or be hauled to a police station.'

His voice was deep, his manner abrupt, and James took an instant dislike to the man.

'Me and the wife are planning on going shopping soon,' he went on as he waved them inside. 'So, please don't drag this out.'

He led them through to a small living room where an open fire blazed, but there was no Christmas tree or any decorations. Mrs Pope was perched on the sofa waiting for them. She managed a tepid smile and invited them to sit on the armchairs.

James reckoned she was in her late fifties, about the same age as her husband. She looked pale and anxious, with bloodshot eyes nestled in tired folds of skin.

Malcom told her who they were before he sat down beside her. He was the first one to speak, but before doing so he cleared his throat, which seemed to James like a nervous gesture.

'We were told you wanted to talk to us about our visit to Kirkby Abbey last Saturday,' he said, his voice rough and clipped. 'And I suppose it's because of what happened to Nigel Booth and his wife.'

James nodded. 'It came to our notice that you went along to the King's Head pub where they were having a drink. And as soon as you saw them you stormed over to their table and said some not very nice things to them.'

'How do you know what was said?'

'You were overheard by other customers and the owners. And for your information, the incident was captured on the security camera in the bar.'

Malcom fixed James with a penetrating stare. 'It's a bit of a bloody stretch to link that with the murders, though, isn't it? Sure, we hated Nigel Booth, but not enough to kill him. And even if we had decided to, we wouldn't have gone on to kill his wife.'

'How much do you know about what happened to them?' Stevens asked.

'As much as most people, I guess. It's been all over the news.'

'And how did you feel when you first heard about it?' James asked.

Malcolm shrugged. 'Shocked, naturally. But to be honest we didn't shed any tears. We lost our son because of Nigel Booth. He chose to believe that bitch over Gabriel even though it was obvious she lied about being raped. She was the one who chatted him up and invited him into her room for sex.'

'It was the jury that convicted him,' James pointed out.

'But he shouldn't have been charged in the first place. He told Booth what had happened, and he told us. We believed him. The woman only decided to accuse him of rape after the bloke she was going to marry found out she'd had sex with someone else on her hen night. Booth didn't press her hard enough. He took her word for it and our boy was punished for something he didn't do.'

He closed his eyes then, clenching his jaw, and his nostrils flared like a bull about to charge.

'And I take it you held Mr Booth responsible for your son's suicide,' James said.

It was Sarah who answered this time, in a voice that was husky with emotion.

'Of course we did,' she said. 'Even before he charged Gabriel, we made it clear to him that our son wouldn't survive in prison. He could barely cope with life on the outside. But Booth wouldn't listen. And he made it much worse for us when he described

Gabriel to the papers as a dangerous and despicable pervert among other things. As his parents we were subjected to abuse from strangers and people we knew. We had to change our phone numbers and even our appearance.

'But the suffering didn't stop there. Eighteen months after Gabriel was convicted, we heard that the woman had been divorced by her husband after he found out she'd been sleeping around. How do you think that made us feel? I even wrote to Booth to make sure he was aware of it.'

She caught her breath then and started sucking on her lower lip as her eyes filled with tears.

Malcolm picked up where she had left off and as he spoke James could see the tension along his jawline and in his neck.

'When we thought it couldn't possibly get any worse, we received the call from the prison telling us that Gabriel had killed himself,' he said. 'The bottom fell out of our world yet again. That's when we decided to let Booth know how we felt and that as far as we were concerned, he was responsible for Gabriel's death and for ruining our lives.

'We already knew that he lived in Kirkby Abbey and it wasn't hard to find their address. But when we called at the house that day there was no one in. We then went into the village and asked around. It wasn't long before we got lucky and someone told us they were in the pub. So, we went there and got it off our chests. But I swear to you that we didn't go back to the village after that.'

'Then what did you mean when you told Nigel that you would make him pay for what he did?' James asked. 'You were overheard saying it.'

A look of concern flashed across the man's features. 'I meant that I was going to make everyone aware that his actions led to my son committing suicide. I wanted to ruin his reputation.

Let people know that he was not the decent, honest copper he pretended to be.'

James felt his stomach clench and a flame of anger flared inside him. But he forced himself not to respond directly to it, and said, 'And now to Christmas Eve. We understand you went to visit friends in Liverpool that day and stayed there until this morning.'

Malcolm's face took on a fiery intensity. 'That's exactly right. We drove straight there and we were with our friends the whole time. I'll give you their address and phone number and you can check.'

'What time did you leave here on Christmas Eve morning?' This from Stevens.

Malcolm had to think about it before answering. 'It was just after ten. And don't get it into your heads that we might have driven to Kirkby Abbey first. Liverpool is in the opposite direction and I'm sure that our car will appear on plenty of road cameras between here and there.'

James and Stevens shared a look and an awkward silence fell on the room. James broke it after about twenty seconds by asking for the names and contact details of the couple's friends in Liverpool.

Malcolm had already written them down, and as he handed the sheet of paper to James, Sarah spoke up again.

'Would I be right in assuming that you both worked with Booth and his wife?' she asked.

'You would, Mrs Pope,' James replied.

'Then I want you to know that we don't believe they deserved to die like that. What happened to them was awful and I for one hope you catch whoever did it. But I can assure you that it wasn't either of us.'

CHAPTER FORTY-TWO

'Did you believe them?' James asked when they got back into the patrol car.

Stevens twisted his lower jaw as he considered his response, and then nodded.

'Right now, I'm inclined to,' he said. 'They must know that it'll be easy for us to check traffic cameras between here and Liverpool. And from here to Kirkby Abbey, for that matter. And I can't imagine they would have discarded the knife in the skip so close to the crime scene if they did do it. Surely, they would have ditched it on the way to Liverpool.'

'I hate to say it, but I think you're right,' James said. 'And I'm now having to swallow down my disappointment because after finding out who they were I really thought we were on to something.'

'They had a clear motive, that's for sure. And I honestly didn't realise that they gave Nigel so much stick over the case. From what I remember, Gabriel Pope failed to convince any of the team that he didn't rape that woman, let alone the jury.'

'It was all done and dusted before I came to work here, so I was never that close to the case,' James replied. 'But I suppose they felt obliged to believe and support their own son.'

'And I can understand why they got worked up when they heard that the woman in question got dumped less than two years into the marriage because she'd been cheating.'

They had plenty to think about and discuss on the way back to Kirkby Abbey. And they were both forced to concede that they were making too little headway.

It wasn't a good sign three days into the investigation and James had to play down the sense of unease that was growing inside him.

It had stopped snowing and the drive back to Kirkby Abbey was uneventful. They arrived just before two, but the two detectives were in for a surprise when they reached the village hall. A crowd of about twenty people had gathered on the pavement in front of the entrance.

As the patrol car pulled in to the kerb, James saw that a flustered-looking DS Abbott was doing her best to answer questions that were being flung at her.

But as he climbed out of the car, the crowd's attention immediately turned to him.

'Detective Walker, what's going on with the investigation?' someone called out. 'You said you would keep us updated.'

'It's been three fucking days and you still haven't arrested anyone,' someone else shouted. 'How worried should we be?'

James raised his hands in the air and took a determined breath to stiffen his resolve.

'Just calm down, everyone,' he pleaded. 'We're working flat out to identify the person who committed the murders. You have to trust me on that. But these things take time.'

They'd moved away from Abbott now and James found himself surrounded. Some of the faces he recognised, some he didn't.

The next question was lobbed at him by the man who ran the barber shop in the village.

'Is it true that you think Liam Booth murdered his own parents?' he said. 'If so, then why isn't he in custody?'

James started to reply but was interrupted by another question from a woman who worked in the village hardware store.

'It's out in the open now that Liam's in debt and wanted their money,' she raged. 'But I for one was told ages ago that he's been giving them grief ever since he moved back here. Elizabeth let slip once that he had a go at her for spending money on holidays abroad. He told her he resented it because it felt like his inheritance was being drunk through straws at one beach bar after another.'

James felt a surge of warm blood into his face. They were fearful and frustrated for a reason he perfectly understood. And he knew that he had to respond, but he also had to be careful not to give too much away. Plus, he didn't want to say something that would antagonise the community that he was a part of.

'I would ask you all not to jump to conclusions where Liam Booth is concerned,' he said. 'The man has suffered a terrible loss and is cooperating fully with the investigation.'

'So, are you saying that his uncle was talking bollocks when he confronted him at last night's vigil?' came the response from someone standing behind him.

Without turning, James said, 'That should not have occurred, and the man has been spoken to. But what happened to Nigel and Elizabeth has devastated their family. They're all in a bad place and emotions are running high. In such circumstances things are said that shouldn't be.'

Another man began to spout a question, but James waved a hand to stop him.

'You all need to appreciate that I can't continue standing here answering questions,' he said, keeping his voice calm. 'There are things I need to do. But I promise you that we have your interests at heart. We will keep you informed of the progress we make. But you have to bear with us. Investigations don't always move at the pace we'd like them to.'

CHAPTER FORTY-THREE

What James had said to the crowd did the trick and as he entered the hall no more questions were fired at him and they started to disperse.

Abbott and Stevens were waiting for him beyond the swing doors.

'They turned up about fifteen minutes ago demanding to speak to you, guv,' Abbott said. 'I tried to answer their questions as best I could, but I was relieved when you showed up.'

'It's hard not to sympathise with them,' James responded. 'They're all scared, confused and upset. And they're desperate for answers that we can't give them. The finger being pointed at Liam has made a bad situation a whole lot worse.'

'All the more reason to lean on him,' Stevens said. 'If we do I think there's a good chance he'll crack.'

In the main hall several tables had been decked out with drinks and snacks that had been delivered by the caterers. Officers and admin staff were tucking into a light lunch, so James held off on calling them together for another briefing. Instead, he helped himself to a sandwich even though he didn't have much of an appetite.

Being subjected to yet another barrage of questions had really got to him. It had made him feel like he was letting them down. Letting the entire village down.

At the same time, frustration was gaining momentum inside him and he could feel the tension clawing its way up his spine.

He was used to difficult cases that raised many difficult questions, but this one was particularly challenging because it was so personal.

He managed only two bites of the sandwich before he realised that he didn't want it and dropped it in the bin. He then poured himself a black coffee, and as he drank it, he pushed the negative thoughts out of his mind and focused on what needed to be done next.

Minutes later he got the team's attention and began the briefing by telling them about the interview with Malcolm and Sarah Pope in Milnthorpe. He then told Stevens to carry out the follow-up enquiries.

'Check out the friends they say they spent Christmas with in Liverpool, and find out if their car was captured on any traffic cameras on Christmas Eve,' he said. 'Start with the roads between Milnthorpe and here.'

'Caroline, have you been to see Zelda Macklin again?'

'Yes, I have, boss,' Foley answered. 'I got nothing new out of her, though. She's sticking to her story. We also had a quick look around her house but didn't come across anything suspicious. However, I did speak on the phone with her GP who confirmed that she was recently diagnosed with lung cancer.

'I've also arranged for a PC to carry out surveillance on Liam

Booth. He's in plain clothes and has access to an unmarked car. I gather he's already watching their house.'

James invited suggestions on how to progress the investigation. Several ideas were put forward and as they were being discussed one of the uniformed officers on duty outside the building entered the hall and approached DS Abbott. After saying something to her, he stepped outside again and she waved her hand to get James's attention.

'We have something, guv,' she said. 'The woman whose house was burgled close to Maple Lane at some point over Christmas is outside. She's come to tell us that she thinks she knows who might have been responsible for the burglary.'

James felt his pulse jump up a notch. Would this turn out to be a genuine breakthrough, he wondered?

'Go and bring her to the meeting room,' he said. 'I'll be waiting there for you.'

CHAPTER FORTY-FOUR

James went straight to the meeting room, but he didn't have time to check his notes before the woman was brought in. He'd forgotten who she was so was glad when Abbott introduced her as Hilary Tyler.

'As you'll recall, Mrs Tyler and her husband went away for Christmas and when they returned on Boxing Day, they discovered that their house in Driscoll Street had been broken into,' Abbott said. 'A sum of money and some jewellery was taken.'

James nodded and shook the woman's hand before she sat down at the table.

She was somewhere in her late forties and had an oval face and dark hair cut into a gentle bob.

'We're still not sure when the burglary took place exactly,' Abbott said. 'But we're working on the assumption that it could have been on Christmas Eve, sometime before or after the murders in nearby Maple Lane.'

Mrs Tyler unzipped her coat and removed her gloves, placing them on the table.

'It was my husband who told me to come and see you,' she said in a high-pitched voice. 'He's at work, but I called him just now to tell him what had occurred to me. I was confused as to what to do and I'm still worried that I might be wasting your time.'

'I'm sure that won't be the case,' James said. 'Just start at the beginning and tell us why you suspect you know who burgled your house.'

She drew in a long breath and then released it slowly. 'As I've already explained, we went to stay with friends over Christmas. We left here the day before Christmas Eve, on the Monday afternoon. When you came to see me, Detective Abbott, you asked me if we had told anyone that we were going away and I answered no. That was because I'd completely forgotten that I did tell one of my closest friends, Kerry Devlin. We had coffee together on the Sunday and I mentioned it to her.'

'And are you now suggesting that she could have broken into your house?' James asked her.

She shook her head. 'No, of course not. But her son was with her, you see. So, he knew that our house was going to be empty. His name is Wayne. He's in his twenties and it came back to me when I saw him in the village a short time ago.'

'Then he's the one you suspect,' James said.

She nodded. 'That's right, but I need to explain why. You see, Wayne was living in Leeds until about a month ago. He moved back in with his mum here in the village after breaking up with his girlfriend. But it's no secret that he's a bit of a reprobate. Not so long ago he was convicted of a burglary and spent some time in prison. He got a few months, I think.'

James exchanged a look with Abbott and said, 'That's worth knowing, Mrs Tyler. Thanks so much for bringing it to our attention. We will certainly follow it up.'

'The thing is, I doubt I'd be telling you this now if it wasn't for the fact that Nigel and Elizabeth were murdered on Christmas Eve,' she responded. 'I would have been reluctant to risk destroying my friendship with Kerry by suggesting it could have been her son who broke into our house. But I know you've been wondering if the burglary and the killings are connected.'

'That's correct. We do believe it is possible.'

'But that's not the only thing that got me thinking and prompted me to phone my husband before coming here,' she added.

James raised a quizzical brow. 'Oh? Then what else was it?'

She made a thoughtful noise in her throat before answering. 'When I saw Wayne walking along the street just now his head was covered with a hood. Straight away, I thought about the man who was spotted in the garden of the empty house in Oak Lane on Christmas Eve. It struck me that it might have been Wayne. I know that I'm probably letting my imagination run away with me. But what if I'm not?'

CHAPTER FORTY-FIVE

After Hilary Tyler left, James let the rest of the team know what she'd told them.

'Mrs Tyler gave us Kerry Devlin's address so Jess and I will go there now and have a word with her son,' he said. 'But first, can someone put Wayne Devlin's name into the database and see what comes up?'

The result came through in no time and they downloaded and printed Devlin's photo, which James immediately pinned to the evidence board. He had a thin, sharp face, bulging eyes, and short spiky hair.

It turned out that he had spent four months in prison at the start of the year after being convicted of two counts of burglary. He'd broken into a house and a nearby shop in Leeds and made the mistake of allowing himself to be caught on CCTV.

But that wasn't the first time he'd fallen foul of the law. Three years ago, he was fined for punching a man who spilled drink over him in a city centre pub.

'This is another interesting line of inquiry,' James said. 'And it sounds quite promising given that Devlin has form. But best not to get too excited. The guy may well be our burglar, but that doesn't mean that he's also the killer.'

'Have you come across him before, boss?' Stevens asked.

James shook his head. 'I've never heard of him. Or his mum. We should speak to our colleagues in Leeds. See what else they have on him. And let's check to see if he crops up on any cameras here in the village.'

A light snow was now falling, so James got the same officer who drove him and Abbott to Milnthorpe to take them to Kerry Devlin's house. He also instructed another uniform to go with them as a precaution, in view of the son's previous convictions.

The address was in a quiet street just off the perimeter road, but on the opposite side of the village to Maple Lane.

On the way there he made a quick call to Annie to ask her if she knew Kerry Devlin, and once again his wife proved to be a useful source of local information.

'I've met her a few times,' she said. 'She's a widow and used to work as a tour guide for visitors to the Lake District. But she was forced to retire several years ago because severe arthritis restricted her movements. The first time I met her was at a coffee morning in the hall and we've chatted since then at various other events and when we've bumped into each other in the village.'

'Do you know anything about her son? His name is Wayne.'

'Sorry, no. I'm aware that she has a son, but he never came up in any of our conversations. Why do you ask?'

'I'll tell you later. How are the little monsters?'

'Good as gold, actually. I was going to take them for a walk before it started to snow again. Now Theo is sleeping and Bella is playing quietly by herself in the living room.'

'That's great. I'll let you know if it's going to be another late one.'

'Okay, love. And I'll let you know if I hear anything interesting on the village grapevine. So far today three people have phoned me and two have dropped by to see what I can tell them. Last night's vigil has really added fuel to the fire and Liam is now the target of a lot of horrid speculation.'

Within minutes of James coming off the phone they were approaching Kerry Devlin's end-of-terrace house. It was in a slightly elevated location overlooking neighbouring properties and the countryside beyond them. They parked the patrol car in a layby directly across the road and James instructed the two officers to remain inside.

As he and Abbott approached the front door, he caught sight of a face staring down at them from an upstairs window.

'That looks like the son,' he said, nudging Abbott's arm and flicking his head towards the window.

Abbott glanced up and glimpsed the face just before it disappeared.

'I expect he's coming down to answer the door,' she said. 'His mum might not be in.'

They rang the bell anyway, but after almost a minute and two more rings, it still wasn't answered, which caused a knot to tighten in James's throat.

'This doesn't bode well,' he said. 'We know there's someone in there.'

'So, what do we do, guv?' Abbott asked.

'You stay here and I'll go and check at the back.'

He dashed around the side of the house and on the way signalled for the two PCs to get out of the patrol car and come across the road.

The terrace backed onto a row of garages and the small rear gardens were enclosed by high fences with gates. The first gate along gave access to the Devlin property and James was only yards away from it when it was suddenly pulled open from inside.

A man then stepped out and froze in his tracks when he saw James approaching. He was wearing a parka, the hood tight around his head, and carrying a black holdall.

James recognised him at once from the photo he'd pinned to the evidence board back in the hall.

'Hello, Wayne,' he said as he stepped up to him. 'Where are you off to in such a hurry?'

Panic seized the man's features and his eyes flared.

For a fleeting moment James thought he was going to reply. Instead, he made a snap decision to turn away and leg it. But he wasn't quick enough and James managed to hurl himself forward and grab the back of his coat with both hands.

'I'm a police officer,' James yelled at him. 'Stay put and talk to me.'

Devlin spun round and used his elbow to push James's hands away.

'Get the fuck off me,' he barked and spit flew off his lips. 'I've got to go somewhere and you can't stop me. I've done nothing wrong.'

He stood there wielding a fierce look of defiance while clutching the holdall against his chest. He seemed oblivious to the snowflakes that were gently falling on his head and shoulders.

'Why didn't you answer the front door to us?' James asked him. 'Is there something in the bag that you don't want us to see?'

Devlin's eyes shifted beyond James as one of the uniformed officers came up behind him.

'My mum's indoors,' he said. 'I thought she'd answer it.'

'Well, she didn't. And it was you we came to talk to.'

Blood vessels were bulging out of his temples now and he was clenching his teeth.

His eyes switched between James and the officer as he struggled to decide what to do.

'If you try to run away again, we'll catch you,' James said. 'You must realise that. And you should also know that if you refuse to cooperate with us, you'll make things much worse for yourself.'

Devlin didn't move other than to take a deep breath that inflated his chest.

'But why the fuck do you want to talk to me?' he said. 'I've told you I haven't done anything wrong.'

James shook his head and clucked his tongue. 'I find that difficult to believe, Wayne. You obviously panicked as soon as you saw the patrol car outside and watched us approaching the house. I'm guessing that you quickly filled that bag with stuff that you didn't want us to find.'

Devlin squeezed his eyes shut then and gritted his teeth.

'We want to ask you some questions about where you went and what you did on Christmas Eve,' James said. 'And you need to understand that we won't be going anywhere until you've answered them.'

Devlin opened his eyes and clamped his top lip between his teeth, giving James the impression that it had at last dawned on him that he'd been caught bang to rights.

'Let's go and do this inside the house, Wayne,' he said. 'It's only fair that we explain to your mum what's going on.'

'But it will only upset her and she doesn't need that kind of shit right now.'

'Well, you should have thought of that before you got up to your old tricks.'

He gave James a sneering look of contempt. 'What's that supposed to mean?'

James shrugged. 'I've seen your criminal record, Wayne. You recently served a stretch in prison after being convicted of burglary. I'm willing to bet that it was you who broke into a house on Driscoll Street at some point over Christmas. And it wouldn't surprise me if that bag contains the jewellery and cash you stole from there.'

James paused, expecting Devlin to issue a denial, but he didn't. He just stood there without moving, his face draining of colour.

'I'm assuming that you were also the man seen loitering in the garden of an empty house on Oak Lane on Christmas Eve,' James continued. 'A house that's just a short walk from Maple Lane where two people were murdered on that same day.'

This time Devlin did react. His eyes bulged to the size of eggshells and indignation rose in his voice.

'Are you fucking serious?' he roared. 'You actually think I killed them? That's crazy. I didn't go anywhere near Maple Lane on Christmas Eve.'

'Then you need to convince us of that,' James told him. 'Because your actions have put you firmly in the frame.'

CHAPTER FORTY-SIX

Wayne Devlin was shocked into silence and complied without making a fuss when James demanded he hand over the holdall. He then chose not to put up any resistance as James and the PC led him back through the gate into the garden.

They were approaching the rear door when it was jerked open by a short, grey-haired woman who was supporting herself on a pair of elbow crutches. Abbott was standing directly behind her and nodded at James when their eyes met.

'What in God's name is happening?' the woman said as confusion flickered across her features. 'Are you arresting my son?'

'You must be Mrs Devlin,' James replied. 'I'm Detective Chief Inspector Walker. And your son—'

'I don't give a damn who you are,' she bellowed, cutting him off. 'Tell me why you're here.'

Before he could answer, she turned to her son and said, 'Have you done something bad again, Wayne? You promised me you wouldn't.'

He just shook his head as a look of grim resignation spread across his face.

His mother's eyes drilled into him while she mumbled an expletive under her breath. After several seconds she abruptly turned and hobbled along the hallway.

'Go on in,' James said to Devlin. 'You need to answer some questions.'

He asked the PC to escort the Devlins into the living room while he had a quick word with Abbott.

'I kept ringing the bell and Mrs Devlin finally answered the door,' she said. 'She was apparently sleeping on the sofa and thought her son was upstairs in his room. But as she was about to call out to him, she saw you two enter the garden.'

'He was trying to slip away,' James said, and held up the holdall. 'I suspect this is full of stuff he nicked.'

'Has he admitted to it?'

'No, but I don't think there's any doubt that he's the burglar and was also the hooded guy seen in the garden of the empty property. When I mentioned the murders in Maple Lane, he said he didn't go anywhere near there on Christmas Eve.'

'Do you believe him?'

James shrugged. 'I'll reserve judgement on that for now.'

In the living room, Devlin was slumped on an armchair looking like death warmed up. His face was ashen, drained of any colour, and he was doing his best to avoid eye contact with his mum, who sat opposite him on the sofa.

James experienced a fierce wave of sympathy for her and he felt it was only fair to explain what was happening.

After placing the holdall on the floor, he said, 'We came here to ask your son some questions about a burglary that took place on Christmas Eve, Mrs Devlin. He saw us approaching your house from an upstairs window, but did not answer the door when we rang it, which made us suspicious. We then caught him hurrying out the back with this holdall, which I believe contains stolen property.'

She switched her gaze from her son to James, her face pinched with concern.

'But that's not right,' she said. 'You can't just assume that he broke into a property because he was stupid enough to do it before. And besides, when he went into the village centre earlier, I asked him to take a few things to the charity shop. But he forgot. So, he probably came back to get them and was on his way out again when you lot turned up.'

'Well, there's one way to find out,' James said as he pulled a pair of latex gloves from his pocket and put them on.

No one spoke as he knelt down, unzipped the bag, and poured the contents onto the carpet. There were items of jewellery, including bracelets and watches, a small pile of cash, mostly five and ten-pound notes, plus an expensive looking bottle of brandy and a mini laptop.

'No wonder it was so bloody heavy,' James said, turning to Devlin. 'How many homes did you break into, Wayne?'

Devlin shot James a cold, hard stare. 'I won't be saying anything until I've consulted a lawyer. I'm not stupid enough to think that you give a toss about homes being burgled. You want to stitch me up for those murders because you're under pressure to get a result and you're struggling.'

His mum reacted to this by gasping, which spiked a loud, phlegmy cough that lasted all of ten seconds.

When she finally had it under control, she gazed at James squarely and said, 'Is this true? Do you seriously believe that Wayne killed Elizabeth and Nigel Booth, who were actually my friends? If so, then you must have lost your mind.'

James shook his head. 'At this stage we don't know who killed them, Mrs Devlin. But we know that someone did, and Wayne has questions to answer because he was breaking into homes in that part of the village when it happened.'

She was lost for words after that and wept into her hands as James explained that her son was going to be taken to Kendal Police Station where he would be formally questioned. And officers would be carrying out a search of her house, with the focus being on Wayne's room.

The poor woman couldn't even bring herself to look at her son as he was led out of the living room.

When he was gone James tried to speak to her, to check that she was okay, but she ignored him, too.

'Stay with her for a while,' he said to Abbott. 'See if she knows more than she's letting on and arrange for the place to be searched. I'll head to HQ and will let you know what transpires.'

CHAPTER FORTY-SEVEN

James arranged for another patrol car to take him to Kendal HQ behind the one carrying Devlin. It was almost 5 p.m. when they set out and darkness had fallen like a blanket over Cumbria. Luckily the snow was holding off and it was an easy drive along the A684.

James made two calls during the journey, the first to DI Stevens to bring him up to date.

'Liaise with Jessica,' he said. 'She's still at the house with Devlin's mother. I've asked her to organise a search of the place. And get someone to check and see if the guy crops up on Christmas Eve CCTV footage.'

The second call was to Annie to let her know that he was having to go to Kendal so would be back late.

'Is there anything you can tell me?' she asked.

'Only that we have a suspect who needs to be questioned under caution and with a solicitor present. But it's too early to say if it will yield a result.'

'Any idea when you'll be back?'

'Not yet, but I'll let you know as soon as I can.'

'Take care then, my love.'

The festive spirit still prevailed in Kendal and the streets were busy with people determined to make the most of the party atmosphere in the run up to the start of the New Year. There were plenty of lights and decorations, and the shops, pubs and restaurants appeared to be doing a roaring trade.

It was half five when James entered the station and the first thing that he did was arrange for Devlin to be taken to an interview room. Then he briefed the duty solicitor and asked him to go and speak to Devlin before the formal process began.

There were several detectives on duty and it was DC Colin Patterson he chose to attend the interview with him. Patterson, who James rated highly, had been liaising with his colleagues in Kirkby Abbey so he was well versed in the case. All James had to do was explain to him why Wayne Devlin had been brought in for questioning.

They were ready to roll within half an hour and when James and Patterson entered the interview room, Wayne Devlin was waiting for them with his appointed brief.

He had removed his coat and had on a tight shirt over his thin frame. The defiant glint had retreated from his eyes and they were now glazed and haunted.

After the two detectives took their seats, James pressed on with the pre-interview formalities, which included explaining for the tape why they were there.

'I've spoken to Mr Devlin and he's happy for me to represent him,' said the duty solicitor, a man named Christian Lee, who James knew to be sharp and thorough. 'He's now prepared to answer your questions, but first he wants to place on record that he had no involvement in the murders of Nigel and Elizabeth Booth.'

James took a deep breath and held it before speaking. 'We'll come to that in a moment. First, I want you to know that it's clear to us that you tried to flee from your mother's house when the police car pulled up outside and you happened to see me and my colleague approaching the front door. It's also pretty obvious that you didn't want us to find the items in the holdall you were carrying. These included cash, jewellery and a mini laptop. It won't take us long to establish where they came from and if they were stolen.

'So, let's start with that, Mr Devlin. Did you break into a house on Driscoll Street on Christmas Eve? Were you the hooded man seen in the garden of an empty property on Oak Lane that same day? And did you burgle any other houses on, before or after that day? If you did, then I strongly advise you to own up now and make things much easier for yourself going forward.'

Devlin looked briefly at his solicitor and then spent several seconds gnawing on his bottom lip. When he finally responded, his voice was low and brittle.

'I don't think I have much of a choice but to admit that yes, I did break into the house on Driscoll Street. I also checked out the place on Oak Lane, but the woman next door scared me off. And I did break into two other empty properties. But I didn't take much from any of them, and I know I shouldn't have done it. But I swear on my mother's life that I did not murder that couple. You have to believe me. I'm a petty thief, not a fucking killer.'

James ballooned his cheeks, letting the air out slowly between his teeth.

'Well, I'm glad you've decided to own up to being a repeat offender,' he said. 'That will save us a lot of time. You will, of course, be expected to provide details of the other properties you burgled.'

Devlin nodded. 'I can do that.'

James leaned forward on the table. 'I'm sure you can. But can you also convince us that you did not go up to Maple Lane because you thought the Booths' house would be empty?'

Devlin knotted his forehead. 'Why would I have assumed that? I didn't know the couple.'

'But your mum did. She told us they were her friends. Which means there's a good chance she told you that Nigel was taking part in the Santa Claus parade and you then jumped to the conclusion that his wife would go along to watch him, leaving their house empty. But it wasn't, was it? Elizabeth was there and confronted you. For whatever reason, things got out of hand and you stabbed her in the kitchen. Then Nigel saw you rushing along the lane and you stabbed him, too.'

Devlin's face twisted in anger. 'But that's complete fucking nonsense. I wouldn't dream of stabbing anyone. And while you're wasting your time trying to stitch me up, the real killer is roaming free and posing a threat to other people.'

'My client has a point there,' his solicitor said. 'You haven't presented any hard evidence linking Mr Devlin to the murders and I take that to mean that you haven't got any. He's confessed to breaking into several homes and he will have to face the consequences. But unless you can prove that he also entered the house on Maple Lane, then I think you should stop this line of questioning.'

James sat back and allowed the solicitor's words to hang in the air for a few moments. He had been in this situation many times before, of course, not knowing how hard to push things when there was no solid evidence linking a suspect to a crime. And it didn't help that he himself wasn't convinced that Devlin had carried out the killings.

'Very well,' he said. 'We'll conclude the interview there. Mr Devlin will be charged with multiple counts of burglary, and he'll remain in custody overnight while we continue our inquiries.'

James turned to Devlin, expecting him to kick up a fuss. Instead, he cupped his face in his hands, closed his eyes, and slumped forward onto the table.

CHAPTER FORTY-EIGHT

James told Patterson to take Wayne Devlin to the custody suite and formally charge him with three counts of burglary.

'Send his clothes and shoes to forensics and find out the addresses of the other houses he broke into,' James said. 'And get someone to log the contents of his holdall.'

James went to his office to call Stevens and get him to update the rest of the team.

'We'll keep Devlin in overnight and I'll get Colin to have another session with him tomorrow,' he said to his DI. 'But instinct tells me that he's not our killer. Is there better news at your end?'

'I'm afraid not, guv,' Stevens replied. 'We've checked with the family who Malcolm and Sarah Pope stayed with in Liverpool. They confirmed that the couple arrived about lunchtime on Christmas Eve and they were with them until this morning. We're still waiting to go through CCTV footage.'

'Have you spoken to Jessica?' he asked, feeling disappointed.

'Yes. She's still at Devlin's mother's house, or at least she was when I spoke to her about ten minutes ago. The place was being searched.'

'I'll call her then.'

'What about tomorrow, guv? Do you want the team to come to the hall or go to headquarters?'

'The hall. We should continue to use it as our base for the time being. It's convenient, and it provides a degree of reassurance to the villagers, which I think is important right now.'

James phoned Abbott and briefed her on the interview with Devlin.

'Well, his mum is also convinced that he didn't do it. But she's in a terrible state. He apparently swore to her that he was going straight, but she feared he might slip back into his old ways because of the split from his girlfriend and the fact that he's been out of work for months.'

'How's the search going?'

'There's nothing to get excited about so far. Mrs Devlin has given her consent for us to take some of Wayne's clothes for analysis. And I've got his phone and laptop.'

'I need you to ask her something for me. Find out if she told Wayne that Nigel would be taking part in the Santa parade on Christmas Eve. If she did, then he might have assumed that their house would be empty. No need to call me back. Just text me her response.'

'No problem, guv. What shall I do when I'm finished up here?'

'Go home. That's what I'm about to do. We'll reconvene at the village hall first thing tomorrow.'

James sent a message to Annie to let her know that he would soon be on his way home. But before setting off, he attended to a mound of paperwork that had gathered on his desk and put in a call to Superintendent Tanner to update him.

'I'm under pressure to stage another media briefing, James,' Tanner said. 'But I'm not keen to unless we've got some good news to impart.'

'Well, I'm sorry to disappoint you, boss, but we're still struggling with this one.'

'So, I gather. It wouldn't be so bad if it wasn't for the continued interest being shown by the media. Some stories penetrate the national psyche and this is one of them. That's why I want it wrapped up as soon as possible. I've been told that at least one TV production company has already decided to make it the subject of a documentary to be included in one of those true crime series. They've already started filming and interviewing villagers.'

James blew out his cheeks in exasperation. 'I haven't come across them yet, but that's all we need. It will just make everyone here even more anxious.'

'Let's hope things pick up tomorrow,' Tanner said. 'And I'll let you know if another presser gets scheduled.'

Minutes later James was back in the same patrol car that had brought him to Kendal. As they headed towards Kirkby Abbey, the tension in his shoulders eased slightly, but he was still groggy with fatigue and his eyes felt like they were burning at the edges.

It had been a frustrating day, and it didn't seem as though they were any closer to getting justice for Nigel and Elizabeth.

He feared they were soon going to run out of suspects and without strong forensic evidence the investigation was likely to stall.

Soon after leaving Kendal, he received a text from Abbott telling him that Mrs Devlin was certain that she had not mentioned to her son that Nigel was taking part in the Santa parade on Christmas Eve.

And she remains convinced that he would not have murdered the couple.

It was approaching 8 p.m. when the patrol car dropped him outside his house and by then his head was beginning to hurt from thinking so hard.

The sight of the doorbell camera they'd had installed three years ago distracted him momentarily. He had come to believe that such devices should be an integral part of a copper's home. But he knew that they weren't. Even members of his own team had admitted to not having them. He was now wondering if he should go a step further and consider installing a full-blown home security system. Perhaps it would have made a difference for the Booths if they had replaced the one in their home.

'You look shattered,' Annie said when he entered the house and saw her standing in the hall.

'That's how I feel, love. It's been a long day.'

'Are you hungry?'

'Of course.'

She gave him a hug and a kiss. 'Then come into the kitchen and I'll heat up the beef stew I made.'

He ate the stew and they had a couple of drinks together while he told her about his day, including his visit to Sarah and Malcom Pope's house in Milnthorpe and to Kerry Devlin's home in the village.

'Her son Wayne confessed to breaking into several homes on Christmas Eve, but he's denying that he went to Maple Lane and killed Nigel and Elizabeth,' James said.

He could tell from her face that she was finding it hard to take it all in. A deep frown scarred her forehead and she kept rubbing at her eyes.

Her voice became low and quivering when she told him about the people who had dropped by or phoned to ask her what she knew.

'Everyone is so unsettled,' she said. 'And I get the impression that some people want the killer to be Liam so that he can be arrested and they can feel safe again.'

They eventually went upstairs, but before going to bed, James looked in on the kids. They were both fast asleep and just seeing them brought a smile to his face.

But he couldn't suppress a rush of guilt for not having spent more time with them over the Christmas period.

CHAPTER FORTY-NINE

Sunday morning came with an arctic blast of wind that whipped up the snow which had fallen overnight.

James was awake at six and out of the door by seven, leaving Annie and the kids in bed.

He'd managed to sleep for no more than four hours, but he felt alert and high on adrenaline as he walked to the village hall.

The case was really getting to him and he was well aware that the longer it dragged on, the harder it would be to solve. He needed to stay on top of things and ensure that the team remained fired up. Plus, he had to do whatever he could to keep the villagers onside.

It was clear that they were already feeling let down as well as deeply concerned. And as they became more impatient, the pressure would inevitably mount.

He had called ahead to let DCs Hall and Isaac know that he'd be in early, and when he arrived, they were ready and waiting to provide him with updates.

'The first thing to report, guv, is that nothing to link Wayne

Devlin to the murders has been found at his mother's house,' Isaac said. 'Some of his clothes and shoes are now with forensics, but there were no obvious signs of blood on them. Second, he gave us the addresses of the other two houses he broke into. Turns out they're second homes and we've informed the owners.'

'We've also had it confirmed that Malcolm and Sarah Pope were caught on road cameras between Milnthorpe and Liverpool on Christmas Eve,' Hall said. 'But their car doesn't appear on CCTV coming north towards Kirkby Abbey.'

'That would suggest they told us the truth then,' James said, feeling disappointed to have his fears affirmed.

Hall nodded. 'That seems likely.'

'We were approached late in the evening by a TV crew who are producing a documentary on the case,' Isaac said. 'They wanted to come into the hall and film the set-up, but we turned them down. I expect they'll be back, though.'

'The Super told me about them,' James said. 'It's no great surprise since there's a huge appetite for real crime docs these days.'

'You're right about that,' Hall said. 'In fact, what we're dealing with here would be a perfect fit for two of the series that a lot of us got hooked on.'

'Let me guess,' James said. '*Killer in My Village* and *Killing Mum and Dad.*'

Hall grinned. 'Spot on.'

James told them to prepare for the full briefing when the rest of the team arrived and he arranged for more detectives at HQ to relocate to Kirkby Abbey for the day. He spent the next few minutes checking the news headlines.

The story was still being given prominence on the rolling news channels, but now the focus was on the concerns being expressed by the villagers who feared that the killer was living among them. Some even complained that the investigation into the murders was making too little progress.

When James checked to see what was being written about the case online, he felt bile rise at the back of his throat. Dozens of social media posts were claiming that the prime suspect was Liam Booth, the victim's only son. Some of them mentioned what took place at the vigil while others pointed out that despite being questioned twice by police, he had somehow managed to avoid arrest.

'This stuff is outrageous and potentially libellous,' he said to Isaac and Hall when he drew their attention to it. 'And it will only serve to make things more difficult for us.'

James felt compelled to check in with Liam. He was quick to answer the call and assured James that he was fine.

'Needless to say, we didn't get much sleep last night,' he said. 'But I'll be going for a short hike soon to clear my head and Colleen's planning to do some shopping.'

James had already decided not to mention the online trolling.

'I'll probably want to talk to you again at some point, Liam,' he said. 'And the family liaison officer will also be in touch.'

'Are you any closer to finding out who murdered my parents?' he asked.

'I can't say for sure. But we're leaving no stone unturned and we will get justice for them. I promise you that.'

After ending the call, James wondered if he'd been right to make such a promise given that they seemed to be getting nowhere fast.

It was just approaching 9 a.m. when the team briefing began. Detectives Abbott, Stevens, Sharma and Foley had all arrived by then and Superintendent Tanner and DC Patterson joined in by video link from HQ. Two more detectives were on their way from Kendal to lend support.

James began with a brief summary of where they were with the investigation and mentioned the online posts that were targeting Liam Booth.

'I spoke to him a short time ago and I don't think he's aware of how bad it is,' he said.

DI Stevens couldn't resist the opportunity to make his point again. 'You know my view, boss. I'd put money on him being our killer.'

James nodded. 'And he may well be, Phil. But I've yet to be persuaded. And for that reason, I'm reluctant to head full blast in that direction when there are other credible suspects in the mix.'

'That's a fair point, James,' Tanner said. 'And I can appreciate why you're holding back given that it's very rare for someone to murder both their parents. But Phil also has a point and I agree with him. I think it's time we started to put more pressure on Liam.'

James blew out a breath and nodded again. 'Okay, I'll think about it. But first let me run through some updates. Wayne Devlin remains in custody having been charged with multiple counts of burglary. Colin will have another go at him this morning and forensics will be examining the belongings taken from his mother's home. But so far, we don't have enough to link him to the killings.

'Malcolm and Sarah Pope might have to be removed from the ever-shrinking list of suspects as there's camera footage of them travelling to Liverpool from Milnthorpe on Christmas Eve, but none showing them heading this way,' he said. 'Of course, that doesn't mean they didn't come here and visit Maple Lane. It just means that we can't prove they did.

'Zelda Macklin remains a suspect. We know that she visited

the Booths on Christmas Eve morning, but she swears they were alive when she left the house. And although there's no evidence to the contrary, I'm not convinced she's told us the truth.'

There followed a discussion about the day ahead and Tanner made it known that a decision had just been taken to stage a media briefing in Penrith at which he would make a fresh appeal for information.

'There's more interest in the case now than when the story broke,' he said, 'so we need to keep the media on our side going forward.'

James made clear that he continued to believe that the killer lived in or near to the village and was probably someone the Booths knew.

'We should therefore have a close look at all the villagers,' he said. 'Intensify the background checks and find out where everyone was on Christmas Eve. But at the same time, I want us to seek out more suspects among the many people who Nigel and Elizabeth arrested during their careers, starting with the years leading up to their retirements.'

This gave DS Abbott the opportunity to express a view that she'd kept to herself until now.

'I think we might be missing a trick by not putting more effort into that line of inquiry, guv,' she said. 'I really do believe the killer could be someone from their past, or even a crazy person who developed a hatred for coppers past and present and has embarked on a mission to put the shits up all of us.'

'Well, given the vitriol that's being expressed online that is something we do need to consider,' James responded. 'But the fact is we have to work within our means. We don't have unlimited resources and therefore have to prioritise, which means focusing for the time being on the suspects who've so far emerged.'

The briefing lasted for another ten minutes before James wound it up. He then started reading back over all the notes he'd made following his encounters with Liam Booth, Wayne Devlin, Zelda Macklin and Mr and Mrs Pope. He was fifteen minutes into it when Sharma approached him.

'There's been a development, guv, and it could be significant.'

His words jolted James out of his thoughts. 'Go on,' he replied. 'Make my day.'

'I just received a call from PC Baker, who's been watching Liam's house. He saw him leave there a while ago in his hiking gear and followed him on foot. But instead of heading into the fields, Liam walked to the car park behind the church. There was an SUV there and a guy was standing next to it. Liam went straight over to him and they had what Baker described as a brief conversation. The guy then got back into the vehicle and drove off while Liam crossed the car park and walked into a field. Baker watched him until he disappeared.'

'Do we know who the other guy was?'

'That's the thing, guv. Baker thought he recognised him, but just to be sure he ran a check on the vehicle registration. And it confirmed he was right. The man Liam met up with was none other than Eddie Kane.'

James felt a shudder run down the length of his spine. 'Do you mean …?'

Sharma nodded. 'Yes, I do. The man we often refer to as Cumbria's cruellest crime boss.'

CHAPTER FIFTY
ANNIE

It was 10 a.m when Annie left the house with Bella and Theo. She'd made arrangements to spend the morning at Janet's place to help break up the day.

Bella was looking forward to teaming up with the twins and Theo would no doubt welcome the chance to crawl around different rooms.

Annie had got up soon after James went out. She'd hoped to have a lie-in, but the kids insisted on being fed. The plan now was to drop them off at Janet's and go on to the general store to get a paper and some snacks for lunch. Janet had suggested chicken nuggets and some ice cream, and Annie had insisted on paying.

It was a cold and breezy day and the streets of Kirkby Abbey were particularly quiet for a Sunday. But as she walked to Janet's house, she passed three uniformed officers.

'Daddy's a policeman, isn't he Mummy?' Bella asked her.

Annie smiled. 'Yes, he is, sweetheart, and that's why we're all very proud of him.'

Bella's face creased into a frown. 'Then why doesn't he dress like they do? Those suits are nice.'

Annie couldn't help but laugh. 'I've told you before that they're called uniforms. And Daddy used to wear one, but now he doesn't have to.'

She expected her daughter to ask a follow-up question, but Bella got distracted by a couple being interviewed in front of their house by a television crew.

Annie found it all so very unsettling. She wanted to believe that the nightmare would soon be over, but it seemed most unlikely.

James and his team were clearly struggling and the strain it was putting on the village was immense. Some people were reluctant to leave their homes, while others were becoming more frustrated by the day and were only too keen to talk to reporters. It was a sad and troubling state of affairs, and Annie feared the community would never fully recover if her husband failed to catch the killer.

The first test of their resilience would come when there was no longer a police presence. It would be hard, if not impossible, to convince everyone that they were safe. And after that a dark cloud would hang over the village and life would never be the same again.

By the time Annie got to Janet's house her pulse was spiking like crazy. Her friend answered the door before she reached it, and said, 'You go on to the store and I'll sort the kids. And can you get another pint of milk for us?'

The general store was part of a traditional limestone terrace close to the village square. As Annie strode towards it, she got a shock when the door opened and Colleen Booth came rushing out carrying a shopping bag.

The woman looked upset and was about to cross the road when Annie called out to her.

'Hey, are you okay?'

Colleen stopped walking and turned to Annie. 'No, I'm not. I just got asked by someone in there if my husband murdered his parents.'

Annie grimaced. 'Oh God. Who was it?'

'Rachel Martell. She used to be a friend of Elizabeth and Nigel.'

'I know her,' Annie said. 'She often says things that she shouldn't.'

'Well, it's really pissed me off and I dread to think how many more people are going to ask me the same question. I just can't …'

Colleen stopped there and put her fist against her mouth to hold back the tears.

Annie instinctively reached out and took her by the arm.

'Where are you going?' she asked her.

Colleen lowered her hand, took a breath. 'Home. I've got all I need.'

'Come on, then. I'll walk with you.'

'There's no need. I'll be fine.'

'But I want to. I can come straight back here.'

Annie held on to Colleen's arm as they crossed the road and headed towards the square.

'Thank you, Annie,' Colleen said. 'It's kind of you.'

'It's no trouble. Honest. Is Liam looking after Rosie?'

'No. My mum is. She came down late last night to be with us. Liam has gone on one of his walks. He's feeling the pressure even more than I am and walking helps him to deal with it.'

Annie squeezed her arm. 'I really feel for you, Colleen. It's awful what you're having to go through, especially after what happened to your in-laws.'

'I can't believe that so many people think that it was Liam who killed them. And that's down to Darren. The bastard had no right to spout off his mouth at the vigil. It was a wicked thing to do.'

The pain on Colleen's face was raw and visible, and Annie didn't know how to respond. So, she remained silent during the rest of the walk to Chapel Road.

'Would you like to come in for a cup of tea?' Colleen asked her when they arrived at her home.

Annie said she couldn't because she had to get back to the kids. But the real reason was that she didn't think James would approve of her going into the house of one of the suspects in his murder investigation.

'Well, thank you again for being so considerate, Annie,' Colleen said. 'You're a good friend. I suppose I will just have to accept that things are going to be difficult for us, at least until your James finds out who really committed the murders.'

Annie waited until Colleen had closed the front door behind her before she started walking back towards the general store.

On the way she tried not to think how devastating it would be for Colleen if her husband did turn out to be the killer.

CHAPTER FIFTY-ONE

As far as James was concerned the investigation into the murders of Nigel and Elizabeth Booth had taken a curious turn.

Their son had met up with one of the most notorious villains in the north of England and it raised a bunch of disturbing questions.

How well did Liam know Eddie Kane? What did they discuss when they got together in the car park behind the church? Was it conceivable that Liam was in some way involved with Kane's nefarious activities?

After DC Sharma told James about the encounter, he called the officer who witnessed it to get a first-hand account.

PC Baker told him that he was in the unmarked police car close to Liam's house when the guy came out wearing hiking gear and carrying a backpack.

'I followed him on foot expecting him to head straight into the fields, but instead he walked to the car park,' Baker said. 'The man I now know to be Eddie Kane was waiting for him there. He was standing next to an SUV and smoking a cigarette. Liam went up to him and I had to hold back so they wouldn't see me. They spoke for about ten minutes before Kane climbed back into the SUV and drove away. Liam then took off across the field behind the church and I came back to Chapel Road. I'm now in the car again and he hasn't returned yet.'

'Well, alert me as soon as he does,' James said. 'I'll need to talk to him.'

Before bringing the team together, James got Sharma to print off a summary of what they knew about Eddie Kane, and to download the latest available photograph. As soon as it arrived, he pinned it to the evidence board.

Surprise was evident on the faces of the other detectives and uniformed officers when he told them what Baker had seen.

'This is unquestionably a bolt from the blue and we need to get to the bottom of it,' he said. 'Let's start by reminding ourselves who Eddie Kane is.'

He pointed to Kane's photo on the evidence board. The man was thirty-five but looked older and had a hard, thin face and shaved head.

'Kane has been labelled Cumbria's cruellest crime boss, and with good reason,' James said. 'We know, even though we haven't been able to prove it, that he heads up an outfit that controls no fewer than three county line drug operations, as well as a prostitution racket. Plus, we're convinced he's involved to some extent in people trafficking. The National Crime Agency have had him in their sights for some time.

'We've all worked on cases where violence and intimidation were attributed to him and the scumbags who are on his payroll. But so far, he's managed to stay one step ahead of us despite our best efforts.'

James went on to remind the team of Kane's criminal record.

His first conviction at the age of eighteen was for shoplifting and he received a fine. Four years later he received a suspended sentence for vandalising the home of a man he'd fallen out with in Penrith.

Then, just days after his twenty-third birthday, he was convicted of possessing with intent to supply class A drugs – namely cocaine – with a street value of over a hundred thousand pounds. He was sentenced to six years and served three of them behind bars and the other three on licence.

'It's also worth noting that Nigel was the officer who led the drugs case against him,' James went on. 'Since I came to Cumbria I've interviewed the guy twice. He's clearly a nasty piece of work, but he's also shrewd when it comes to concealing what he's up to. That's how he's managed to build his little empire since coming out of prison.

'His last known address was in Carlisle, but from what I remember he's in the habit of moving around and not staying in one place for long. So, the first thing we need to establish is where he's currently residing. Ahmed, I'd like you to check the files to see if Nigel, or Elizabeth for that matter, had any other dealings with him.'

'And so, the plot thickens,' DI Stevens said. 'Is it possible that Kane was behind the killings because he wanted to settle a score with one or both of them? And if so, did he team up with their son to get it done?'

'That seems highly unlikely to me,' James replied. 'But it is something we have to consider. We know that Liam was in debt, so perhaps Kane paid him to do something for him. Or maybe Liam has been on the gang's payroll for some time, despite the fact that his parents were coppers. After all, he has a legit job delivering parcels and Kane might well be using him to move drugs around.'

James halted the briefing there so that the team could get moving on this new line of inquiry.

Determining the whereabouts of Eddie Kane was a priority, along with confronting Liam when he returned from his hike.

James informed Tanner of the development.

'We should keep this to ourselves for now,' he said. 'It'll cause an enormous distraction if the papers get wind of it at this early stage. But I will bring it to the attention of the Chief Constable, who might well decide to alert the NCA.'

It didn't take the team long to come up with Eddie Kane's current address as it was still listed on the database as being in the city of Carlisle. James gave instructions for the local team to find him and then to bring him down to Kendal HQ to be questioned.

Shortly after that, word came through that the warrant to search Liam's place had been signed off, and PC Baker called to say that Liam had returned home from his hike.

'Then I'll come straight there,' James said. 'Has anyone else entered or left the house this morning?'

'Only his wife,' Baker said. 'She went out briefly and I think it was to do some shopping. When she came back, she was accompanied by a lady who I'm pretty sure was your wife.'

James couldn't conceal his surprise. 'Annie?'

'That's right. You introduced me to her not so long ago when she popped into HQ so I don't think I was mistaken. And it's no secret that she and Colleen Booth are friends.'

James felt his heart skip a beat. He should have told Annie to steer clear of Colleen while her husband remained a prime suspect in the murder investigation. Them being seen together at this time was without a doubt somewhat inappropriate.

It was a stupid mistake on his part and one he hoped he didn't come to regret.

CHAPTER FIFTY-TWO

James asked DC Sharma to go with him to interview Liam and bring along a copy of Eddie Kane's photograph.

'It's started snowing again outside so arrange for a lift,' he said. 'We'll leave in five minutes. I just need to make a quick call first.'

He went into the small meeting room and phoned Annie. When she answered, she explained that she was at Janet's house and she would be there until after lunch.

'Are you able to talk?' he asked her.

'Sure. I'm in the kitchen making tea. The kids are in the living room with Janet and her mum. What's up?'

James cleared his throat. 'The officer who's been keeping an eye on Liam Booth's home has told me that he saw a woman arrive there earlier this morning with Colleen. And he's sure it was you.'

'It was. I bumped into her coming out of the village store. She was ever so upset over something that had happened to her inside, so I offered to walk to Chapel Road with her.'

'And I'm sure that she was grateful, love. But it's best to avoid her while Liam remains a suspect in the killings. It's my fault because I should have flagged it.'

There was a brief pause before Annie responded. 'No, you're not to blame. I acted on impulse without thinking. But when she invited me in for a cuppa, I did turn her down because I thought you'd probably disapprove.'

'It can't be helped, Annie,' he said. 'I know she's your friend, but it doesn't look good with me, your husband, being the senior investigating officer on the case.'

'I can see that and I'm sorry. I'll steer clear of her from now on. It won't be easy, though, because I feel so sorry for her and I don't expect she'll get much sympathy or support from the other villagers.'

'You said she was upset over something that happened to her. What was it?'

'When she was in the store a woman asked her if Liam had murdered his parents. It really got to her and she now fears being asked the same question by other people who think that he did. What she's going through is heartbreaking.'

James chose not to tell her about the latest development involving Colleen's husband, but he did let her know that he was going to pay Liam another visit.

'I expect Colleen will be there,' he said. 'And at least if she mentions meeting up with you earlier it won't come as a surprise.'

'Well, I'm glad of that,' Annie said. 'But before you go can you tell me if you've made any progress?'

'All I can say is that there's been an interesting development, but I can't go into the details. Hopefully, I'll be able to fill you in on it when I see you later.'

Only a light snow was falling, but it was enough to settle across the village.

On the short drive to Chapel Road, James spotted two TV crews at work. One was interviewing a group of villagers and the other was filming a reporter in the square speaking into a camera.

They served to remind him that the case was still high up in the news agenda even though three days had passed since the bodies of Nigel and Elizabeth Booth were discovered.

Three days during which their killer had remained free. And even now there was a degree of uncertainty as to whether that person was a local resident.

James's assumption that the killer lived in the village was based on nothing more than instinct and weak circumstantial evidence, which included the murder weapon being discarded in the skip.

But it was entirely possible that the killer not only fled the scene, but also the village, and was now watching events unfold from afar, safe in the knowledge that the police wouldn't be able to trace them.

Despite that, James wasn't yet ready to move the focus of the investigation beyond Kirkby Abbey, especially now that a link had emerged between one of the suspects and a notorious criminal.

It was a significant development which called into question the integrity of Liam Booth and gave weight to DI Stevens's view that he was the killer. But still, it was hard for James to imagine why the son of two former police officers would get involved with the likes of Eddie Kane. James was therefore looking forward to hearing what he was going to tell them when he was put on the spot.

It was approaching 11 a.m. when the patrol car turned into Chapel Road, but James and Foley were unprepared for the sight that greeted them.

A violent scuffle was taking place between Liam and another man in front of Liam's rented house. A third man, who James immediately recognised as PC Baker, was struggling to pull them apart, while Liam's wife was screaming for them to stop.

Two other men were watching the brawl from a few feet away and choosing not to intervene. And as the patrol car screeched to a halt against the kerb, James was sure that he saw one of them grin.

CHAPTER FIFTY-THREE

By the time James and Sharma were out of the car, PC Baker had managed to break up the fight.

He was standing between the pair, blood vessels bulging out of his neck, a determined expression on his face.

To his left, Liam was taking deep, loud breaths, his eyes filled with a cold fury, and a distressed Colleen was clinging to his arm.

To Baker's right stood the other man, who James knew as Walter Green, the village butcher. He was short and stout, and in his late sixties. Behind him were the two other men, both around the same age, and no doubt his pals. James had come across all three of them in the village on numerous occasions.

'What the bloody hell was all that about?' he yelled, looking from Liam to Green.

Baker began to speak, but Liam beat him to it.

'Isn't that fucking obvious?' he spluttered. 'These pricks believe I killed my mum and dad and they came here expecting me to confess. Instead, I told them to piss off and when they wouldn't go things got physical. Sure, I threw the first punch, but it was nothing more than a light jab against his shoulder. Then he back-handed me across the face.'

'You deserved it,' Green shouted as he turned to Liam, his stare intense and full of aggression. 'Your dad was one of my best friends and he told me more than once that you wanted him and Elizabeth to put their freedom aside so that you could use them as a cash cow. You're an ungrateful, money-grabbing dirtbag, so it came as no surprise when Elizabeth's brother let it be known what you'd done.'

'Okay, that's enough,' Baker said, pushing the pair further apart. 'Let's end this here before things get further out of hand.'

'PC Baker is right,' James said, flicking his head towards Green. 'You need to leave here right now.'

'I will, but first tell me why he hasn't been arrested,' Green said. 'Nigel and Elizabeth were great people and everyone in the village respected them. Except him. All he wanted was their money and he made that clear time and again. Then, when they told him they were moving abroad, he panicked and killed them. Everyone knows it. And so do you, otherwise you wouldn't have one of your people watching the house from a car across the road.'

James felt the blood stir inside him, a hot flush through his veins. 'Mr Booth's home is under surveillance for his own protection,' he pointed out. 'We were concerned that something like this would happen and it turns out we were right to be. A thorough investigation into the murders is being conducted and wild speculation of this kind serves only to impede progress. So, leave now, Mr Green, before I have you forcibly removed.'

This time Green responded with alacrity by turning and walking away, followed by his two pals.

'And don't come back here,' Liam called after them, which prompted his wife to start crying.

James signalled for DC Sharma to lead the couple back into the house before he turned to Baker.

'I'm guessing those three arrived just before we did,' he said.

Baker nodded. 'I saw them walk up to the front door and ring the bell. There was a brief conversation, which quickly turned into an argument. Then Liam pushed Green back onto the pavement before punching his shoulder, and Green retaliated. I came running across as things started to kick off, but they didn't stop when I told them I was police, so I had to step in.'

'I'm glad you did, otherwise it could have turned into something much worse.'

'I don't doubt that, sir. At least no blood was shed or bones broken.'

'And it's a relief that we're not required to take any further action.'

'I take it you're here to ask Liam about his encounter with Eddie Kane?'

'That's right. And I'm assuming it's going to come as yet another unwelcome surprise for him.'

CHAPTER FIFTY-FOUR

PC Baker returned to the unmarked police car across the road and James walked up to the front door, which had been left ajar.

DC Sharma was standing at the far end of the hall when he entered, and as James approached him, he said, 'Liam, Colleen and Colleen's mum are in the living room. I've told Liam that we want to speak to him, but I didn't say what about.'

The three of them were sat together on the sofa. Colleen had stopped crying, but was still shaking. Her mother had an arm around her shoulders, while Liam stared down at the floor, his hands balled into fists on his knees.

'Are you all okay?' James asked as he sat on one of the armchairs. 'That was very unpleasant and should never have happened.'

Liam lifted his head and aimed unblinking eyes at James. 'But it will keep on happening until you find out who did carry out the murders. The longer you take, the worse it will get for me and my family. People like Green are jumping to the wrong conclusion simply because I fell out with my parents. It's not fair. It wasn't me who killed them and I'm sick of having to say it.'

'People have also started asking me if Liam was responsible,' Colleen said. 'It happened in the store this morning. I met your wife afterwards and told her about it. She was kind enough to walk home with me.'

'Yes, I know,' James said. 'She mentioned it. And I realise how uncomfortable it must be for you both.'

'Then isn't there something you can do about it?' Colleen's mum said. 'Stage a press conference or issue a statement making it clear that Liam is not a suspect.'

James shook his head. 'But he is a suspect, Mrs Vine, along with everyone else who lives here in the village. And I'm afraid I can't publicly rule anyone out until we've exhausted every avenue of inquiry. In fact, that's why we're here. We need to ask your son-in-law some questions relating to a new development.'

Liam released a slow breath and gritted his teeth. 'What is it, Inspector? There's nothing I haven't already told you.'

Just as James was about to speak the sound of a child crying came from upstairs.

'That's Rosie,' Colleen said. 'I'd better go …'

'No, you stay here,' her mother told her. 'You should listen to what they have to say. I'll go and take care of Rosie.'

As Mrs Vine shuffled out of the room, James gestured for Sharma to close the door behind her. He then took his notebook from his pocket, along with the warrant to search the property and the photo of Eddie Kane.

Before showing them to Liam, he said, 'When I spoke to you on the phone earlier this morning you told me that you were going on a short hike to clear your head.'

Liam nodded. 'And I did just that. It helped.'

James held up the photo. 'But what you didn't tell me was that you were planning to meet up with this man in the car park behind the church. One of my officers followed you there and saw you speaking to him. I'm sure you don't need me to tell you that his name is Eddie Kane and he heads up one of Cumbria's biggest crime gangs.'

A flash of panic passed over Liam's face and he stared at James in slack-jawed disbelief.

After several seconds he twisted his mouth, searching for words, but before they came out, Colleen turned to him and said, 'Is this true? You didn't tell me about meeting anyone. And how on earth do you know someone like that?'

Liam looked at her and placed a hand on her knee, but she pushed it away.

'Just tell me, Liam,' she said, a sharp note of irritation in her voice. 'What are you keeping from me?'

Liam swallowed hard and sucked in a long breath. 'I didn't tell you about Kane because I didn't want to worry you, Colleen. And I was hoping that I would never have to.'

Colleen cocked her head to one side and frowned. 'Now you're scaring me, Liam. What's been going on?'

'That's what I'd like to know,' James said.

Liam swept a hand through his hair and turned to James. 'I knew Eddie Kane when we both lived in Carlisle and went to the same school. We were mates for a while, but then lost touch after my parents moved here. Years later I heard that he'd turned to a life of crime. His name often came up in the papers and then my dad got him sent down for dealing drugs.'

'Why didn't you tell me that you knew him?' Colleen asked.

Liam shrugged. 'It never occurred to me. Honest. For three

years after we got together, I didn't think about him. But then, six months ago, we met up by chance when I delivered a parcel to someone's home in Carlisle and he happened to be there. We remembered each other and got talking, and I made the mistake of telling him something that I shouldn't ...'

The words dried on his lips and guilt suffused his features.

'Don't stop there, Liam,' James prodded. 'What did you tell him?'

Flicking his eyes back towards his wife, Liam replied, 'I told him that I'd recently moved from Manchester where I got myself heavily in debt to a loan shark.'

Colleen gasped and covered her mouth with her hand.

'It was a stupid mistake, love,' Liam said. 'But at the time it was the only choice open to me. The debts were piling up and my credit rating had fallen through the floor so I couldn't borrow any more money from the banks. And we had to get by. I didn't tell you because I knew you would freak out.'

'So, how much are we talking about?' James asked him.

After a brief hesitation, Liam said, 'Just over fifty grand. It built up over a long period and every time I borrowed from my parents, I spent the money on something else or gambled it away. I accept now that I really fucked up.'

Colleen squeezed her eyes shut and sucked in a breath.

'I was given the name of the loan shark by a friend in Manchester,' Liam went on. 'I knew he was a shady character, but he was up for it and he convinced me that it would be easier and cheaper in the long run to pay off one lender rather than a bunch of 'em. So, I did the deal with him and he paid off the money I owed and I got a few grand on top. We agreed on an interest rate and monthly repayments, and things were fine until he upped the rate and I struggled to pay. It meant I borrowed more on credit, which made things worse. That was when I suggested we move back here to Cumbria. I hoped that if I lived nearer to my parents, I'd be able to get them to bail me out.'

'And you told all this to Kane?' James said.

'That's right. He asked me how I was doing and it all came out. But I said I planned to pay the guy off by getting the money from my parents. Kane then let me know that lending money was one of the things he did as part of his business. He knew the guy in Manchester and offered to take the loan on until my parents sorted things for me. I thought it would be easier paying him back rather than the other bloke, so I agreed. But months after the deal was done, he started to put on the pressure and said he wanted the whole amount paid off because he had some cash flow problems. I've no idea if that was true, though. It was my own fault for leading him to believe that my parents were ready to give me my inheritance early. I think he saw it as a way of getting back at my dad for putting him in prison all those years ago.'

That was a lot of information to take in so James reflected on it for a few moments. But he was inclined to believe the man.

Leaning forward, he said, 'Did you tell Nigel and Elizabeth that you'd become indebted to Eddie Kane?'

A shake of the head. 'Of course not. I just pleaded with them for more money to keep things ticking over. They helped out in the beginning when I went to them asking for it, but then I took the next step, which was to try to persuade them to downsize and give me enough to buy a home of our own. My plan was to then take out a loan against the property to pay Kane off.'

'But that's not how things worked out,' James said.

Liam shook his head. 'Mum and Dad suddenly revealed to

me that they'd decided to sell up and use the money to retire to Spain. It screwed everything up for me. When I told Kane about it, he said it wasn't his problem and if I didn't sort it out quickly, I'd come to regret it.'

'So, he threatened you,' James said.

'He never actually told me that he would hurt me, but it was implied. He phoned me three times in the run up to Christmas and by the Monday I was in a right state and got so upset that I almost confessed to Colleen.'

'You should have,' she blurted. 'I just thought you were worked up over falling out with your parents. That was why I begged you to go and speak to them, and for us to spend Christmas with them.'

'I couldn't tell you,' Liam said. 'I was too ashamed.'

A howl of anguish suddenly escaped Colleen's throat and her face collapsed in a flood of tears. She managed to compose herself after a few minutes and when she did it was James who broke the silence.

'Now tell me, Liam, why Eddie Kane came here to Kirkby Abbey this morning,' he said.

'He called me yesterday to tell me that he'd heard what had happened to my parents,' Liam replied. 'He wanted to talk to me face to face. He made it clear that he expected me to pay off the debt, with a bonus on top, as soon as I got my hands on my parents' house and money. He also wanted to know how much cash they'd left me and how much the house was worth. I agreed to meet him in the car park, but it was mainly because I had a question for him. I wanted to know if he was the one who had killed them, or if he'd got someone to do it for him.'

'And what did he say to that?'

249

'He claimed he had nothing to do with it and even said that he'd been wondering if I'd done it myself to get my hands on their money. I told him that I hadn't.'

'Did you believe what he said?'

'I didn't know what to believe then, and I still don't. But what I do know is that the guy is not going to thank me when he finds out what I've told you and that's now a big, fucking worry on top of everything else.'

CHAPTER FIFTY-FIVE

Liam Booth's confession that he'd got into debt with two crooked moneylenders came as a surprise to James. But the impact it had on Liam's already shell-shocked wife was far more significant.

Unable to control the flow of tears, she had to get up and leave the room. James felt really sorry for her. First her life had been hammered by the murders of her in-laws. And now she was having to deal with knowing that her husband had been keeping so much from her.

He might well insist that it was for her own good, but that was unlikely to encourage her to forgive him, at least in the short term.

There was also the fact that this new information served to heighten his status as a suspect, and would bring even more pressure to bear on both of them.

After the door was closed behind Colleen, Liam rubbed his hands over his face and said, 'I know this all looks really bad. I let things spiral out of control and I shouldn't have. And I don't want to believe that my parents might have been killed because of me.'

'Why didn't you tell us about Kane at the outset if you suspected he could have been responsible for their murders?' James asked him.

The man's jaw tightened. 'It was because I was shit-scared. You see, I've been praying that it wasn't Kane who did it and that you'd quickly find out that it was someone else. I feared that if he was arrested then he might claim that I was involved. Or he might even take steps to stop me revealing that he put pressure on me to come up with the money to pay off what I owed.'

'But that makes no sense, Liam. You know you've been a suspect from the start because of the breakdown of the relationship with your parents. What if we had arrested you before today?'

'Then I would have told you everything. I'd have had to. But I'd still have ended up right where I am now, with a cloud of suspicion hanging over me. I know Kane well enough to be sure that he won't go down without a fight. He'll use all means available to him to distance himself from what happened. And you can be sure that if he had decided to take my parents out of the picture, then he wouldn't have carried out the killings himself. He would have got someone on his payroll to do it for him.'

It was a valid point and one that James would have to consider when they got to question Kane.

'For your information, we've already dispatched a team to what we believe to be Kane's home in Carlisle,' James said. 'But I'm not sure we have his phone number, so I'd like you to give it to us. In fact, in view of what we now know, you'll need to hand over your phone and other digital devices.'

Liam took a breath and let out a long sigh. 'Are you serious?'

James nodded and held up the search warrant for him to see. 'We also have a warrant to search the house. And for your own sake I advise you to cooperate fully with us on this. You insist that you did not murder your parents. If that's true then the sooner we can establish who did, the sooner you and your wife can get on with your lives.'

'That's not going to be easy, Inspector,' Liam responded. 'My parents are dead, my relationship with Colleen might never be the same again, and Christ only knows how Kane will react when he discovers that I've grassed on him. He'll still want his money and he's bound to go to any lengths to get it, even if he's banged up.'

'And on that note, would you be prepared to testify against him if we charge him with illegal moneylending?' James asked. 'It's an offence that can carry a prison sentence as well as a substantial fine.'

Liam sat in frozen silence for several seconds, sweat beading on his forehead. Then he said, 'I'm not sure if I could. It'd be too risky. There's no way you'd be able to protect me and my family.'

James had some sympathy for Liam on that particular issue. Illegal moneylending was big business and organised crime gangs used it to launder their ill-gotten gains. Borrowers who went to them as a last resort were often subjected to a cycle of fear, intimidation and violence as their debts spiralled out of control.

'I do understand why it's something that concerns you, Liam,' James said. 'But it goes without saying that we would do whatever is necessary to protect you.'

Liam started to massage his temples with his fingertips.

'I'd have to talk to Colleen before I decide what to do,' he said. 'This is all so fucking crazy and messed up. It feels like I'm trapped in a nightmare that will never end.'

'I have a final question for you,' James said. 'Have you ever done any jobs for Kane as a way of paying off some of the debt?

It occurred to me that since you deliver parcels for a living, he might have got you to move drugs for him.'

Liam shook his head. 'No, never. I would never have done something like that.'

He suddenly dissolved into tears and James saw no point in continuing with the conversation. He told Sharma to call headquarters and arrange for a forensics team to come and search the house.

'You stay here and oversee things,' he said. 'Bag up his phone and other devices and once he's given you Kane's number send it to me. And get the keys to his van and check that, too. I'll head back to the hall and see where we're at.'

He explained to Liam what was going to happen next and advised him to speak to his wife and mother-in-law.

'Before I go there's something that I need to make clear,' he said. 'If you're holding back anything else then that would be a big mistake, because we will find out.'

Liam rubbed knuckles into his eyes and shook his head. 'There isn't anything,' he said. 'I promise. But do you realise what's going to happen when your lot turn up and start searching this place? Every bugger in the village will assume that the police believe I did murder my parents.'

James felt a cold flush wash over his skin. 'I realise that it won't look good, Liam, but it can't be helped. You do have the option of relocating. Temporarily, of course.'

'I thought about that, and Colleen's mum wants us to go and stay with her in Shap, but I don't want to. This is our home and I'm not going to let a bunch of gossip-mongers drive us out of it.'

CHAPTER FIFTY-SIX

An adrenaline rush took hold of James's body as he stepped back out onto the street. It made him almost oblivious to the snow that was still falling across the village. There was no patrol car to take him back to the hall, but he was happy to walk because it would give him a chance to think through what had happened.

The investigation was suddenly picking up pace and things were starting to unravel. The involvement of Eddie Kane added a disturbing dimension to what they were dealing with. Did he murder Nigel and Elizabeth in their home on Christmas Eve? Or did he get one of his gang members to do it for him?

It was certainly plausible since James was pretty sure that the man already had other people's blood on his hands from all the years he'd been involved in organised crime. And he harboured a serious grudge against Nigel, who got him sent to prison.

But at the same time James couldn't be sure that Liam was being entirely truthful. It was clear now that he had got himself into a financial mess that he was desperate to get out of, so when his parents refused to abandon their plans to sell up and buy a villa in Spain, he might well have resorted to murder in order to save his own skin.

The streets of Kirkby Abbey remained more or less deserted, but James did spot a few uniformed officers hanging around. It made him appreciate yet again that the force was deploying considerable resources in a bid to make the villagers feel safe. But he doubted that even that was enough. Normality and a sense of security was not going to be restored until the case was solved and the killer was in custody.

Until then it was going to be a real struggle trying to dispel people's fears.

Back at the hall, the rest of the team were waiting anxiously to hear what James had to tell them. But first he was given the news that Eddie Kane was no longer living at the address they had on the database. He had apparently moved out several months ago.

'We've rolled out an alert across the county and beyond,' DI Stevens said. 'The National Crime Agency are also on the case. Assuming he hasn't gone into hiding, I don't anticipate that it will be long before we trace him.'

Just then James's phone pinged with an incoming text message. It was from DC Sharma and contained Kane's mobile number taken from Liam Booth's phone.

James chose not to call it straight away and instructed one of the support staff to pass it on to forensics in the hope that they'd be able to locate it. After that, he briefed the team on what Liam had revealed.

'Ahmed stayed at the house to oversee the search,' he said. 'I'm not sure there's anything to be found, but if Liam is our killer, he might have made a mistake and left some evidence there.'

Although the focus of attention was very much on the latest developments, other updates were brought to James's attention.

DC Patterson, on video link from Kendal HQ, said he had formally interviewed Wayne Devlin a second time and nothing new had emerged.

'The items taken from his mother's house are still being examined,' Patterson said. 'But I'll be surprised if they contain anything incriminating. It's my belief that the guy is a burglar and not a murderer.'

DS Abbott then told the team that, so far, no other credible suspects had been flagged during the search through cases that Nigel and Elizabeth had been involved in before they both retired.

'It's still a work in progress,' she pointed out. 'But it's quite time consuming, so we shouldn't expect anything to turn up any time soon.'

Next on James's agenda was a call to Superintendent Tanner to bring him up to speed.

'Perfect timing,' Tanner said when he answered. 'I'm just about to front a media briefing here. Is there anything new I can put out there?'

'There is indeed, boss,' James answered. 'You can make it known that we're keen to speak to a man named Eddie Kane who we believe might be able to assist us with our inquiries. His last known address was in Carlisle, but his current whereabouts are unknown.'

'Are you referring to Eddie Kane, the crime boss?'

'That's right.'

'My God. How the hell does he fit into the picture?'

'Well, in addition to being a notorious drug dealer, he's also a loan shark and Liam Booth is heavily in debt to him. It could be that he had Nigel and Elizabeth killed so that Liam could get access to his inheritance and pay him off.'

'Well, that's not something we expected,' Tanner said. 'I'll be sure to include it then.'

After the briefing was over, James sat down for a few minutes to collect his thoughts before turning his attention to the media briefing that was aired live on the TV from Constabulary headquarters in Penrith.

He watched as Tanner addressed the reporters who were gathered. The Super began by stressing that the investigation into the murders remained a priority for Cumbria Police and that progress was being made.

He then appealed for information on the whereabouts of Eddie Kane and a photo of the crime boss was flashed on the screen.

'All I can say about the man is that he's recently been residing in Carlisle and he might have information that could help detectives leading the investigation.'

A stream of questions followed, but Tanner was careful not to be drawn on whether Kane was a suspect or had been known to the victims.

As James continued to watch, his face scrunched up in concentration, he was unaware that Stevens was trying to attract his attention until the DI resorted to tapping him on the shoulder.

'We've got a visitor, guv,' Stevens said. 'A guy named Ben Blake. I just had a brief word with him in reception and I think you should hear what he has to say.'

James frowned. 'Who is he?'

'He lives here in the village and he's just turned up to speak to you. He was one of Nigel's friends and he took part in the Santa Claus parade with him on Christmas Eve.'

'The name is vaguely familiar,' James said. 'What does he want?'

'To pass on something that Nigel told him that morning before he returned to his home after the parade.'

'Does it have a bearing on the case?'

Stevens nodded. 'Quite possibly. If he's to be believed, then Zelda Macklin lied to us about what happened when she paid the Booths a visit that day.'

James felt his heart jump. 'Is he still in reception?'

'No. I took him to the meeting room.'

'Then go and wait for me there. I want to check my notes first to remind myself what Zelda Macklin told us.'

CHAPTER FIFTY-SEVEN

James was more than a little confused. Was it really possible that Zelda Macklin had lied about what happened when she visited Nigel and Elizabeth on Christmas Eve?

She claimed that the couple had given her a warm welcome and even offered to help her cope with the lung cancer she'd recently been diagnosed with. She also said that she didn't volunteer the information about her visit because she feared the police would jump to the wrong conclusion.

She certainly hadn't lied about the cancer diagnosis because her doctor had confirmed it. So James was intrigued to know what Ben Blake could possibly say that called into question Zelda's account of what had happened that day.

James recognised Ben Blake as soon as he entered the meeting room, but only as someone he had seen out and about in the village during the past four years. He was reasonably sure that he'd never had a conversation with the man.

Blake was in his late sixties with a fleshy, nondescript face and unruly, tousled hair. He was sitting at the table opposite Stevens.

'Mr Blake, this is my boss, Detective Chief Inspector Walker,' Stevens said.

Blake smiled, showing a large gap between his front top teeth. 'You've been pointed out to me on a number of occasions, Detective Walker. It's a shame that we finally get to be introduced as a result of something bad that's happened.'

Only then did James notice that the guy's left wrist was in a splint beneath his jacket sleeve.

'Well, I'm pleased to meet you, Mr Blake,' James said as he sat down next to Stevens. 'I gather you have some information for us relating to something that Nigel Booth said to you shortly before he was murdered on Christmas Eve.'

Blake nodded. 'We both took part in the Santa Claus parade, just as we had in previous years. We were good friends, you see, and did a lot of stuff together. Anyway, I thought I ought to let you know what he told me after the parade ended.'

'Before you do, can I ask why you haven't come to us before now? Nigel and Elizabeth were found dead on Boxing Day.'

'Because on that very morning I was involved in a road accident and I wasn't discharged from hospital until late last night. My wife didn't tell me about the murders until then because she didn't want to add to my woes.'

'I'm sorry to hear that,' James said. 'How badly were you hurt?'

He held up his left hand. 'I suffered a fractured wrist, concussion, whiplash and a badly bruised back. I was in and out of consciousness for twenty-four hours, but I count myself lucky because it could have been much worse.'

'What happened?'

'I was driving to Ambleside to spend the day with my son from my first marriage when I swerved to avoid a stray dog and smashed into a tree. Fortunately, my wife wasn't with me. The car's a write-off, though.'

'But thankfully you lived to tell the tale,' James said. 'Now, tell us about the conversation with Nigel after the parade.'

'Right, yes. Well, it came to mind when I heard on the news this morning that you were trying to find out who he and Elizabeth came into contact with on Christmas Eve. And it occurred to me that you might not be aware that a woman named Zelda Macklin paid them a visit that morning. Do you know Zelda, Detective Walker? She lives here in the village.'

'As a matter of fact, I have met her. She runs the charity shop.'

'That's right. Well, it's no secret that she hasn't been on speaking terms with the Booths for years because Nigel ended a relationship with her and took up with Elizabeth. But on Christmas Eve she turned up at their house in Maple Lane because she wanted them to know that she had cancer. Nigel said that came as a big surprise and they expressed sympathy for her. But then they got another shock when she apparently lost her rag and blamed them for her illness.'

James felt a shiver of unease. 'What do you mean? How were they meant to have been responsible?'

'Exactly. It was ridiculous. But according to Nigel, Zelda reckoned she only started smoking cigarettes because he ended their relationship to be with Elizabeth. She said it helped her cope. And she claimed that over the years she smoked too many fags as well as cannabis joints because they made her life hell by not talking to her.

'Nigel said she got into a right old strop. She called them a pair of nasty bastards and told them that she wanted them to know how she felt before she died.'

'Did this go on for long?'

'About half an hour apparently, because she refused to leave the house. Eventually Nigel had to grab her by the arm and march her to the door before pushing her outside. To his relief she then walked away, but it really upset both him and Elizabeth. He even considered not taking part in the parade. Elizabeth managed to persuade him to, but she was no longer in a mood to come and watch him so she stayed at home and missed it.'

'That does surprise me because I was actually at the parade and Nigel looked as though he was enjoying himself,' James said.

Blake shrugged. 'It was an act. He told me that it was all a bit of a strain and that he wanted to get home to Elizabeth to see if she was all right. Nigel also told me not to mention it to anyone else.'

'So, why did he open up to you?'

'No doubt because I sensed there was something wrong and asked him if he was okay. He did hesitate at first, but he must have felt the need to share it with someone.'

'Have you told anyone else about this?'

'No, I haven't. I might have done so if not for the accident. And I probably would have confronted Zelda about it. What she said to them was appalling. They were a decent couple and it was absurd and hurtful to blame them for her cancer.'

'Can I ask you to please keep this to yourself, Mr Blake?' James said.

'Of course. But talking about it like this has made me wonder if Zelda might have done more than just accuse them of causing her cancer. Do you think it's possible that she actually went back to the house and killed them?'

James knew he had to choose his words carefully and said, 'It seems highly unlikely. However, we will speak to Mrs Macklin to see what she's got to say for herself. But for now, I'd like to thank you for bringing it to our attention and I wish you a speedy recovery from your injuries.'

CHAPTER FIFTY-EIGHT

The team had been thrown yet another curveball and it was one that James was struggling with.

He didn't disbelieve what Ben Blake had just told him, but it was hard to accept that Zelda Macklin might well have committed the murders.

However, the woman did lie to him about the real reason behind her visit to the house in Maple Lane. It wasn't to try to rekindle her relationship with Nigel and Elizabeth. It was to make them feel bad about her cancer diagnosis.

But was it really possible that after being forced out of the property by Nigel, she got so worked up that she decided to go back there when Elizabeth was by herself?

If so, then perhaps Elizabeth let her in, or maybe she entered through a door that wasn't locked. A fierce argument might have ensued during which Zelda grabbed the knife and stabbed Elizabeth. Then, as she fled the scene, she bumped into Nigel and stabbed him as well.

It was all conjecture, of course, because there was a total

lack of any physical evidence. But James was of the belief that if Zelda was guilty of murder, then it wouldn't be hard to draw a confession out of her if they put her under enough pressure.

During that first interview she had come across as vulnerable and somewhat fragile, which he assumed was on account of her illness. He had therefore been relatively gentle with his questions. But the next time he wouldn't be.

He remained in the meeting room, running through it all in his mind, until Stevens returned from showing Ben Blake out of the building.

'What was your take on it, guv?' Stevens asked. 'I don't think there's any doubt that what he told us was true.'

James nodded. 'Me neither. If it wasn't the truth, then I very much doubt he would have bothered coming here. The woman had me fooled. She lied about what happened when she went to the house. But I'm not entirely convinced that she returned there to commit murder.'

'Well, from what Nigel said to Mr Blake, it sounded as though she was really fired up. Dangerously so. Therefore, we shouldn't rule it out.'

'I agree. She lives in Badgers Lane. Can you go straight there and take some uniforms with you? If she's in then call me and we'll whisk her up to HQ to be formally questioned. I'll brief the rest of the team.'

The news about Zelda Macklin surprised everyone else in the team, particularly DC Foley as she had been with James when he first questioned the woman on Friday, and then carried out a second interview with her yesterday.

'I'm truly gobsmacked,' she said. 'I really believed what she told me, and I felt so sorry for her.'

'You're not alone there, Caroline,' James said. 'She spun us a convincing tale. We do know that she was being honest about her cancer, though.'

'But she may well have used the diagnosis as an excuse to get even with the Booths for a perceived wrongdoing before the illness restricted her movements.'

James nodded. 'That is a credible theory, and it reminds me of a case I headed up in London many years ago. A guy who was given less than a year to live with a terminal illness decided to seek revenge against his ex-wife before he died. He blamed her for all the bad things that happened in his life after she divorced him.'

'What did he do to her?' Foley asked.

James raised his brow. 'He broke into her home one night and hacked her and her second husband to death with a machete while they were in bed.'

Several other examples of murders committed by men and women with life-limiting illnesses were brought up. And in each case revenge was the motivating factor, the perpetrators unable to abide the thought of dying while individuals they felt had wronged them went on living.

They were still discussing the issue when DI Stevens phoned James to let him know that he was outside Zelda Macklin's home in Badgers Lane, but she didn't appear to be at home.

'One of her neighbours saw her leave the house earlier but didn't see her return,' Stevens said.

'Then stay there for a while,' James told him. 'We'll pass on her description to patrols in the village and get them to look out for her.'

James gave Foley the task of liaising with uniform and then switched the conversation to Eddie Kane. The first thing he was told was that the crime boss had still not appeared on the radar.

'A few known associates of his have been approached, but they all claimed that they don't know where he is,' DS Abbott said. 'And forensics haven't been able to trace his mobile phone using the number that Liam Booth gave us because it appears to be switched off.'

A support officer who'd been monitoring news coverage of the story spoke up then to reveal that it was back at the top of the bulletins following Superintendent Tanner's media briefing earlier.

'The potential involvement of Eddie Kane has sparked even more interest in the case,' she said. 'His photo is being posted all over the internet and our own press office is being inundated with calls. Plus, some of the anti-police online trolls are even suggesting that Nigel and Elizabeth might have been corrupt coppers who used to do business with Kane before they retired. And he may have had them killed because he feared they were about to expose him.'

James let his breath escape in a slow whistle and shook his head. The frustration was now like a raging storm inside him. He just wished there was some way to control or contain the misleading crap that was put out there for all to see. But there wasn't, not as long as so much of the media continued to be unregulated.

He motioned towards the evidence board, which had been filling up with new information, and said, 'So, we have three prime suspects in Eddie Kane, Liam Booth and now Zelda Macklin. Until Ben Blake turned up my money was on either Kane or Liam. But now I'm not so sure. I really didn't think that this case would have so many twists and turns.'

'I don't reckon any of us did,' Abbott said. 'And it does concern me that if those three turn out to be innocent then we'll be right back to square one. And that will bring more pressure to bear from the manic media and people living here in Kirkby Abbey.'

James knew that Abbott was right to worry. Having multiple suspects didn't necessarily mean that you were on course to wrap things up. What was needed was irrefutable evidence or a confession, and right now they had neither.

After checking his watch, and noting that it was already 5 p.m. and dark outside, he told the team to take a break.

'Afterwards we'll start giving thought to how we should approach the interviews with Kane and Zelda when we eventually get them in a room,' he said.

He then decided to call Annie to let her know that he was likely to be late home again.

'I'll probably have to go to Kendal shortly to interview someone,' he said. 'How are things with you?'

'All fine,' she replied. 'The kids enjoyed themselves at Janet's and we stayed longer than I planned to. At least it was a distraction from all that's going on. I don't suppose there's anything else you can tell me?'

'Not right now, love. But hopefully we'll have time to chat when I eventually get home.'

'I got some ready meals at the store today so you'll have a choice if you're hungry.'

After hanging up, James called Sharma to check on what was happening at Liam's house.

'We'll soon be finished here, guv,' Sharma told him. 'We've bagged up plenty of Liam's belongings, including his phone, laptop and some clothes. I have to say though that nothing so far has struck me as suspicious.'

'Is he cooperating?'

'Sure, but he's mostly spending his time trying to console his wife and mother-in-law. They're both in a terrible state. And quite a few of their neighbours are gathered outside on the street watching despite the snow.'

James went to get himself a coffee and as he started to drink it, he took another call from Stevens.

'Zelda Macklin still hasn't returned home,' Stevens said. 'And uniform haven't spotted her in the village. It could be that she's gone on a trip and won't be back today. Or maybe she's actually in the house and too scared to answer the door to us.'

James felt a twist of alarm and came to a quick decision.

'In that case I'm giving you the go-ahead to force your way in,' he said. 'In the circumstances I'm sure we can justify it.'

He finished his coffee before reconvening the meeting. But just as James began to speak, his phone rang again. Another call from Stevens.

'We're inside the house and it's not good, guv,' the DI said. 'Zelda Macklin is here and I suspect she has been for most of the day. But I'm afraid she's dead.'

CHAPTER FIFTY-NINE

'It appears that she killed herself,' Stevens said. 'An overdose.'

James felt his spine stiffen and a wave of heat suddenly rose up his neck.

His mind took him back to when he met Zelda Macklin and how he was struck by her pale, listless skin and rheumy eyes. And that was before she told him she had cancer.

'There's a suicide note,' Stevens continued. 'But before you jump to the wrong conclusion, it's not a confession to murder. Do you want me to read it out to you?'

James coughed against the dryness in his throat. 'No. I'd rather read it myself. I can be there in minutes. Seal the place off and I'll alert forensics and the pathologist.'

The rest of the team could tell from the look on his face that he'd received some more disturbing news.

'Brace yourselves for another shock,' he said. 'That was Phil. I told him to force entry into Zelda Macklin's home because there was no answer there. He did and they've found her dead inside. Almost certainly suicide.'

Foley was the first to respond by letting out a loud gasp. 'Oh, my lord. That's terrible. How did she do it?'

'Looks like an overdose. There's a note, which I'll read when I get there, but Phil says it's not a confession. That doesn't mean that she didn't kill the Booths, though.'

'She was already facing a death sentence,' Foley said. 'Maybe she just decided not to wait for the cancer to consume her.'

'Did she have any next of kin?' James asked.

Foley shook her head. 'I asked her that when I last spoke to her. As you know, her husband Graham died about four years ago. They had no kids. Her parents are no longer alive and she was an only child.'

After a long, thoughtful pause, James asked Foley to arrange for forensics and the pathologist to go to the house.

'I'll head there myself now. Stick around until I come back. Dawn and Kevin should be here soon to start the night shift so pass on everything to them, including your thoughts on how we should deal with Eddie Kane when we eventually bring him in.'

James decided to go on foot to Badgers Lane in the hope that it would ease the tension that had seized him.

By the time he stepped outside of the hall barely any snow was falling and the streets were virtually empty, but as he walked at a steady pace every muscle in his body continued to feel taut and the blood pounded in his ears.

His head had also begun to ache from the flow of unsettling thoughts rushing through it. Zelda Macklin's death was more than just a tragedy. It was going to impact the investigation in several ways.

The team would need to find the answers to a bunch of new questions. And when it became public knowledge that she had been a suspect in the killings, it would heighten the pressure from the febrile media. Plus, his fellow villagers were bound to become even more concerned and confused. Two murders and now a suicide in less than a week would be enough to make some of them believe that Kirkby Abbey was cursed.

It took him less than ten minutes to get to Zelda's small detached house. There was a patrol car parked outside and several curious neighbours had gathered on the pavement. James was well aware that if they didn't already know what was going on, then they soon would because it wouldn't be fair, or indeed possible, to keep the woman's death a secret.

There was a uniformed officer standing in the doorway and when he saw James's face beneath his woollen hat he waved him inside.

In the hall James called out to Stevens as he pulled on a pair of latex gloves.

'I'm in the living room,' Stevens called back, and as James stepped in there, he felt his stomach muscles clench.

He saw Stevens first. He was standing in front of the television scribbling notes on a pad. To his right was the sofa and Zelda was lying on top of it in her dressing gown, with her eyes closed and her mouth open.

The sight of her hit James like a cattle prod and robbed him momentarily of air.

'There's a box of all kinds of medication on the coffee table over there,' Stevens pointed out to him. 'It looks to me as though she made herself comfortable before overdosing on both paracetamol tablets and anti-depressants. There's nothing I can see to indicate foul play or that anyone else has been in the house recently. It's my guess she's been dead since late this morning.'

She looked so peaceful to James, as though she were sleeping, and he couldn't help wondering if she had contemplated taking her own life for some time. Or had she only just decided to?

'You should read the note she left,' Stevens said. He reached behind him and picked it up from on top of a sideboard. 'It appears to answer a couple of questions for us. I've compared the handwriting with various documents I came across in her bedroom drawers and I'm pretty sure she wrote it.'

He handed the note to James. It was scrawled neatly and carefully on a sheet of lined white paper. As James read it the words sent a chill through every fibre of his being.

To whoever is unlucky enough to find me.

By the time you read this I should be long gone thanks to all the tablets I've taken. I see no point in waiting for the cancer to kill me. I have nothing to live for and no one to love and now guilt has made me even more miserable.

My behaviour towards Nigel and Elizabeth on Christmas Eve was unforgivable and I deeply regret it. I also regret lying to the police by not telling them why I really went to their house. It was to make them feel bad because they'd had it so good.

They were still together and enjoying life while I was ill and desperately unhappy. I made myself believe that it wasn't fair and so I said some horrible things to them. They didn't deserve it.

I still can't believe what happened to them later that day and it serves to compound my guilt. But I was being honest

with the detective who spoke to me when I told him that I
did not kill them and I have no idea who did.

I have one last wish before I die and it's that the police find
the murderer so that whoever it is will be made to suffer
the consequences.

I'm now going to lie back and close my eyes and hopefully
find peace in death.

Zelda

James was really moved by Zelda's words and he felt all twisted up inside.

'What do you think?' Stevens asked him.

James rolled his shoulders. 'I think that if she had murdered Nigel and Elizabeth then she would have confessed to it. She'd have had no reason not to.'

'That's exactly what I think, too, guv. But it does mean we're down another suspect.'

CHAPTER SIXTY

James saw no need to hang around in Zelda Macklin's house since he was as sure as he could be that it wasn't a crime scene.

Like many other terminally ill people before her she had sought to end her own life before it became progressively unbearable.

He didn't leave the property until he'd taken photos on his phone of Zelda lying on the sofa and the suicide note. He wanted to show them to the rest of the team. He also got Stevens to show him the other examples of her handwriting, and came to the same conclusion as his DI, that Zelda had most definitely written the note.

A forensics team arrived just as he was stepping outside, and he was told that the pathologist wasn't far behind.

A sense of unease gripped him as he made his way back to the village hall. His mind was racing, throbbing, buzzing. A drink. That was what he needed, but it was going to have to wait until he got home. First, there was one more briefing to attend to.

It was unlikely to last very long unless there had been some other breakthrough, which he very much doubted. He would have to let Superintendent Tanner and the Constabulary press office know about Zelda, of course. They would need to pull together a response to the questions that were going to be hurled at them once the news of her death broke.

It was sure to fuel the media firestorm that was already raging out of control following the appeal for information on the whereabouts of Eddie Kane.

James could well imagine the feverish activity taking place in newsrooms across the country. Journalists would be digging out the files on Kane and calling in favours from contacts in the force. And they'd soon be searching for information on Zelda Macklin, the elderly widow who had taken her own life soon after being questioned about the murders of the two retired police officers.

The latest shocking developments would almost certainly arouse even more interest among viewers and readers. But at the same time life for the residents of Kirkby Abbey was set to become even more stressful. A third villager found dead. The involvement of a high-profile figure associated with organised crime. Yet another home being searched by police. In addition, they were faced with the chilling prospect that the investigation could drag on for days or even weeks.

James found it impossible to switch off the negative thoughts and by the time he got to the hall his mind was on fire.

As expected, the team had nothing new to report. There was still no word on Eddie Kane's whereabouts and the search of Liam Booth's house had concluded without anything being found to link him to the murders.

James described the scene in Zelda Macklin's home. He showed them the photo of her body and read out the suicide note she'd written.

'I think we have to conclude from this that she did not kill Nigel and Elizabeth,' he said. 'Yes, she lied to us about what happened that morning, but I'm pretty sure that she would have owned up to the murders in the note if she had committed them.'

The others agreed with him and they were still discussing it when DCs Isaac and Hall arrived to start their overnight shifts. James quickly briefed them on the developments before he put in a call to Tanner.

The Superintendent was none too pleased to hear about Zelda and he took it upon himself to liaise with the Constabulary press office.

'We have to make it clear that she was interviewed because she visited the house in Maple Lane on Christmas Eve morning,' he said. 'It was therefore likely that she was the last person to see them both alive. We should also stress that she most definitely wasn't put under excessive pressure.'

'She wasn't, sir,' James said. 'We certainly didn't give her the impression that we thought she was our killer.'

Tanner then told James that there had been a significant response to the appeal for information on the whereabouts of Eddie Kane.

'We suspect that some of the calls that have come in were from time wasters who really have no clue where Kane is. But some sound legit and are being followed up. Meanwhile, I have a meeting first thing tomorrow with the powers that be, including the Chief Constable and the county's Crime Commissioner. They want me to give them a full update and they're bound to express their disappointment that we still haven't solved the case. So, if something comes in overnight be sure to pass it on to me.'

When James came off the phone, he shot his cuff and consulted his watch. It was almost eight o'clock. It prompted him to send a short text to Annie telling her that he'd be home sooner than expected because he had no need to travel to Kendal.

By now he was more than ready to call it a day. His eyes felt heavy and gritty and he was finding it harder to concentrate.

Before leaving the hall, he had a brief conversation with the team about how they would handle Eddie Kane when he eventually turned up. DC Isaac was tasked with pulling together a file on the suspect and DC Hall with drawing up a list of all his known associates in the underworld.

'Kane is now our main suspect for reasons other than the fact that he's a vile lawbreaker,' he said before drawing the meeting to a close. 'He wanted Liam to get his hands on his parents' money and assets. He had a grudge against Nigel for getting him put in prison. And now he's suddenly gone awol. So, let's hope that it won't be long before we're able to bring him in.'

CHAPTER SIXTY-ONE
ANNIE

It came as a huge relief to Annie that James would be home sooner than expected. She really didn't want to go to bed without speaking to him first.

The last couple of hours had been dreadful. A few of their neighbours had turned up on the doorstep asking if she could shed light on what was going on in the village. And she'd received three phone calls from friends, including Janet.

They all asked the same questions. Was it true that Zelda Macklin had been found dead in her home? Since police officers were searching Liam Booth's home, did that mean he did kill his parents? And what the hell did an infamous gangster have to do with anything?

Annie had been too busy making the kids their tea and putting them to bed to devote any time to catching up with the news. And James hadn't been feeding her bits of information.

She therefore had to tell the callers that she honestly had no idea what was happening, but she wasn't convinced that they all believed her.

Now, as she sat at the breakfast bar hunched over a mug of coffee, a feeling of despair clawed at her, and checking the news on the phone didn't make her feel any better.

There were still reporters in the village and they were constantly providing updates to their online news feeds. Annie had seen a clip of Superintendent Tanner's latest media briefing and the photo of Eddie Kane, the man they wanted to trace. She had also seen a short video clip of police and forensic officers entering and leaving Liam and Colleen's home.

The news that Zelda Macklin had been found dead hadn't been confirmed by police yet, but one of her neighbours had called the BBC to tell them that she'd seen police officers force their way into the woman's home and had then heard one officer tell another that it appeared Zelda had committed suicide.

Annie was floored by the news and she was finding it increasingly hard to make sense of anything. As with everyone else in the village, this whole rotten business was really getting to her. It was as though their normal lives had been put on hold. Emotions were running high and it was proving impossible for people to talk about anything else.

Janet had told her about the retired couple living next door to her who had decided to move into a rented caravan in Whitehaven until the killer was caught. And one of the Walkers' own neighbours had said that she was now too afraid to allow her fifteen-year-old daughter to go out in the village after dark.

It was enough to make Annie wonder if anyone was safe right now, and this and the other thoughts that were filling her head were giving rise to a mounting sense of trepidation.

It was just before nine when James arrived home. His face was taut and sullen and he looked exhausted.

After he had slipped off his coat, Annie put her arms around him and gave him a kiss. She could feel the tension in his body and it was obvious that he'd had a rough day.

'Would you like me to make you something to eat?' she asked as she eased herself away from him.

'It's a drink I need and maybe some crisps,' he replied. 'I know I probably should be famished since I've hardly eaten anything since this morning, but I really couldn't face a proper meal.'

He didn't bother to go upstairs to change. Instead, he went into the living room and dropped onto the sofa.

Annie prepared him a large whisky with some ice and Coke, and poured crisps into a bowl.

'Thanks, love,' he said as she handed him the glass and placed the bowl on his lap. 'It's been a shit day.'

'I gathered that,' Annie said. 'I didn't realise that so much had been going on until the neighbours started arriving here and friends began calling. Is it true that Zelda is dead?'

James downed a mouthful of whisky before nodding. 'She killed herself. I saw her body and read the note she left. It was horrible.'

Annie felt a cold weight settle in her chest. 'Do you want to talk about it?' she asked him.

His face slipped into a grimace. 'Not really, but I think it's only fair that I keep you abreast of events since everyone else in the village seems to know what's happening.'

And so he told her about his day, and as she listened Annie felt the emotions well up inside her throat.

'It's no wonder you don't have an appetite,' she said.

James asked her how her day had gone and she decided to open up to him.

'I got really anxious this morning after meeting Colleen,' she said. 'What that poor woman is going through is beyond belief. And when I was at Janet's place neither of us could stop talking about the murders and wondering who was responsible. Then, after I put the kids down, the calls started. Now I'm far more worked up. It's even got me wondering if life here in the village will ever return to normal. And if it doesn't then should we actually consider moving away for Bella and Theo's sakes?'

The question surprised him and his eyeballs popped out on stalks.

'That's the last thing I expected to hear, love,' he said. 'Do you mean it?'

A deep furrow entrenched itself in her brow. 'That's just it. I don't know. All I do know is that I'm not sure I want to stay in a place where I don't feel comfortable.'

James took her hand and gently squeezed it. 'I will get to the bottom of this, Annie. I promise you. And once it's behind us we can decide what happens next. But I'm confident that Kirkby Abbey will recover from this, just as it did after that first bout of bloodshed turned all our lives upside down four years ago.'

CHAPTER SIXTY-TWO

Troubled thoughts kept James awake for much of the night. They veered between the investigation and the impact it was having on his wife and the other villagers.

Before they got into bed, he tried to reassure Annie that once the case was solved things would slowly but surely return to normal. But she didn't seem convinced, and he wasn't even sure he believed it himself.

The truth was the village had never fully recovered from the serial killer rampage four years ago. Some families moved away because of it and a few of the elderly residents were too afraid to step outside of their homes for months afterwards.

Journalist Gordon Carver even wrote an article for the *Cumbria Gazette*, which was published just over a year ago, in which he revealed that dozens of villagers were still struggling to go to sleep at night because of what had happened.

What was going on now was different in many respects, but it would be wrong to underestimate the effect it was having on the community.

'What time is it?' Annie croaked beside him.

'I didn't realise you were awake,' he said as he leaned over to glance at the bedside clock. 'It's only half five. I'm going to get up. Do you want me to make you a cup of tea?'

'No thanks. I had an awful night. I'm going to try and drop off again before the kids have me up. If I'm lucky I'll get an hour's sleep. Just be quick and quiet if you can.'

'I will,' he said. 'And I'll use the downstairs bathroom.'

He kissed her on the forehead before rolling out of bed and grabbing the clothes he'd left out. Once downstairs he tried to focus his mind as he shaved and showered, but it wasn't easy. There was just too much going on inside his head.

When he was dressed, he went into the kitchen and made himself a coffee and some toast. He then used his phone to go online and check Monday morning's newspaper headlines.

Two of the tabloid front pages carried a photo of Eddie Kane with headlines saying that Cumbria Police wanted to speak to him in connection with the murders in Kirkby Abbey. On one of the papers, it appeared alongside a picture of Nigel and Elizabeth Booth.

Prominence was also given to the death of Zelda Macklin. The *Sun* ran the story on an inside page with the headline: *Another mystery death shocks Lake District village.* It then claimed that a source within the Cumbria Constabulary had told one of its reporters that they believed she had committed suicide after the police questioned her about the killings.

It never ceased to amaze James how quickly news spread. In this era of mobile phones and social media it was becoming increasingly difficult for the police to withhold information, or even delay it from being released.

After downing the coffee and toast, James got moving. It

wasn't snowing outside and the forecast was for a dry but cold day. On the brisk walk to the hall, it suddenly occurred to him that tomorrow, Tuesday, would be New Year's Eve.

He very much doubted that many people in the village would want to celebrate. But he knew that elsewhere in the county hordes of revellers would take to the streets, filling the pubs, bars, restaurants and event venues. As usual, it was going to put enormous pressure on Constabulary resources. It would probably mean fewer officers being deployed to Kirkby Abbey in order to patrol the streets and help villagers to feel safe. And James feared that it would serve to heighten the sense of insecurity that already had the community in a vice-like grip.

As James entered the village hall it struck him that this was the day his Christmas break officially ended. Yet again it had been seriously disrupted by horrific events that were completely out of his control.

Would something similar happen next year if he and Annie remained in Cumbria, he wondered? It was a question they would have to give thought to when they sat down together to discuss the future.

But for now, it was all about bringing this current nightmare to an end. And he feared that it wasn't going to happen any time soon unless they got a break in the case.

The makeshift incident room was already bustling and he was surprised to find that two of his detectives – DI Stevens and DC Foley – had arrived before him. They were standing in front of one of the TV monitors with DCs Hall and Isaac.

On the screen, GB News was running video footage of police and forensic vehicles outside Zelda Macklin's house in Badgers Lane. And they showed a short interview with one of her neighbours, who described Zelda as a kind lady who ran the village charity shop.

'I just saw myself coming out of the house yesterday,' Stevens said when James joined them. 'I hadn't realised I was being filmed.'

'There are cameras all over the village,' Isaac pointed out. 'TV crews were prowling the streets throughout the night and interviewing anyone who was willing to provide a sound bite. I gather they also did some filming in the King's Head pub before they upset a couple of locals and were thrown out.'

'This is a story that keeps on giving and the hacks are lapping it up,' James said. 'That's why we need to step up our game before we run out of leads and suspects.'

He quickly convened a meeting that included uniforms and support staff. But he soon learned that there had been no positive developments overnight. Isaac and Hall had spent much of their shift pulling together notes relating to Eddie Kane. A list of his underworld associates had been circulated and shared with the National Crime Agency. But the guy still hadn't appeared on the radar.

James was given various updates. The post-mortem on Zelda Macklin would be carried out by Pam Flint later in the morning, but it wasn't expected to throw up any surprises. And officers were continuing to delve into Nigel and Elizabeth's case files, looking for felons who might have decided to seek revenge against them.

He was also told that family liaison officer Samantha Cooper would soon be visiting Liam Booth and his wife to check on them.

As more of the team began arriving, James received a call from Superintendent Tanner, who was about to go into his meeting with the Chief Constable and Crime Commissioner, among others.

James informed him that there had been no further developments during the night.

'That's a shame but it's what I expected,' Tanner said. 'I'll let you know how the meeting goes, but I can tell you now that one of the issues on the agenda is deployment of resources tomorrow. They're going to insist that we drastically reduce the number of uniforms being sent to Kirkby Abbey. I can completely understand why. Last New Year's Eve was one of the busiest ever across the county, with a shooting, three stabbings, and at least a dozen drunken brawls during which a number of people were hurt.'

'It's something that I've already thought about, guv,' James said. 'We'll just have to cope.'

'And I'm sure you will, James. I'll get back to you as soon as I can. Make sure that I'm alerted to any developments in the meantime.'

When the call ended James got everyone together for a briefing. But just as he was about to start talking, the doors leading to the reception area were thrown open and a group of angry-looking people stormed into the hall. It was immediately obvious to him that they were villagers, as some of them he recognised.

He felt his heart leap into his mouth and a blast of heat spread through his body. Then he drew in a ragged breath and steeled himself for what he knew was about to follow.

CHAPTER SIXTY-THREE

There were about fifteen of them and they were followed into the hall by the PC who had been on duty out front. It was clear to everyone that they'd forced their way past him to gain access to the hall.

James stepped forward quickly and gestured for his team not to react.

'Just stay put and let me handle this,' he said to them.

The familiar figure of Walter Green, the village butcher, had led the charge. The last time James saw him was when he'd grappled in the street with Liam Booth, who he had openly accused of murder.

Now he stood in front of James with the other villagers spread out behind him. He was wrapped in a thick black duffle coat and the expression on his face was openly hostile.

'We didn't want to have to resort to this, but you've given us no choice,' he said, his voice loud and clear. 'We're all living in fear in our own village while being kept in the dark as to what the hell is going on. The same thing happened four years ago when lots of stuff was kept from us as a killer stalked around the village. We don't want to go through that again, so we came here to demand some fucking answers.'

James held up his hands, palms out, fingers splayed. 'I can appreciate why you all feel so frustrated, but you shouldn't be doing this,' he said. 'The building is closed off to the public for a reason. It's being used as the base for our investigation and as such …'

'We're not stupid, Detective Walker, we know that,' Green cut in. 'But we decided that this was the only way to really get your attention. It seems like you're prepared to confide in those press vultures, but not with us, even though we're the ones who live here.'

'That's exactly right,' someone else spoke up. 'I couldn't believe it when I saw on the news that some guy who is known to be a gang leader is involved. And what about Zelda, who I've known for years? Did you actually accuse her of killing Nigel and Elizabeth? Is that the reason she decided to top herself?'

Green mouthed off again before James could respond to the question. 'I don't get why you're not arresting their son. You must suspect him otherwise you wouldn't have sent a team to search his home. So surely he has to be a threat to the rest of us and ought to be locked up.'

The air in the hall was suddenly loaded with tension and James had to take a breath before responding. He spoke slowly, measuring his words so as not to further alienate his aggrieved audience.

'The investigation into the murders is ongoing,' he said. 'We're therefore unable to share with you all the information we gather. There are procedures we have to follow. Unfortunately, in a close-knit community such as this, that can cause problems and make some people feel uncomfortable. But I'm afraid that can't be helped.'

'That's not good enough,' bellowed a man who James recognised as one of Kirkby Abbey's two resident taxi drivers. 'You can't expect us to say and do nothing while people we know are dying, homes are being searched, and police feel the need to patrol the streets to keep us safe. We have a right to know what's behind all this and if everyone living here does face a serious threat.'

'He's right,' Green added. 'And in case you've forgotten, tomorrow is New Year's Eve. What are we expected to do? Is your advice to stay at home or will it be perfectly safe for us to go out and celebrate?'

James listened with mounting irritation as more questions were fired, but at the same time guilt nudged at him because he could also see it from their point of view. They had all been dealt a shocking blow with the murders in Maple Lane. But it hadn't ended there and the unnerving events that followed had stoked up their anxiety.

'Look, I really am sorry that it's come to this,' he said. 'But you must understand that there are many questions that we don't yet know the answers to. And that includes who murdered Nigel and Elizabeth. I've said before that we don't think the killer will strike again. But it's our duty to encourage everyone to be cautious. That doesn't mean you shouldn't go out and celebrate the New Year.'

'But what about Liam Booth?' Green fired back. 'Are we supposed to act as though he's done nothing wrong?'

'We haven't come across any evidence to indicate that he has,' James said. 'Mr Booth is one of several people we've spoken to, but I can't say more than that. However, I can tell you that we do not believe that Zelda Macklin carried out the killings. She was interviewed because she visited the Booths at their home on Christmas Eve before they were killed. It was to tell them that she had sadly been diagnosed with terminal lung cancer. We now have reason to believe that she committed suicide because she didn't want to prolong her own suffering.'

The news of Zelda's illness obviously hadn't spread because there was a collective intake of breath and glances were exchanged.

The news was still being processed when Green said, 'What about this bloke Eddie Kane whose picture is being plastered all over the news? Most of us had heard of him before now, but is he actually a suspect? And why?'

'Again, I can't disclose why we want to speak to him,' James replied. 'And you really shouldn't expect me to. During the course of any investigation, it's essential that we respect the privacy of individuals who we talk to.'

A heavy silence fell over the room as the questions dried up.

James took it to mean that they'd got the message and accepted that there was only so much he was able to tell them.

'Can I ask you to please leave the building now?' he said. 'My colleagues and I need to get on with the job. But I want you to know that I've taken on board the concerns you've raised and will give serious thought to them going forward.'

They all seemed reasonably satisfied with his response, even Walter Green, who said, 'Well, I suppose that's fair enough for now. But please don't let us down, Detective Walker. You need to share information with us so that we know if we should or shouldn't panic.'

Green and the others then filed out of the hall, accompanied by several uniforms. James experienced a blast of relief as he watched them go.

'That could have gone a lot worse than it did,' he said to the rest of the team, who all nodded in agreement.

He then followed the group out onto the street to make sure they dispersed. But they didn't do so straight away because a TV news crew happened to be filming the front of the building and quickly seized the opportunity to approach them.

James thought about intervening but quickly decided not to and went back inside. As he re-entered the hall he could feel the blood throbbing in his temples. What had just happened had left him perturbed and somewhat demoralised. The level of disquiet among the villagers was continuing to rise and it was clear that he was losing their trust.

It wouldn't have mattered so much if these people were not his friends and neighbours. But they were and this case could potentially damage his relationship with them.

The thought played on his mind as he gestured for the team to get together again so they could pick up where they'd left off with the briefing.

But before he began to speak his phone rang. The caller was DC Patterson and the news he wanted to pass on took James's breath away.

'You're not going to believe this, guv,' he said. 'But Eddie Kane has just turned up here at headquarters with his lawyer. He's saying he heard that we've been trying to contact him in connection with the Booths' murders and he's eager to find out what it is we want.'

CHAPTER SIXTY-FOUR

So, Eddie Kane had surfaced at last. But the fact that he'd turned up voluntarily at the station with a lawyer gave James some cause for concern.

Did it mean that he was confident the police wouldn't be able to link him to the murders? It was certainly possible. After all, almost twenty-four hours had passed since Superintendent Tanner had made a public appeal for information on his whereabouts. That had given him plenty of time to construct a credible alibi.

'When did they actually arrive there?' James asked Patterson.

'About fifteen minutes ago,' the DC replied. 'I had a brief conversation with them and the lawyer insisted on speaking to you as the senior investigating officer on the case. When I explained that you were in Kirkby Abbey, he said that he and his client were prepared to wait for you to get here.'

'Where are they now?'

'In the canteen. I told them that you could be here in less than half an hour.'

'And I will be,' James said. 'Prepare an interview room and let them know I'm on my way.'

James swiftly passed on the news to the rest of the team and despite his misgivings a glimmer of hope blossomed in his chest.

'Keep all the other wheels turning,' he told his colleagues. 'I very much doubt that the guy is going to confess to murder or make it easy for us to get to the truth, whatever that is. But even so, this is a big step in the case. Meanwhile, Liam Booth remains firmly in the frame. We need to find out what forensics gets from his phone and laptop, and get the FLO to advise him not to go out hiking by himself for the time being. Tell him it's for his own good.'

'PC Baker is still by himself outside the house in Chapel Road,' DC Foley said. 'I think maybe we should provide some backup.'

James nodded. 'Good idea, Caroline. You sort it and if he ignores our advice about going out then we should have him followed.'

James told DI Stevens to take charge in the hall and instructed DS Abbott to go with him to Kendal HQ.

Finally, to one of the uniforms, he said, 'Can you call up a patrol car for us? We might have to rely on blues and twos to get us there in under half an hour.'

The roads were clearer than James expected them to be so they made good time travelling to Kendal, but there was some congestion along the A684, which prompted the driver to switch on the siren and flashing blue lights.

James's heart was racing in anticipation of what lay ahead, but he tried not to build his hopes up too much. Eddie Kane was no fool. Far from it. In his capacity as a successful crime boss, he had to be smart as well as ruthless.

He'd served only one three-year term in jail, thanks to Nigel Booth, but that was back when he was in his twenties. Since then, he had managed to keep a clean slate despite his involvement in a wide range of criminal activities, including drug trafficking, people smuggling and illegal moneylending.

DS Abbott had never had the dubious privilege of meeting the man so she asked James what she should expect.

'I've interviewed him twice before,' James told her. 'The first time was after one of his rival drug dealers turned up dead having been shot in the head. I'm convinced he did it or arranged for it to be done, but the evidence against him didn't stack up. The second time was when a snitch told us he was keeping a haul of drugs in the basement of his then home in Windermere. We got a search warrant but there was nothing to be found. And I'll never forget the grin that lit up his face when we left the house.'

'So, was the snitch lying?' Abbott asked.

James shrugged. 'I doubt we'll ever know for sure. He wasn't there when I went to his rented flat in Penrith to follow up. He'd vanished along with all his belongings, and no one has heard from him since. So, in answer to your question of what to expect, I think we can expect Kane to put on a good show. The man is a slippery, immoral bastard who has an army of foot soldiers at his beck and call.'

CHAPTER SIXTY-FIVE

On the drive to Kendal, James called Tanner to tell him about Eddie Kane, but he'd already been informed.

'The message came through a few minutes ago,' the Super said. 'I look forward to hearing what he has to say, although I don't expect him to own up to anything, especially not a double murder.'

'Me neither,' James said. 'But if it's obvious that he's lying to us then at least we'll know to throw all our resources in his direction.'

Just before the patrol car arrived at headquarters, James phoned DC Patterson and told him to take Kane and his lawyer to the interview room.

Five minutes later, at just after eleven, he and Abbott entered the building. Patterson had been alerted and was waiting for them.

'Who is Kane's brief?' James asked him.

'Someone you'll be familiar with, guv,' Patterson said. 'Gideon Strong, the go-to lawyer for crime lords and bent politicians.'

James had often faced Strong across a table. The guy was unscrupulous at the best of times, and unfortunately, he was also very good at his job.

There was a uniformed officer standing outside the interview room when they got there and James acknowledged him before stepping inside.

Strong and his client were sitting next to each other and the sight of them caused the skin on James's face to stiffen.

They could not have looked more different. Strong, a tall man with a stooped posture, was smartly dressed in a bespoke grey suit, white shirt and red tie. He had a narrow face with high cheekbones and a large, beak-shaped nose.

Kane was much shorter and wore a leather jacket over a polo sweater. His dark brown hair was longer than it had been the last time James saw him, but he had the same hollow, menacing eyes.

'I don't suppose there's any need for me to introduce myself,' James said as he pulled out a chair from under the table. 'But I don't believe that either of you have met my colleague, Detective Sergeant Abbott.'

Strong stretched his face into something resembling a smile while Kane merely gave her a disdainful look.

When he and Abbott were seated, James went through the motions of explaining that the interview was being recorded.

In response, Strong said, 'Then let me begin by stating that my client is here of his own accord. He had no idea the police wanted to speak to him until that outrageous public appeal was brought to his attention. The clear implication was that he's suspected of murdering those two former detectives in Kirkby Abbey on Christmas Eve. For the record, he vehemently denies any involvement and is now considering lodging an official complaint with the Cumbria Constabulary.'

Kane grinned, cocky and confident, and James felt the blood stir in his veins.

'My client is nevertheless willing to cooperate with the investigation,' Strong continued, his tone of voice professional, detached. 'But afterwards we will expect you to make it clear through the media that he is not a suspect.'

James pressed his mouth into a tight line as he fought down the urge to laugh. True to form, the lawyer had decided to go on the offensive from the start, but it was a tactic that rarely fazed experienced coppers like James.

'Then let me begin by making it clear that we issued the appeal because we were unable to locate Mr Kane,' James said. 'We needed to speak to him as a matter of urgency, but discovered that he was no longer living at the address we had on file.' James turned to Kane. 'So, why don't we start there, Eddie? Where are you currently living?'

Kane wet his lips with the tip of his tongue and said, 'Not far from here. I'm renting a place in Staveley Village. Have been for the last couple of months.'

'Why do you keep moving around?' This from Abbott.

He shrugged. 'Because you lot have made people believe that I'm some kind of villain, which I'm not. It means I don't feel safe staying in one place for very long. And for your information, I still make my money by doing odd jobs and from gambling.'

James clicked his tongue against the roof of his mouth and shook his head.

'Sometimes I think you actually believe the crap that comes out of your gob, Eddie,' he said. 'You're up to your neck in everything from dealing drugs to trafficking people. We managed to put you away for it once and mark my words we'll do it again. It's only a matter of time.'

'I insist that you retract that remark,' Strong reacted. 'My client is not—'

Kane raised a hand to cut him short. 'Forget it, Gideon. He's trying to wind me up and if you object to everything he says, then this farce will drag on forever.'

Kane then thrust his jaw at James. 'Let's get on with it, shall we? For some reason you seem to have got it into your heads that I killed Nigel Booth and his wife. Well, it's just been made clear to you that I didn't. So, can I suggest that you start spending your time trying to find out who did.'

He sat back in his chair and folded his arm across his chest.

James tugged out his notebook and placed it on the table between them.

'It's probably best if I tell you what we know before I put questions to you,' he said. 'Let's start with the fact that you went to Kirkby Abbey yesterday morning to meet Nigel and Elizabeth's son, Liam. One of my officers saw you speaking to him. And Liam has told us that you wanted to know when he'd be able to pay off the money that he owes you, which amounts to about fifty thousand pounds.

'He explained that the two of you used to be friends and when you met up again recently, he confessed to being in debt to a loan shark in Manchester, who happened to be someone you knew. And since one of your lines of business is moneylending, you agreed to take on the debt so that he could pay you instead.

'We also know that Liam made you believe that his parents were going to gift him his inheritance before they passed on. But they suddenly changed their minds and when you heard about it you weren't happy. You told him that you had cash flow problems and that if he didn't sort things out and pay you off then you'd make him regret it.'

A nuance of uncertainly flickered behind Kane's eyes, but he remained silent as he fixed James with a hard stare.

'It therefore occurred to us that you might have decided to solve the problem yourself by killing the Booths or getting one of the lowlifes on your payroll to do it for you. That way you'd be able to get your hands on the fifty grand, or maybe more, and also get your own back on Nigel for getting you sent down.'

Kane threw a glance at his lawyer before letting out a sneering laugh.

'I've always regarded you as a competent plod, Detective Walker,' he said. 'But this is total bullshit and smacks of desperation. I'm not a fucking loan shark and there's no way you'll be able to prove that I am. And no way did I threaten Liam. I don't know why he told you I did. I took on his debt as a favour to an old friend. He'd got himself into a right mess and I agreed to help him out. Secondly, I never harboured a grudge against his dad, either. The guy was just doing his job. Sure, I got banged up, but I had only myself to blame. And to really make your day, I have a foolproof alibi for Christmas Eve when those murders took place.'

'And what is it?' James asked him.

'I spent all of that day in Maryport with three of my mates. We arrived the night before for a stag do and stayed until Boxing Day when I went straight back to Staveley.'

Strong then whipped a piece of paper out from his inside pocket.

'I've compiled a list of my client's friends who were with him throughout the visit to Maryport,' he said. 'The names, addresses and phone numbers. And they're all happy to speak to you. Plus, there's the address of the house they stayed in, the pub where they partied and my client's current address in Staveley.'

'Would I be right in assuming that those mates all work for you, Eddie?'

Anger suddenly blazed in Kane's eyes and his voice dropped to a hard-edged whisper.

'Listen, copper. Whether you like it or not I was nowhere near Kirkby Abbey on Christmas Eve. And I'm sure there'll be plenty of CCTV footage of me and the guys in Maryport. Also, you're bang out of order to suggest that I might have paid someone to kill the Booths so that Liam could get his hands on their money. Despite what you think, I'm not some Mafia don.'

By now James's insides were as tight as a clenched fist. As expected, Kane and his lawyer had come well prepared to rebut any and all allegations. And James was in no doubt that his alibi would stand up. But he wasn't yet convinced that Kane hadn't had some involvement in the murders.

'During your chat with Liam yesterday, I gather you asked him if he had killed his parents?' he said. 'Do you think it's possible that he did?'

A shake of the head. 'No, I don't. I believed what he told me and I don't know why I bothered asking him. The guy would never do something like that. He doesn't have it in him.'

James kept the interview going for another half an hour in the hope that Kane would slip up and say something that he'd come to regret. But he didn't, and in the end, James was forced to concede that there was no point continuing.

Before he called time, he made it clear to Kane that his alibi would be checked out and that they might well want to speak to him again.

Before he showed the pair of them out, he warned Kane to stay away from Liam Booth.

'I'm sure that the issue of the money he owes you will eventually get sorted,' he said. 'But if you harass, or worse still threaten him, then I'll make sure that you're the one who comes to regret it.'

CHAPTER SIXTY-SIX

James got DC Patterson to show Kane and his lawyer out of the building. He then asked Abbott for her reaction to the interview.

'Well, you were right to describe Kane as a slippery, immoral bastard,' she answered. 'That's exactly how he came across. But it does sound like he's got a watertight alibi for Christmas Eve, guv.'

James nodded. 'I don't doubt that he has. However, I'm not convinced that he didn't get one of his henchmen to kill Nigel and Elizabeth. And did you notice the way he jumped to Liam's defence by saying there was no way he would have murdered his parents?'

'I did, but then the last thing he wants is for Liam to go down for it while still owing him money. And if the pair of them colluded in the killings, then Liam would be sure to drag him into it.'

James took a deep breath and let it out in a long, tuneful sigh.

'Can I leave it to you to check out the alibi?' he said. 'We need to speak to the three guys on the list the lawyer gave us. And get our people in Maryport to visit the pub they went to and the house they stayed in. Let's dig up as much CCTV footage as possible, especially from Christmas Eve.'

He and Abbott went to the office where the team gathered round with a shared sense of anticipation. James waited until the others joined by video link from the hall in Kirkby Abbey before beginning the briefing.

Nobody seemed surprised that Kane had sought to distance himself from the murders with what appeared to be a credible alibi. But there was clear disappointment when James explained that there weren't enough grounds to hold him in custody.

'All we can do at this stage is to try to pick holes in his story,' he said. 'That'll include putting pressure on the pals he says went to Maryport with him. I'm guessing they've been well briefed, but that doesn't mean they won't slip up when questioned. At the same time let's try to build up a case in respect of the moneylending. We've never gone down that road with him before, but it could well prove to be a weakness. It'll help if we can persuade Liam to testify against him, but right now that looks unlikely.'

'Do we know if forensics have found anything interesting on Liam's phone and laptop?'

'It seems that he hadn't deleted text exchanges between him and his parents,' DI Stevens replied. 'We've already seen the most recent ones, but others go back months and in them he either pleads for more money or thanks them for giving him some. In addition, there are lots of calls registered between Liam and Kane, but no text messages and nothing incriminating so far. The service provider is going to be asked if any deleted messages can be retrieved.'

'That reminds me,' James said. 'We should apply for a warrant to search Kane's current address in Staveley and get access to his phones.'

'I'll sort that,' Stevens said.

The next update came from DC Foley. 'The post-mortem report on Zelda Macklin has just come in and it's as we expected, guv. Dr Flint is a hundred per cent sure that she died from an overdose of various prescription drugs. There are no signs of foul play on the body. She'll issue a death certificate when she gets the first toxicology results through.'

The briefing was short and sweet, and James drew it to a close after announcing that he would soon be returning to Kirkby Abbey.

He then went to his office and called Superintendent Tanner to let him know what was happening with Eddie Kane.

'We'll be checking out his alibi, but he put on a good show as usual,' he said. 'How did the meeting go with the Chief Constable and Commissioner?'

'They expressed concern that the case is dragging on while attracting so much attention,' Tanner said. 'Plus, they're insisting that we reduce the number of uniforms in Kirkby Abbey for New Year's Eve. They want them deployed in places where things are likely to kick off. It was difficult for me to argue with that.'

James felt the thud of dread in his stomach when Tanner went on to say that of the fifteen uniformed officers currently on duty in Kirkby Abbey, ten would be sent elsewhere. It concerned him because he feared that it would anger and further alienate the villagers.

'That's assuming, of course, that the village remains crime free overnight and into tomorrow,' he added.

James spent the next half an hour in his office catching up on paperwork. It was his least favourite part of his job, but the bigger the case, the more of it there was.

Before leaving headquarters, he had a bite of lunch with Abbott in the canteen. He was happy for her to remain at headquarters until the end of her shift, but asked her to report to the village hall again tomorrow.

'Working from there is still our best option,' he said. 'Kirkby Abbey is where the murders occurred and where clues that will lead us to the killer are most likely to be found.'

It was half three in the afternoon when he headed back south in a patrol car and he was dropped off outside the village hall at four, by which time darkness had descended.

As soon as he was inside, he began yet another conversation with the team about where to go next with the investigation. And he received assurances from his detectives and support staff that any plans they'd had for seeing in the New Year had been cancelled.

James expressed his gratitude and told them that after the meeting they could all go home.

'I don't expect we'll be in for any more unpleasant surprises today,' he said.

But it turned out that he'd spoken too soon because just five minutes later the uniformed officer who'd been on duty outside the building came rushing into the hall.

He was carrying a sheet of paper in his gloved hand and the startled expression on his face brought the team to an abrupt halt.

Looking squarely at James, he said, 'You need to see this note, sir. It's just been picked up from a post box here in the village. And if it's not a prank, then it's pretty disturbing.'

He advised James not to touch it with his bare hands and held it up for him to read.

The words were in big, bold letters on a single sheet of paper. And they caused every muscle in James's body to go stiff.

CHAPTER SIXTY-SEVEN

The note was clearly going to have an impact on the investigation. But it was also going to raise concerns among every copper in the Constabulary.

As James read it a second time, he felt his breath catch in his throat.

To the Filth

No one who is serving or has served as a police officer in Cumbria is safe now. You're all scum and I've decided to make some of you pay for what was done to me. I started with Nigel and Elizabeth Booth because they were easy targets. Others will soon follow until I'm satisfied that I've got my revenge against the force.

Mr Anonymous

'The local postman brought it straight to us after collecting mail from the box on the square,' the officer said. 'It wasn't in an envelope apparently and so naturally he read it and got the shock of his life.'

'Is he still here?' James asked.

'Yes. He's in reception. His name is Noah Sullivan. I said you'd want to speak to him.'

James nodded. 'I know the guy and I do want to have a word.'

He got the officer to hold the note up again and took a photo of it on his phone before inviting the rest of the team to read it.

DI Stevens was the first to react. His eyes ballooned and he said, 'Holy fuck. Should we take this seriously?'

Next came DC Foley, who shook her head as her face ran through a gauntlet of emotions from surprise, to shock, to total disbelief.

'We can't afford to ignore it,' she said. 'If whoever wrote it means business then we have a serious problem.'

As the others read the note, James hurried into reception. Noah Sullivan was waiting for him, dressed in his distinctive red Royal Mail jacket.

He was a dour-faced man in his fifties with short grey hair and a stocky frame. He'd been collecting and delivering the post in Kirkby Abbey for years and also lived in the village.

'Hello Noah,' James said. 'Thank you for bringing the note to our attention.'

'I knew you'd taken over the hall so it made sense to come straight here with it,' he said. 'It struck me as odd as soon as I saw it because it was folded over and not in an envelope. It made my blood run cold when I read it.'

'Mine, too,' James said. 'But we can't be sure that it's not from some sick prankster so I would ask you to keep it to yourself for now. We will, of course, be looking into it.'

'You have my word, Detective Walker. If it gets out it's going to cause a lot of distress whether it's true or not.'

'Exactly. Before you go, I just need to ask you a couple of questions.'

'Fire away.'

'Okay. I gather you just picked it up with the mail from the post box in the square.'

'That's right. There are two boxes in the village. The other one is in Oak Lane. On weekdays we aim to collect from both around half four. There's no collection on Sundays and on Saturdays we pick up about mid-day.'

'So, this would have been put into that box at some point after Saturday lunchtime.'

'Yes, and it was easy for me to spot because there were only two letters in there with it.'

'One final question,' James said. 'Did you touch the note with your bare fingers?'

Sullivan shook his head. 'I've had gloves on the whole time.'

James thanked him again and took down his mobile phone number before going back into the hall and asking DC Sharma to go and see if the post box in the square was covered by CCTV.

Then he gathered the team around him again and told them he would have to send the note up the chain of command.

'I'm not sure what our leaders will make of it, but Caroline is right in saying that we have to take it seriously, at least to begin with,' he said. 'For us it's another line of inquiry to follow up and not an easy one. But for the Constabulary as a whole, it's an issue that will sure as hell cause a high level of alarm.'

CHAPTER SIXTY-EIGHT

James instructed a support staffer to arrange for the note to be handed to forensics in the faint hope that whoever was responsible had left their prints on it. But first he had copies run off for the team.

The more he thought about it, the bigger the ball of anxiety in his chest grew. He wanted to believe that it was a hoax, the work of some pathetic knobhead who thought it would be fun to use the murders of Nigel and Elizabeth Booth to try and instil panic among police officers across the county of Cumbria.

Anonymous threats against individuals and organisations had become far more common in recent years. Most of them occurred online, but there had also been a significant increase in malicious communications through postal services.

There were two other possible scenarios, however, both of them far more ominous. One was that the person behind the note did murder the Booths and now intended to continue the killing spree in order to get revenge against Cumbria Police in general.

Or perhaps it was a blatant attempt by someone who was desperate to divert attention away from Kirkby Abbey and those who were currently suspects – namely Liam Booth and Eddie Kane.

James mentioned all three possible scenarios to Tanner when he called him after emailing over the photo of the note.

'I have no idea what to make of it or how to react to it,' the Super admitted. 'We've received anonymous threats before, but nothing like this. Even if it is the work of a prankster we may not find out for weeks or months. And in the meantime, do we go public with it and put the shits up the more than fifteen hundred officers in the Constabulary and the thousands who've left or retired from the force?'

It was a good question and one that James wasn't sure he could answer. On the one hand it was only right that officers like him should be made aware of any threats against them, however tenuous. But on the other hand, there was always the risk of causing excessive stress and panic when it was unnecessary.

'I'll have to take it straight upstairs,' Tanner continued. 'The decision on where to go with this is above my pay grade. But let's hope it doesn't leak before they've worked out how to respond. If it does, it will put us on the back foot and things could get really messy. I'll get back to you after I've spoken to the Chief Constable.'

James's mind was now raging in all directions and acid was churning in his stomach. He eyed his watch and saw it was almost six. Going home was not an option yet, so he sent a text to Annie to let her know that once again he'd be late.

He then helped himself to a coffee from the machine and looked around the hall as he drank it. His colleagues were keeping themselves busy, speaking into phones, tapping at keyboards and discussing the case among themselves. DCs Isaac and Hall had turned up for their overnight shift and were being updated by DS Abbott.

But James could see that the strain was beginning to show on the faces of every member of the team. That was hardly surprising, though, given the pressure they were under and the hours they'd been putting in.

He was still drinking the coffee when DC Sharma returned from the square to confirm that the post box there was indeed in the range of a CCTV camera.

'It will take a bit of time to access the footage, guv,' he said. 'And then more time will have to be spent going through it.'

'I'll leave that one with you, Ahmed,' James said.

The team discussed the latest developments for another hour and stacked up a bunch of new questions that would need to be answered. Among them was just how many people felt they had a score to settle with the Cumbria Constabulary and would it be easy, or even possible, to identify them all?

If the team chose to pursue that particular line of inquiry, then it would mean taking the investigation in an entirely different direction and James had serious concerns about that.

It got to the point where he had to accept that not much more was going to be achieved by hanging around in the hall. He wanted his team to get a good night's sleep and be refreshed and ready to crack on tomorrow. The few immediate tasks that had been set would be carried out by Isaac and Hall.

Tanner got back to James as he was getting ready to leave the building. He said he'd spoken to the Chief Constable and that a meeting to discuss the anonymous note with the Police and Crime Commissioner would take place first thing in the morning.

'Until we know what they're going to do we keep it under wraps,' Tanner said.

James was walking home when he received another call, this time from PC Baker, who was still keeping Liam Booth's home under surveillance in Chapel Road.

'I'm sorry to bother you, sir,' he said. 'But my shift's about to end and I thought you should know that a short time ago a BBC News crew turned up here and did a brief interview with Liam on his doorstep. When I saw them approach the house I rushed over and asked them what was going on. Liam told me that he wanted to speak to them about his parents and I didn't think I had the authority to stop him.'

'What happened?' James asked.

'I stood back and let them get on with it. It only lasted a few minutes and I was too far away to hear what was said. I did approach the reporter after he was done though, and he told me that it would go out on news bulletins this evening.'

'Did he also tell you what Liam said?'

'Only that the guy came across as angry as well as upset. And that he was quite critical of the police.'

CHAPTER SIXTY-NINE
ANNIE

Annie's phone rang just as she returned downstairs after putting Bella and Theo to bed.

She answered it, expecting James to be calling, but got a shock when a familiar voice said, 'Hi Annie. It's me, Colleen. Can you talk? There's something I need to tell you.'

Her friend sounded quite anxious so Annie felt she had to ignore what James had said about not engaging with the woman.

'Of course,' she replied. 'What is it?'

'I feel I have to apologise for something that Liam has just done. I told him not to, but he ignored me, partly because he'd been drinking and got himself into a wretched state.'

Annie felt a sudden tightness in her chest. 'What did he do, Colleen?'

'He got a BBC News crew to come to the house and interview him,' Colleen said. 'He wanted me to take part, but I refused because I thought it was a bad idea. I wouldn't let them in the house so they did it on the doorstep and I heard every word from inside. Liam said some things that I'm sure he's going to regret when he watches it back.'

'Such as?'

'Well, he claimed that he can't believe that the person who killed his parents is still at large and questioned whether your husband and his team are up to the job. That's why I felt I had to say sorry to you before you see it later on the news. He's now sulking in another room over me having a go at him.'

Annie thought it wise to maintain a neutral position and held back from criticising Liam.

'I do appreciate you calling me, Colleen,' she said, 'but I'm sure that my husband and his colleagues are used to such criticism. It goes with the job.'

'It struck me as grossly unfair, though,' she replied. 'I know that James is doing everything he can to solve the murders and that it's proving challenging for lots of reasons, including the fact that Liam stupidly held things back from both of us.'

'Did Liam want to do the interview just so that he could have a dig at the police?' Annie asked.

'If only. No, he also rounded on people in the village and online trolls who are spreading false rumours that he's the one who committed the murders to get his hands on Nigel and Elizabeth's money. It's absurd, but you know yourself that it's happening. Liam made it clear that he's now living in fear after being threatened and then attacked outside our own home. He also said that he was verbally abused at the vigil, but didn't name Elizabeth's brother.'

'The BBC may decide to edit it down so as not to cause offence to anyone,' Annie said.

'Oh, I very much doubt it. For them it will be seen as good television. Reporters have been clamouring for an interview with him since the bodies were found and until today, he's resisted. But all the stuff that's happened has really got to him and after he was confronted by James about his link to Eddie Kane, he's been a total mess. I'm really worried about him and I fear that spouting off on television will make him more of a target. And me as well.'

'I can only imagine what you've gone through, Colleen,' Annie said. 'It must be hard.'

'It is. I should be grieving the loss of my in-laws, but I haven't been able to. I'm so terrified that I might lose my husband, too, if he's attacked again, but far more severely next time. And you probably know that it's not just his spending that he can't control. It's also his emotions. He's always suffered from bouts of depression and finds it hard to cope when he's under pressure. That's partly why he had a difficult time accepting that Nigel and Elizabeth were planning to retire to Spain. He got in a panic because they'd always been there to support him.'

'Do you think it would help if he saw a doctor?'

'He doesn't believe he needs to. He's already on anti-depressants and they were pretty effective before the problems with his parents got out of hand. And now he's having to come to terms with losing them before he was able to make amends.'

Colleen paused there and Annie heard her sniff back tears. After a few beats she said, 'I shouldn't be going on like this. I didn't intend to. I'm so sorry.'

'Don't be,' Annie said. 'I really don't mind. And it was kind of you to alert me to the interview.'

'Will you pass my apology onto James?' Colleen asked. 'I know that he still regards my Liam as a suspect, but I don't want this interview to work against him.'

'That won't happen,' Annie said. 'I can assure you.'

'Well, before I leave you in peace, is James any nearer to

unmasking the monster who killed Nigel and Elizabeth and ruined all our lives?'

'I honestly don't know, Colleen. There's only so much he's able to tell me. He'd get in serious trouble if he gave me a running commentary of the investigation.'

'I can understand that, Annie. Thank you again for listening to me. You're a good friend and I won't forget it.'

When Annie came off the phone it felt like her heart was swelling up. The conversation had shaken her to the core, but she was glad that Colleen had taken the trouble to warn her about the interview, and to apologise.

Being slagged off by Liam on the television was bound to piss James off, and she wouldn't blame him. All senior police officers were sensitive to criticism, especially when it wasn't justified, and her husband was no exception.

He led a team of highly rated officers with a proven track record. For Liam to accuse them of not being up to the job was unfair and she very much suspected that it was because they'd exposed the secrets he'd been hiding from them, as well as his wife.

Annie was obviously keen to see the interview herself and decided to pour herself a glass of wine before switching the TV on. As she headed for the kitchen, she heard the front door open and James called out, 'It's me, love. I'm home.'

CHAPTER SEVENTY

James was so glad to be home. As he walked through his front door a wave of tiredness crashed over him.

It had been a challenging day and he was eager to wind down, even though he wasn't sure he'd be able to.

Annie stepped into the hall as he was removing his coat.

'I thought you were going to be back much later,' she said. 'I've only just put the kids to bed. I could have kept them up for a while longer if I'd known.'

'Sorry, love. I forgot to send another text. But no matter. I doubt they'd find me much fun anyway.'

Annie walked into his arms and said, 'I can see that this case is really getting to you. You look frazzled.'

'I feel it. A lot's been happening and we've all been at it non-stop. Then, to top it off, I've just been told that Liam Booth has given an interview to BBC News in which he apparently has a dig at our handling of the investigation. It'll be going out this evening.'

Annie pulled back and screwed up her face. 'It's funny you should mention that.'

She went on to tell him about the call from Colleen and in response he let out a sullen sigh. 'Well, I suppose we'd better go and watch it and see how bad it is.'

'Do you want something to eat first? I ate with the kids.'

He shook his head. 'I've been snacking throughout the day and I'm not hungry. But I am thirsty.'

Annie grinned. 'Wine or whisky?'

He smiled back. 'I'm surprised you have to ask.'

Minutes later they were on the sofa, James with his whisky and Annie with a glass of wine. The TV was tuned to the BBC News channel and while they waited for the story to come up, Annie told him that she had received more calls and visits during the day from concerned neighbours and friends who were desperate to know what was going on.

'And I heard about the group storming the hall,' she said. 'That must have come as quite a shock.'

James nodded. 'It's one of the downsides of setting up a temporary base in a small public building. Some people think it's okay to ignore the restrictions and enter it uninvited.'

Inevitably, Annie wanted to know if they'd made any progress with the investigation. James briefly wondered how much to tell her, but after some lip-chewing he decided not to hold back.

'We're still struggling to nail this one down,' he said. 'But there have been two significant developments today. And one of them, if it isn't a sick prank, has far wider implications.'

He began with the news that Eddie Kane had turned up at Kendal HQ with his lawyer in tow and had denied any involvement in the murders.

Annie listened to that with interest, but when he told her about the anonymous note dropped in the village post box, and showed her the picture he took of it on his phone, her brow shot up and her face lost colour.

'The issue now confronting us is how seriously we should take it,' he said. 'The problem is the note could just be a straightforward hoax written by a nutter who thinks it's funny. Or it could be a deliberate attempt by someone to make us believe that Nigel and Elizabeth were the first victims of a serial killer who has decided to target both serving and former Cumbrian police officers.'

Annie was clearly confused. 'But why would anyone want to do that? I don't understand.'

'The obvious reason would be to get us to shift the focus of our investigation away from the likes of Liam Booth and Eddie Kane,' he said. 'We would then have to spread the net wider and look at lots of other potential suspects. People who for one reason or another have made it known in the past that they have a grudge against the force. And there could be hundreds of them depending how far back we go.'

Annie's mouth dropped open. 'My God, James. Does that mean you actually think that Liam or this other bloke might have written the note and put it in the post box?'

'It's not what I think, but it can't be ruled out. It'd be a way of taking the heat off themselves and landing us with a lot more work and pressure.'

Annie considered this for a few moments, then said, 'I see where you're coming from, but at the same time it must also be possible that it's not a hoax or a diversionary tactic, and that the note is the work of someone who does intend to carry out more murders.'

James pressed his lips together and gave a sharp nod. 'That's why there's no easy answer to where we go with this,' he said.

CHAPTER SEVENTY-ONE

James and Annie discussed the anonymous note for another five minutes before their attention was drawn to the TV as the BBC News presenter announced an update to the Lake District double murder story.

She revealed in her intro that there had been two developments, the first being that police had questioned a man they'd been seeking in connection with their investigation.

'We understand that Mr Edward Kane, who lives in Cumbria, was interviewed at Kendal Police Station by Detective Chief Inspector James Walker, who is leading the hunt for the killer of retired police officers Nigel and Elizabeth Booth,' she said. 'A Constabulary spokesperson has told us that Mr Kane left after helping officers with their inquiries. Meanwhile, the BBC has secured an interview with the son of the two murder victims who were stabbed to death on Christmas Eve in Kirkby Abbey. The very latest now from our reporter Colin Fleming.'

The recorded package began with the reporter voicing over a photo of the dead couple and then moved on to various video clips, including shots of the Booths' home in Maple Lane, the village hall and police patrolling the streets. He explained that there was a great deal of disquiet among villagers who feared that the killer could be living among them.

But it was the interview with Liam that James and Annie were anxious to see and the reporter linked into it by explaining that Mr Booth also lived in Kirkby Abbey with his wife and young daughter. He then cut straight to Liam standing on the doorstep of their home in Chapel Road.

Reporter:
Thank you for speaking to us, Mr Booth. I know that it can't be easy for you after what happened to your parents.

Liam:
It isn't, but I feel I should say and do what I can to help find their killer. Mum and Dad were good, kind people and I loved them dearly. They did not deserve to die that way.

James noticed that Liam's face was tight with tension and he appeared to be struggling to get the words out. In addition, his eyes were glassy with tears and there were spots of sweat on his forehead.

Reporter:
So, what would you like to say to our viewers, Mr Booth?

Liam:
Well, we've been told that there's a strong possibility that the killer lives here in the village. If so, then surely someone must know or suspect who that person is. And they should

come forward with that information right away. And just for the record, I had nothing to do with what happened to my parents despite the vile rumours that are circulating both here in the village and on the internet. It's got so bad that I've been threatened and even attacked right here on my own doorstep. For my family's sake it has to stop.

Reporter:
Have the police been made aware of what's happening to you?

Liam:
Of course, but I'm not sure they care. In fact, I get the impression they'd like it to be me so that it will save them a lot of time and effort. Truth is, I'm not convinced that the team investigating this is up to the job. They're certainly not doing enough to make me and other people in the village feel secure. They even stood by while I was verbally abused at the vigil to honour my dead parents.

And at that point they cut away from Liam and the reporter signed off after telling viewers that the BBC would continue to follow the story.

Annie spoke first after letting out a long, dramatic breath.

'Well, that was totally uncalled for,' she said. 'And that last snide remark of his was blatantly untrue. You didn't stand by when his uncle harangued him at the vigil.'

James was annoyed, but he wasn't prepared to let it get to him, not while he had so much else on his plate.

'Yeah, he was out of order, but I suppose it could have been a lot worse,' he said. 'And I doubt that many people would have paid much attention to it.'

324

Annie frowned. 'Are you really not that bothered by what you just heard?'

He shrugged. 'I can't afford to be. It'll be an unnecessary distraction if I let it get to me. And I've got more important things to worry about.'

He downed some more whisky, savouring the gentle burning sensation in his gullet.

Annie leaned across and kissed him on the cheek. 'Do you want me to top up your glass or is it time for bed?'

'I'm up for another drink if you are. In fact, we could offer up a toast to the new year just in case we don't get the chance to tomorrow night.'

Annie chuckled. 'Good idea. I keep forgetting that it'll be New Year's Eve. I'm just glad we didn't have anything planned.'

As Annie got up to fill their glasses, James massaged his eyes with his forefinger and thumb while he reflected on Liam's interview. He wondered if the guy really meant what he'd said or if he'd just wanted to hit back at James for making him a prime suspect and for revealing the true measure of his debts to his wife. Whatever the case, James was determined not to allow it to cloud his judgement or become an issue when he next questioned Liam.

Annie came back into the room and handed him his whisky. They clinked glasses and she said, 'Here's to a happy and prosperous new year, my darling.'

'The same to you,' he replied. 'And to be clear, this doesn't mean that we won't be doing this again tomorrow night if I manage to get home.'

She laughed. 'Absolutely. And with any luck we'll be able to have more than just two tipples before going to bed.'

They took their time enjoying each other's company and at last

James began to feel his mind and body relax. He was reminded yet again that they had missed out on so much during this Christmas break. Just as they did last year and the three before that. He told himself that he would make it up to Annie, Bella and Theo at some point, perhaps by taking them on a holiday early in the new year.

It was approaching ten o'clock when they finished their drinks and decided to head for the bedroom.

But just as James started to mount the stairs a text came through on his phone from Superintendent Tanner.

Did you see the interview that Liam Booth gave to the BBC? If not, check it out. We need to respond and I want us to do it by holding another media briefing tomorrow in Kirkby Abbey. It won't be until after my meeting with the Chief. And it will give us a chance to address some of the other issues that have come up.

James replied with a thumbs up emoji, though he wished he hadn't seen the message until the morning. The thought of having to front another bloody media briefing simply added to the string of worries that were going to make it hard for him to sleep.

CHAPTER SEVENTY-TWO

James woke up at the ungodly hour of 4 a.m. and couldn't get back to sleep. He stayed in bed listening to Annie's heavy breathing while his mind wrestled with uncomfortable thoughts about the day ahead. The same thoughts that had taunted him throughout the night.

The prospect of fronting what promised to be a difficult media briefing filled him with dread, especially off the back of Liam Booth's comments during the BBC interview.

But it wasn't just that. He was also going to have to explain why a full week after Nigel and Elizabeth were murdered, and five days after their bodies were found, the killer was still on the loose.

And he wasn't going to be able to reassure the baying media mob that an arrest was imminent, because it wasn't. Sure, they were chasing some promising leads and had a short list of potential suspects, but that was it. Plus, the investigation was set to get even more problematic thanks to the anonymous note dropped into one of the village post boxes.

He finally hauled himself up at five without waking Annie and that was no doubt thanks to the sleeping pill she'd taken before getting into bed.

After he was showered and dressed he made himself a coffee and drank it while checking the headlines on his phone. There had been no updates to the story overnight and he was pleased to see that Liam's BBC interview hadn't been picked up by the other news outlets.

He checked on Annie before leaving the house and she was still spark out so he chose not to disturb her. But it suddenly occurred to him that he hadn't engaged with Bella and Theo since Boxing Day.

For a brief moment he considered peering into their rooms, but the fear of waking one or both of them up stopped him doing so. Instead, he made a mental note to find the time during the day to pop home for a surprise visit with a gift for each of them from the store. He wanted the little rascals to know that he was still very much a part of their lives.

It was another snow-free morning and James was pretty sure that it wasn't as cold as it had been. During the walk to the hall, he didn't even bother to put on his woollen hat.

When he arrived, the first thing he noticed was that there were only two uniformed officers inside with DCs Isaac and Hall.

'The others who were due to come here first thing this morning have been redeployed elsewhere,' Isaac told him. 'There'll be fewer uniforms patrolling the streets today so it's possible we'll have some villagers turning up here asking why.'

'We tell them that we still have sufficient numbers on hand to keep them safe,' James replied. 'Even if that's not strictly true.'

There were more discouraging updates from overnight. The

three men who Eddie Kane said were with him in Maryport on Christmas Eve had confirmed his alibi. However, there was no CCTV from the pub where they attended the stag do because the system hadn't been working.

Also, no prints had been found on the anonymous note from the post box in the village so there was still no way of knowing who had put it there.

'There is one piece of positive news, guv,' Isaac said. 'More people have returned to their homes here after spending Christmas elsewhere. We've been reliably informed that a number of those properties have door-cams, so we'll be rounding up the footage this morning to see if anything helpful was recorded while they were away.'

The full briefing got going at eight when the rest of the team arrived. To begin with, the discussion was dominated by Liam Booth's interview. They'd all seen it and were none too pleased.

But there were also expressions of concern over the anonymous note warning that the murders of Nigel and Elizabeth were just the start of a killing spree targeting serving and former police officers in Cumbria.

James explained why he thought it was either a hoax or an attempt by someone to divert attention away from their two key suspects.

'If we treat it seriously now then the whole investigation will be turned on its head and it'll be like starting over again,' he said. 'So, I propose we wait for guidance from upstairs. When the Superintendent arrives here to front the media briefing with me, he should be able to tell us what's been decided.'

Word soon came through from the press office at Constabulary headquarters in Penrith that the media briefing had been arranged for ten-thirty in front of the village hall.

But shortly after that Tanner called James to tell him that his meeting with the Chief Constable to discuss the anonymous note had been delayed.

'I'm afraid it means that I won't be able to come down to Kirkby Abbey,' he said. 'You'll have to handle the briefing by yourself. But I'm sure that won't be a problem.'

CHAPTER SEVENTY-THREE

James was given only forty minutes to prepare for the media briefing and he pulled his thoughts together with the help of the rest of the team.

At ten-thirty sharp he slipped on his coat and adjusted his tie. As he stepped outside, his unease mounted along with his heart rate.

In no time at all he was standing in front of a bevy of reporters, photographers and camera crews. A couple of flashes went off as he welcomed them with a nod and a smile.

He only recognised two of the faces in the group and they belonged to *Cumbria Gazette* reporter Gordon Carver and Colin Fleming, the BBC reporter who'd interviewed Liam Booth.

'I'd like to start by thanking you all for coming at such short notice,' James said. 'I just wanted to take the opportunity to keep you updated on the investigation into the murders of Nigel and Elizabeth Booth. I'll be happy to take questions in a moment, but first let me make clear that I am aware of the criticism that's been levelled at myself and my colleagues by those who've been hoping for a speedier resolution to this case. I can appreciate that there's a degree of frustration among people in the village, but I want them to know that we're doing everything possible to find the person who carried out the murders.'

Eager to get a few points across before the questions began, he went on to say that it was still not known if the killer lived in or near the village or had been someone the Booths knew.

'We're still keen to hear from anyone who has information that might be helpful to us,' he said. 'Nigel and Elizabeth had many friends, but during their careers on the force they would have made more than a few enemies. We're working hard to identify as many of those individuals as we can.'

He then said that he was now able to confirm that the large kitchen knife recovered several days ago was almost certainly the murder weapon.

'We believe that it belonged to Mr and Mrs Booth and was taken from their home by the killer,' he added.

The first question came from Gordon Carver, who wanted to know if Zelda Macklin had committed suicide because she had become a suspect.

James sucked on his top lip and shook his head. 'Mrs Macklin was never a suspect. But she did visit the Booths on Christmas Eve and so we had to speak to her. And that was when she revealed to us that she had terminal cancer. In a note she left she made it clear that she'd decided to take steps to end her suffering.'

Next up was Colin Fleming, who said, 'Detective Walker, would you care to respond to the claims made by Liam Booth in an interview with me yesterday? I'm sure you're already aware that he said he doesn't believe that you and your colleagues are up to the job of finding out who murdered his parents. He also said that he'd been physically attacked and verbally abused because of false rumours that he's the one who did it.'

James straightened his back and thrust out his chin. 'I did indeed see the interview, but it wouldn't be right for me to comment on all the points he raised. You must appreciate that Mr Booth is not only grieving, but is also under a considerable amount of stress. And naturally he's frustrated, just as we all are, because he's desperate for whoever killed his parents to be brought to justice. But I can assure you that we're aware of his situation and are already providing him with a level of personal protection. I'd also like to say that the detectives and uniformed officers who are working with me on this are fully committed and I can't praise them highly enough.'

James denied Fleming the opportunity to ask another question by inviting someone else who had their hand up to do so. A bunch of other questions followed, including: *Why was Eddie Kane questioned and how was he connected to the Booths? Are you still investigating the string of burglaries that took place in the village on and around Christmas Eve? Will it be safe for villagers to go out tonight to celebrate New Year's Eve?*

James responded to every question either with an answer or by saying, 'I'm sorry, but I'm not at liberty to disclose that information at this stage.'

After another fifteen minutes he made a show of checking his watch before abruptly ending the briefing. He thanked the group again for coming and was pleased to see that they all appeared to be reasonably satisfied with what he'd told them.

CHAPTER SEVENTY-FOUR

James received plenty of praise when he went back into the hall and even a couple of slaps on the back.

'It was a laudable performance, guv,' DI Stevens said. 'And thanks for throwing in a compliment to the rest of us.'

'I'm just glad it's out of the way,' James replied. 'And I hope that the next time I face that lot I've got some better news to pass on.'

The next hour was spent tossing ideas around and going back over all the information that had already been gathered.

News also came through that the warrant to search Eddie Kane's place in Staveley had been signed off. Stevens volunteered to go there with a forensics team and James told him to get right on it.

DS Abbott then announced that she had started compiling a list of potential suspects from Nigel and Elizabeth's case files.

'The aim has been to identify individuals who might have harboured a grudge against them,' she said. 'Unsurprisingly, they both worked on lots of cases that involved people who were jailed for violent crimes, including murder. We know that some of these offenders were released from prison in recent months, so we're using them as a starting point. But it'll be a slow process trying to find out where they are now and where they were on Christmas Eve.'

'Well, keep at it,' James said. 'And flag up anyone who you think we should home in on.'

James decided to tell the team to break for lunch, but just then DC Sharma called everyone over to the table where he'd been working on his laptop.

'Take a look at this,' he said, pointing at the screen. 'I finally got access to the footage from the CCTV camera that points towards the post box in the village square. The one the anonymous note was collected from.'

James and the others gathered around, peering over his shoulder.

The image on the screen was of the red post box situated on the pavement between two benches.

'The postman, Noah Sullivan, told us that there were two letters alongside the note when he collected from there yesterday evening,' Sharma said. 'Well, I've seen one of the letters being posted on Saturday afternoon by an elderly man. The envelope was most definitely brown. Then, on Sunday, a woman walking past got her young son to post a letter or card. And then there's this from yesterday at two o'clock in the afternoon.'

He pressed play and they watched a figure in a light grey hooded jacket walk into shot, take what looked like a folded sheet of paper from his inside pocket, and then push it into the box. Sharma paused it there and expanded the image.

'You can just about make out the face,' he said. 'And I don't think there's any doubt that we're looking at a fella who is probably in his thirties or forties.'

James felt a flare of excitement sweep through him. 'It's a shame his features are blurred. But I think it's safe to say that it's most definitely not Liam Booth or Eddie Kane. Where does he go from there?'

Sharma pressed play again and the man walked out of shot to the left.

'We need to carry out another trawl of CCTV and door-cams in the village,' James said. 'Let's see if we can find him elsewhere, perhaps getting into a car or entering a building. He cuts quite a distinctive figure in that coat and should stand out.'

'So, is he our killer or someone who wants us to think he is?' Abbott said.

James continued to stare at the screen, his eyes wide and unblinking.

'That's what we need to find out,' he told her.

A few minutes later the team received another shock when James called Tanner to let him know about the footage, only to be told by the Superintendent that copies of the same anonymous note had turned up elsewhere in Cumbria.

'It's only just been brought to my attention,' Tanner said. 'Collections were made this morning from post boxes in Ambleside and Bowness-on-Windermere. The same note was among the mail in both. Local police were alerted and photos taken, which I've compared to the one you sent to me. They're a match.'

'Then we need to check CCTV cameras to see if the same guy is responsible,' James said. 'We'll circulate the footage from down here.'

'If it is the same person then one has to assume that he's driving between towns and villages to spread them around.'

'Or maybe the notes were posted by different people and it's all part of a plan to mislead and confuse us.'

'That is possible.'

'What about the meeting you had with the Chief Constable and the Commissioner? How do they want to handle it?'

'They decided we should hold fire on making it public until we're certain that it's not a prank. And they don't believe it's a credible enough threat to alarm every officer on the force. And every former officer, for that matter.'

'But that was before these other copies turned up,' James said. 'Do you reckon it will make them think again?'

'I doubt it, but I will be discussing it with them. Meanwhile, a quick thank you for fronting the media briefing by yourself. I haven't seen it yet, but I've been told that you did a good job.'

'I just wish I'd had more to tell them.'

'Me too, but the involvement of a high-profile villain like Eddie Kane has got everyone talking. And I wasn't the only one who was surprised to learn that you let him walk straight after the interview.'

'We didn't really have a choice. He was lawyered up and he gave us an alibi for Christmas Eve, which has subsequently checked out. But he's still in the frame and we're about to search his latest address in Staveley. We'll also see if we can get him for moneylending.'

'It's about time the bastard was taken down,' Tanner said. 'But I've had dealings with him myself and so I know how artful he is.'

James came off the phone and helped himself to a Coke and sandwich, courtesy of the caterers.

Looking around the hall, and seeing how busy everyone was, made him wonder what he should do next. There were no more interviews lined up, no new leads to pursue, and nothing to convince him that they were making significant headway.

At the same time the questions were piling up in his head.

Had they overlooked any vital clues or dismissed them as being irrelevant? Were they right to focus so heavily on Liam Booth and Eddie Kane? Was it possible that the killer did not actually live in the village? And should they take the anonymous note put in the post boxes at face value?

'Have you got a second, guv?'

DC Foley's voice came from behind him, and he turned to face her.

'Sure, Caroline. What is it?'

'There's something I want to show you on my laptop. And trust me, you will want to see it.'

'Then lead the way.'

As they crossed the hall, Foley added, 'It's just that I've been going through some of the door-cam recordings that have been recovered from several of the homes that were unoccupied when we last went trawling for footage in the village. And one of them is from a home in Chapel Road, close to where Liam Booth and his family live.'

'I'm sure we've had some door-cam footage from a house along there,' James said.

She nodded. 'We have, but nothing showed up from Christmas Eve. This latest footage, however, is from a house at the other end of the street and there's something on it. Something that struck me as bloody odd.'

When she was seated in front of her laptop she pointed to the screen, which showed a freeze frame of several houses in Chapel Road.

'Now, I was with you when we went to Shap and broke the news to Liam that his parents had been murdered,' she said. 'He told us that on Christmas Eve he went for a hike between about eleven in the morning and two.'

'I remember. Does he appear in this?'

'No, he doesn't, but according to him the route he took starts just across the road so he wouldn't have been caught on either camera.'

'I see. So, what's got you so excited then?'

'Watch and you'll see.'

After she pressed play, James saw a woman appear on the screen steering a pushchair along the pavement. She then paused it again.

'If I'm not mistaken, that's Liam's wife, Colleen. This was recorded at half eleven on Christmas Eve morning, so presumably she'd just left their house.'

James felt his body grow rigid. 'Oh fuck. I see where you're going with this. She told us that she didn't go out that day.'

Foley nodded. 'That's right. I distinctly recall her saying in answer to your question that she stayed in until Liam got back and then they drove to her parents' home in Shap. She said she had to sort things out for the trip.'

Foley then scrolled the footage forward to a point where Colleen was seen walking back along the road.

'This is her returning home,' she said. 'She was out for an hour. I've checked a map of the village and noticed that she didn't head towards the centre and the shops. Instead, she headed in the other direction, towards Maple Lane.'

CHAPTER SEVENTY-FIVE

James felt the air leave his lungs as though he'd been kicked in the chest.

Colleen Booth had lied to them. The door-cam footage was proof that she'd left her house on Christmas Eve morning. And yet she'd told him that she didn't. She'd said she'd stayed in the house while her husband was out hiking.

'This looks bad, guv,' Foley said. 'Colleen went for that walk at about the same time we believe Nigel and Elizabeth were murdered. If she had gone to any of the shops then I'm sure she would have turned up on one or more of the cameras we've checked before now.'

'It could be that she went out to get some fresh air or maybe it was the only way to get her baby to sleep,' James said.

Foley shrugged. 'Or she could have walked to Maple Lane. And if she had, then Elizabeth wouldn't have thought twice about letting her into the house. I've checked, and Chapel Road merges with Forge Avenue, which leads to the outer perimeter road, which intersects Maple Lane.'

James blew out a long breath through pursed lips as he tried to process this unexpected development.

His instincts screamed at him to take it seriously, even though he found it hard to believe that Colleen Booth would have stabbed to death her own in-laws.

'You and I will go and talk to her,' he said. 'Send a still and the relevant clip from the footage to our phones. And while I brief the others, can you call PC Baker, or whoever is currently watching their house, to make sure that Colleen's home?'

The rest of the team were totally thrown by what James told them and as he was speaking an image of Colleen with her pushchair arrived on their phones attached to a group email from Foley.

'Let's not get over excited,' he warned them. 'She did lie to us, but it may have been unintentional. We'd just delivered some devastating news and she was in shock. It could be that she forgot that she went out, even though that does seem unlikely.'

He thought back to their Boxing Day visit to the home of Colleen's parents in Shap.

'She seemed genuinely upset when we told her and her husband what had happened to Nigel and Elizabeth,' he said. 'She broke down and had to go outside for a spell because she thought she was going to be sick.'

'It's worth noting, guv, that when their house was searched, it was Liam's belongings we focused on and took away,' Abbot said. 'Not hers. Perhaps we should have.'

'At that time, we had no reason to suspect that she might have had something to do with the killings,' James replied. 'But if it now turns out that she did, then the question arises as to whether she acted alone. Or were others involved? After all,

341

we still can't be sure where Liam was when the murders took place. And we shouldn't forget that two other men are still in the frame, the reprobate Eddie Kane and the hooded guy who's been posting notes warning of a forthcoming killing spree. When you take them into account the mystery deepens still further.'

CHAPTER SEVENTY-SIX

James and Foley left the hall as soon as they received confirmation that Colleen was at home. It was two o'clock by then and a patrol car dropped them outside the house in Chapel Road five minutes later.

James's thoughts were still burning like a fuse and the questions were continuing to mount. The investigation had taken another unexpected turn and he had no idea where this new road would lead them.

It was Liam who answered the door and he was clearly surprised to see them.

'I hope you're here to tell me that you've finally found out who killed my parents, and not to lecture me over what I told the BBC reporter,' he said.

James shook his head. 'I'm afraid we still haven't solved the case, Liam. And we're not here regarding the interview. We're reviewing everything we have relating to what took place on Christmas Eve. And as part of that review, I need to ask you some more questions.'

'But I've already told you what I did and where I was.'

'I'm aware of that, but there are some points that need to be clarified. This shouldn't take long.'

After a couple of beats, Liam begrudgingly stepped aside and waved them in.

He told them to follow him through to the living room where Colleen was sat on the sofa watching the television. When she saw them, her eyes narrowed and her body visibly stiffened.

'What is it?' she said. 'Have you got some news for us?'

She was wearing a navy polo sweater and black leggings, and her hair was gathered up and pinned at the back.

'They want to ask more questions,' Liam told her. 'It must mean that I'm still a ruddy suspect.'

'Is that true, Detective Walker?' she responded. 'Surely it's obvious by now that Liam had nothing to do with it.'

'I just explained to your husband that we're reviewing all the information we've gathered in respect of what happened on Christmas Eve,' James said. 'The aim is to make sure that we haven't missed something. And as part of the process, we need to ask further questions and clarify certain points. We'll be as quick as we can.'

'You'd better sit down then,' Liam said before joining Colleen on the sofa. 'Rosie's upstairs asleep, but she'll be awake soon and when she's up we plan to drive to Shap to spend New Year's Eve with Colleen's mum and dad.'

The two detectives perched themselves on the armchairs after taking off their coats. They'd already decided how they were going to play it, with James asking the questions while Foley took down notes.

James immediately got the impression that Liam was more angry than anxious. His eyes fixed on James and his jaw was tightly clenched. Colleen, on the other hand, looked nervous and kept licking her teeth with the tip of her tongue.

To Liam, James said, 'We know that you both travelled to Shap at about five o'clock on Christmas Eve, which we believe would have been several hours after the murders took place in Maple Lane. And you told us that you went out hiking between about eleven in the morning and two.'

Liam nodded. 'That's because I did. It wasn't a lie.'

'But it seems that nobody saw you and much to our surprise you didn't appear on any CCTV cameras in the village.'

Liam gave a derisive snort. 'I didn't walk through the village. I crossed the road here and went straight into the field, just as I always do. And believe it or not, there aren't any cameras out there keeping tabs on people.'

James gave a crisp nod and let the heavy silence hang between them for a few beats before turning to Liam's wife.

'And what about you, Colleen? Can you remind me what you did with yourself while Liam was out walking?'

She replied without any hesitation. 'I stayed in. I told you that. I was too busy to go out anywhere. Liam had left me to do the packing and it was one of those mornings where Rosie was craving attention.'

'And you're absolutely sure of that are you?' James asked.

This time she did hesitate, but only briefly before giving a vigorous nod. 'Of course, I am. It wasn't that long ago and my memory's not failing me.'

James experienced an icy shiver as she flashed him an uncertain smile.

He reached into his pocket for his phone and when he pulled it out her eyebrows drew together.

'There's something I want to show you,' he said, bringing

up the photo of her with the pushchair. 'This image is from a door camera on this very road. It recorded you leaving here on Christmas Eve shortly after your husband went on his hike. You returned about an hour later.'

He stood up and stepped closer to the sofa, holding the phone for her to see the screen. When her eyes settled on the photo, a shocked expression froze on her face.

Liam reacted by grabbing the phone from James. 'What the fuck are you on about?' he snapped through gritted teeth. 'This can't be …'

His throat seized up the moment he saw the picture and his mouth fell open.

'That is most definitely your wife, Liam,' James said. 'And she was captured on camera at eleven-thirty on Christmas Eve morning.'

'But it can't be her,' Liam insisted. 'It's a mistake. You heard what she said.' He then turned to Colleen. 'Tell him, love. This isn't you, is it?'

For a moment James thought that she was going to tell him what he wanted to hear, but she obviously realised there'd be no point. Instead, she shook her head and held up her hands.

'I honestly don't recall going out, but that's definitely me so I must have done,' she said in a small, pitiful voice. 'I probably went to the store to get something we needed and forgot all about it. I still can't remember and that's scary.'

Liam handed the phone back to James.

'What's the big deal anyway?' he said. 'We all forget things.'

'The big deal is that we were led to believe that your wife was here in this house when your parents were murdered,' James said.

Liam started to respond, but Colleen spoke over him. 'Are you insane? Are you actually suggesting that it was me who killed them? I don't believe it.'

'And I find it hard to believe that you can't remember going out,' James said. 'And we can't ignore the fact that you were caught on camera heading in the direction of Maple Lane, not the village store.'

James sat back down then, but Liam shot to his feet.

'Okay, that's enough,' he shouted. 'I want you both to leave now. This is uncalled for.'

James stayed where he was because he wasn't buying what Colleen had told him. He could see the fear bundling up inside her. She was shaking and the tendons in her neck were so tight they looked ready to snap.

He could almost see the guilt distorting her features and sensed that she was on the brink of confessing. If he didn't push her over the edge now, he might not get another chance before she'd got her act together and her confidence back.

'Are you bloody listening to me, detective?' Liam yelled. 'I told you to get out of my house.'

And that was when an idea popped into James's head. A way that might get her to open up. It was something he'd tried before on suspects. It wasn't illegal or unethical and it was rarely successful, but he decided it was worth a try.

'Please calm down, Liam,' he said. 'We're not going anywhere yet.' He turned back to Colleen and despite the shiver of doubt that swept through him, he gave in to impulse and asked a hypothetical question in the hope that in her fragile state she might misinterpret it as a statement of fact.

'What if I was to tell you that we also have CCTV footage of you in Ruskin Street, Colleen? What if we can place you at the skip where the murder weapon was dumped?'

There was a moment, just a moment, when James feared that she would see the questions for what they were, and he felt a flash of disappointment. But then suddenly her face creased up, a cry flew out of her mouth, and he realised that she'd fallen for it.

Her shocked husband reached out and put his hand on her shoulder, but she pushed it away.

She then fixed her eyes on James and he felt a ball of emotion well up inside him even though he'd got what he wanted by deploying an element of trickery.

'I didn't mean for it to happen,' she shrieked. 'I went to the house to plead with Elizabeth to end the feud with Liam that was tearing the family apart. But it all went wrong when she lost her temper with me and I made the mistake of picking up the knife.' She looked up at her husband then and said, 'I'm so, so sorry.'

But Liam just stared down at her, tears forming at the corners of his eyes. He didn't move, not even to blink.

And that was when Colleen broke down in a paroxysm of tears.

CHAPTER SEVENTY-SEVEN

Colleen continued to cry uncontrollably and Liam made no move to comfort her. He sat on the armchair vacated by DC Foley who had left the room to arrange for a van to come and take his wife to headquarters in Kendal.

He was in a state of total shock, his expression a mixture of pain, anger and confusion.

James tried to persuade him to leave the room, but he refused, saying he wanted to hear what else Colleen was going to reveal.

James wanted to hear it, too, and when she finally regained her composure after about five minutes, he asked her why she had killed Nigel and Elizabeth.

She took a deep, stuttering breath and her eyes swivelled between the two men. Her mouth opened, her lips trembled, but no words came out.

In a voice laden with emotion, Liam said, 'I need to know, Colleen. I need to know why you did it. Why did you kill my mum and dad?'

More tears started running down her cheeks and James feared

that her composure was on the verge of deserting her again. But after a few seconds she pushed her shoulders back, then cleared her throat to find her voice.

'I killed Elizabeth by accident and Nigel out of desperation,' she said. 'You were never supposed to find out, but it was stupid of me to think that I could keep it from you.'

Liam just sat there burning over her words while shaking his head in disbelief.

'Start at the beginning, Colleen, and tell us again why you went to the house and exactly what happened when you got there,' James said just as Foley came back into the room and signalled to him that the van was on its way.

Colleen swallowed hard and released a breath in a loud gasp. Then she turned to Liam and said, 'I went there that morning because I knew that your dad was at the Santa parade and your mum would be alone in the house. I thought it would be best to talk to just her. I wanted to urge her to reconsider retiring to Spain because I feared that if they did then it would destroy you and make life unbearable for us going forward.'

Liam clenched his jaw and bared his teeth. 'But I told you to stay out of it. I didn't want you to fall out with them as well.'

'And I tried to, but you were becoming more and more angry by the day. It got to the point where I felt I had to do something to help get us out of the financial mess you'd got us into. I was thinking of our future. Of Rosie. And like you I came to realise that our only hope was for them to stump up your inheritance early instead of spending it on living the high life in Spain.'

'So, you did go to their house with the intention of killing them,' Liam said.

She shook her head. 'Of course not. I wanted to beg her

350

to think of you and me and their granddaughter instead of themselves.'

'But I don't understand. What made you stab Mum? It makes no sense.'

By now Colleen was on the verge of losing it again and blood vessels were bulging out of her temples. But to James's surprise she responded to Liam's question, her voice dropping to almost a whisper.

'As soon as she opened the door to me, I realised that she was in a foul mood,' she said. 'Rosie was asleep in the pushchair so I left her in the hallway and followed Elizabeth into the kitchen. I asked her what was wrong and she said that Zelda Macklin had turned up earlier and they'd had a terrible argument. She didn't want to talk about it, and then asked me why I'd dropped by. When I told her, she said that she didn't want to talk about that either.

'But I persisted and she agreed to listen to what I had to say while she prepared lunch. But her response was to bad mouth you and say that she and Nigel were tired of bailing you out. She even accused me of being partly to blame for our situation because I hadn't done enough to stop the debts from spiralling out of control.

'We ended up screaming at each other. Then she turned her back on me and told me to leave the house. It made me really mad so I used the back of my hand to knock the mug from the worktop and it smashed onto the floor. She turned around then and called me a crazy bitch. Then she slapped my face and pushed me back against the sink. My right hand landed on top of one of the kitchen knives and I instinctively picked it up and waved it at her. I didn't intend to hurt her with it, but she rushed forward to grab it from me and slipped on the broken mug. She lost her balance and I was still holding up the knife as she stumbled forward. Before I could jerk my hand back, she fell onto it and the blade lodged in her throat. I let go of it then and she fell backwards and hit her head on the worktop. As soon as she landed on the floor, I knew that she was dead.'

Liam just stared at her, his face set in stone, and James could see the fire growing in his eyes.

'What happened next?' James asked.

She turned to him and after another long, strained pause, said, 'That was when things went from bad to worse. I panicked because I knew that nobody would believe that I hadn't meant to do it. I thought about my husband and my daughter, and that if I went to prison and never saw them again, I wouldn't want to go on living. So, I told myself to focus on the future and let everyone think that Elizabeth had been killed by someone else.'

James was struck by the way the words were now flowing so quickly and clearly out of Colleen's mouth and how determined she seemed to get it all off her chest. It was something he had experienced before with other people who'd felt the need to cram as much information as possible into their initial confession.

'It made me sick to my stomach when I pulled the knife out of her throat and wrapped it in the tea towel, but it had to be done,' she carried on. 'I left the house and intended to dump it on the way home. I was heading along the lane when I saw Nigel coming towards me in his Santa Claus suit. He waved and when he drew close, he asked me if I'd been to see Elizabeth. I tried to answer him but I couldn't and at the same time he saw blood on my face and coat and asked me what had happened.

'I knew that I couldn't tell him, and I also couldn't let him go to the house. The survival instinct kicked in and I reached under the pushchair and pulled the knife out from the towel and stabbed him in the chest. But he grabbed my arm and so I stabbed him again in the stomach. When he fell to the ground I waited until I was sure he was dead and pulled him into the bushes. Then I wrapped the knife in the towel again and headed for home. I didn't think it would be wise to dump it close to the body and looked out for somewhere else.

'There were more people around when I crossed the perimeter road so I took a different route along Ruskin Street and that's when I saw the skip. Before I dumped the knife in there, I rubbed it clean and soaked the towel in a puddle.'

Liam leapt to his feet again and yelled at her, 'That's all I can take. If I stay here listening to you for a second longer, then I won't be able to control myself. And if I hurt you there'll be nobody to take care of our daughter. She's all I've got now and I'm all she's got.'

With that he turned and stormed out of the room, and James signalled for Foley to go with him.

CHAPTER SEVENTY-EIGHT

Colleen didn't try to stop her husband from leaving the room. She just stared after him and James could tell from the stricken look on her face that she knew she'd lost him forever.

Despite what she had done, he felt sympathy for her. He didn't believe that she was an intrinsically bad person, but having succumbed to a moment of madness she was going to have to suffer the consequences.

'Is there anything more you want to tell me?' he asked her.

She breathed in deep through her nostrils and looked at James.

'Only that I wish God would strike me down right here and right now,' she said. 'I've lost everything. My husband, my daughter, my in-laws. And I'm sure that even my own parents will never forgive me for what I've done.'

'I'll make sure your parents are informed of what's happened,' he said. 'But first I need to make it clear that I'm arresting you on suspicion of murder. I know you've already confessed, but I'm obliged to say that you do not have to say anything more unless you wish to do so, but anything you do say will be taken down and may be given as evidence. You will be transported to Kendal Police Station where you'll be held in custody and charged. A formal interview will then take place, most probably tomorrow.'

Just as he finished speaking, Foley appeared in the doorway to tell him that the van had arrived outside.

'And Mr Booth is upstairs with his daughter,' she added.

Within seconds two uniformed officers entered the room and Colleen was led away. James asked Foley to go with them to Kendal and to formally charge her with two counts of murder.

'On your way there will you arrange for a forensics team to come here along with a family liaison officer?' he said. 'And also get someone to alert social services to the situation. Liam may well need help coping with this.'

James went upstairs and found Liam sitting on the floor next to where his daughter was sleeping soundly in her cot. His face was creased up and tears were spilling from his eyes.

The sight of the poor man brought a lump to James's throat. His pulse quickened and the rhythm of his heart seemed to change.

'Is there anyone you would like me to call, Liam?' he asked.

Liam shook his head. 'I need to be alone with my baby. It's just the two of us now.'

'I'm arranging for a family liaison officer to come here. And I'm going to have to inform social services. Help will be there if you need it.'

'Is my wife still downstairs?'

'No. She's being taken to Kendal where she'll spend the night and be formally charged.'

Liam squeezed his eyes shut and pinched the bridge of his nose. 'I had no idea what she'd done,' he said. 'She told me she didn't go out on Christmas Eve and I believed her. She didn't say or do anything after that to make me suspect she'd lied. But I can't help blaming myself for what's happened. It was me who got us into debt and then gave my parents hell for not bailing me out. They would still be alive if I hadn't acted like a complete prick. And my wife and the mother of my daughter wouldn't be destined to spend years behind bars.'

James heard sounds from downstairs and assumed that more officers had arrived.

'You should know that a forensic team will soon be here,' he said. 'They'll want to take away some of your wife's belongings, including her phone and some clothes.'

Liam shrugged. 'They can take whatever they want to.'

'Are you comfortable staying here or would you like to go elsewhere?'

'I've got nowhere else to go and this is my home, so we're staying.'

James took out his phone and swiped it open.

'There's one more question I need to ask you, Liam. Have you any idea who this man is?'

He showed him the image of the hooded guy placing the anonymous note into the village post box.

Liam squinted at it and shook his head. 'I can't see his face clearly, but I don't think I know him. Why?'

'Well, the note he's depositing carries the claim that someone else murdered your parents and that more serving and former police officers are also going to be killed.'

Liam drew in a chest full of air. 'A few minutes ago, I might have believed it. But now we both know that it has to be a hoax.'

James nodded silently and left the room.

There were now four uniformed officers downstairs, plus

DS Abbott, who'd come straight to the house when the team received word that Colleen had been detained. She was going to coordinate things until DC Hall arrived to relieve her at the start of his night shift.

'Forensics should be here soon, guv, and the FLO is on her way,' she said. 'How's the husband?'

'Shell-shocked,' James answered. 'Keep an eye on him. I'll go back to the hall. I need to speak to the Super and set things in motion.'

'Well, there's something else you need to be aware of. DI Stevens just called in to say that they'd executed the warrant on Eddie Kane's place in Staveley, but while they were there, things kicked off and Phil arrested him for assaulting a police officer.'

James felt his heart flip. 'This is proving to be an eventful New Year's Eve.'

CHAPTER SEVENTY-NINE

As soon as James stepped outside the house, he was confronted by a group of people that included several hacks and snappers.

The police presence in Chapel Road had alerted neighbours to the fact that something was happening and word had quickly spread. And Colleen Booth had obviously been seen being bundled into a van.

'Why has Mrs Booth been arrested, Detective Walker?' someone shouted. 'Do you believe that she murdered her in-laws?'

James chose to ignore that and the other questions that were thrown at him. And as he headed straight back to the village hall, the adrenaline was searing his senses.

He found himself struggling to accept that the case had been solved and that the person who killed Nigel and Elizabeth Booth was none other than their own daughter-in-law. If not for the door-cam footage they might never have uncovered the truth. He didn't feel good about it, though. Just relieved. And he was sure that all the villagers were also going to be relieved when the news reached them.

He was back at the hall just after five and the first thing he did was grab a coffee because his mouth was as dry as burned toast. Before calling the team together for a briefing, he rang Tanner to give him the news.

The Super congratulated James and said he would speak to the press office about issuing a statement.

'I take it this means that we can stop worrying about those anonymous notes threatening a killing spree?'

'I suppose so,' James said. 'But it's a loose end that we still need to tie up. Among the questions I want answers to is whether the same man delivered the notes to boxes in Ambleside, Bowness and here in Kirkby Abbey.'

When the team got together, he told them what Colleen had said and also let it be known how he'd managed to get her to open up by deploying a method that was cunning but completely by the book. They were surprised and impressed and even gave him a brief round of applause.

They were still discussing her shock confession when DI Stevens called with an update on Eddie Kane's arrest.

'I brought him here to Kendal to be charged and couldn't believe it when Caroline turned up with Colleen Booth,' Stevens said. 'She's about to fill me in.'

'To be honest, it still hasn't sunk in with me,' James said. 'Now, what about Kane?'

'Well, he was at home when we turned up with the warrant and had clearly been drinking. He tried to stop us entering the flat and punched one of the uniforms in the process.'

'But I take it you managed to search the place.'

'Sure we did. We found three burner phones and a laptop and they're already with forensics. But there were no drugs or other contraband.'

'He's not stupid enough to store that stuff in his own home. But it'll be interesting to see what you find on the phones and laptop.'

James stayed in the hall for another hour attending to paperwork and answering calls. Foley let him know that Colleen had been processed and was now in a cell, and her parents had been informed.

Abbott also called to tell him that the FLO was with Liam and forensics officers were bagging up some of his wife's belongings.

Before leaving for home, James put in a call to Darren Hanson, Elizabeth's brother, who expressed profound shock at the news.

'I reckon I owe Liam an apology,' he said. 'I really thought it was him who killed my sister and Nigel.'

The one person James wasn't looking forward to breaking the news to was Annie. Colleen had been her friend and Annie had felt such sympathy towards the woman following the murders on Christmas Eve.

But as soon as he walked through the door, he sensed from her stiff expression that she already knew. She confirmed his suspicion by saying, 'Is it true about Colleen?'

James swallowed, trying to moisten his throat, and then nodded. 'It is, I'm afraid.'

She bit down on her bottom lip as the blood drained from her face.

'Janet called me about half an hour ago,' she said. 'She'd been told that Colleen's neighbours saw her being taken away in a police van and it's already all over the village that she killed Nigel and Elizabeth. As soon as I came off the phone, I thought it best to put the kids straight to bed.'

She started to quietly weep then, and as James put his arms

around her, it felt like his own heart was trying to pump its way out of his ribcage.

When she stopped crying, she wanted him to tell her what Colleen had confessed to doing. He saw no point in holding back, but it gave him no pleasure to see the sheer pain reflected in her eyes.

They sat down for the rest of the evening and for much of the time Annie remained silent, as though lost within herself.

James had actually forgotten that it was New Year's Eve and only remembered when fireworks started to go off in the village at the stroke of midnight.

CHAPTER EIGHTY
NEW YEAR'S DAY

The new year began with another early start for James. First stop on his rapidly pulled together schedule was a trip to Kendal in the back of a patrol car.

On the way he scanned the online news sites and saw that Colleen Booth's arrest was dominating most of them. There were soundbites from people living in Kirkby Abbey who spoke about how shocked everyone there was.

He arrived at HQ just in time to address the media briefing that had been set up. It lasted only about fifteen minutes, during which time he read out a prepared statement explaining that Colleen Booth had been charged with murdering her in-laws on Christmas Eve. He took a few questions but was careful not to say anything that might prejudice the future trial.

Then he sat down with Colleen and her lawyer and carried out the formal interview.

She looked dreadful after a night in the cell. Her skin was deathly white, her eyes inflamed from crying.

Before the session began, she asked James how Liam and Rosie were and he told her that he hadn't seen them since yesterday.

'When you do, please can you tell Liam that I completely understand why he won't want to ever see me again,' she said, 'but I want him to know that I still love him and Rosie with all my heart.'

She then managed to hold it together and answered every question that was put to her. She admitted to killing Nigel and Elizabeth and basically repeated what she had already said to him.

At the end of it her lawyer indicated that they might use diminished responsibility as a defence at her trial.

James stayed in Kendal for the rest of the day as the makeshift incident room in Kirkby Abbey's village hall was being dismantled.

While he was there, another mystery relating to the case was solved. The hooded man who put the note into the post box in the village had also been caught on cameras doing the same thing in Ambleside and Bowness on the same day. And one piece of footage showed him getting into a car. The registration was clear to see and it was quickly established that it belonged to a man named Richard Grimes who worked for Eddie Kane.

But even better news followed when the digital forensics team gained access to Kane's laptop. They discovered that it was him who had written and printed off copies of the anonymous note that claimed the Booths were the first victims of a planned killing spree in Cumbria. He'd foolishly forgotten to delete the document.

When confronted by James with the evidence late that evening, Grimes caved and admitted that Eddie Kane had instructed him to post the notes. The revelation, along with what was found on

Kane's computer, gave the crime boss no option other than to confess.

'I was convinced that Liam killed his parents to get their money,' he said. 'Naturally, I didn't want him to go down for it before he paid off his debt to me, so I tried to make you believe that the Booths were the victims of some nutter out for revenge against the entire Constabulary.'

EPILOGUE
ONE MONTH LATER

For the third weekend running Cumbria was being lashed by strong winds and heavy snow. But James didn't care because he was comfortably ensconced in a smart hotel with Annie, Bella and Theo.

He was now watching all three of them splashing around in the children's indoor play pool while he sat on one of the loungers enjoying a nice cool beer.

Bringing them here for a three-night break had been his way of making up for spending so little time with them between Christmas and New Year's.

It had been an eventful January during which a date had been set for Colleen Booth's murder trial and Eddie Kane had pleaded guilty to perverting the course of justice by producing and distributing material aimed at interfering with a police investigation. He was awaiting sentence on that but was also on course to face a charge of illegal moneylending.

Liam Booth had agreed to testify against Kane and only three days ago had entered the witness protection programme to keep him and his daughter safe.

Liam had decided he no longer wanted to live in Kirkby Abbey and his aim was to start a new life abroad, perhaps even in Spain. He hadn't made contact with his wife since her arrest and had no intention of doing so.

For James, the most emotional event was the double funeral for Nigel and Elizabeth. Dozens of police officers joined villagers at the ceremony and scores more lined the streets of Kirkby Abbey to watch the solemn procession up to the church.

Their son found the strength to read out a very moving eulogy in which he made no reference to his wife.

It was now time for James to look ahead. Another year had begun and it was bound to throw up a whole bunch of new challenges. Plus, he and Annie were going to have to make some important decisions. Chief among them was whether to remain in Cumbria or move to a place where Christmas didn't always come with such a large dose of mischief, mayhem and murder.

THE END

ACKNOWLEDGEMENT

Once again, I'd like to thank the excellent team at Avon/ HarperCollins for their continued support with this series. They've made writing the books such an enjoyable experience. And a special thank you to my editor, Amy Mae Baxter, whose hard work and commitment has been very much appreciated.

If you've enjoyed *The Killer in the Cold*,
then why not head back to DI
James Walker's first case?

A serial killer is on the loose in Kirkby Abbey.
And as the snow falls, the body count climbs …

One farmhouse. Two murder cases.
Three bodies.

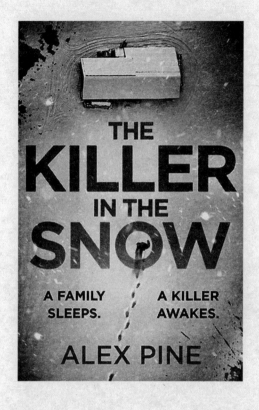

DI James Walker knows that to catch
this killer, he needs to solve a case
long since gone cold …

**Christmas has arrived in Cumbria, and
wedding bells are ringing.
But an ice-cold killer is waiting in the fells …**

Something old, something new.
One guest is a killer.
The question is: who?

This Christmas, the hunters become the hunted …

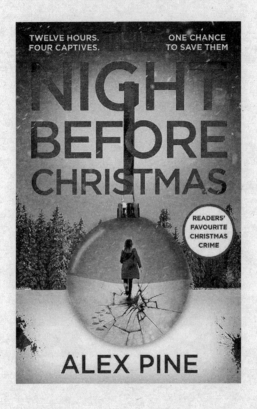

As a snowstorm descends, three lives hang in the balance. But can the killer be caught before the trail goes cold?